Mary V.

# The Cat Who Came to Breakfast

## ALSO BY LILIAN JACKSON BRAUN

# The Cat
# Who Came
# to Breakfast

## Lilian Jackson Braun

G. P. PUTNAM'S SONS
*New York*

G. P. Putnam's Sons
*Publishers Since 1838*
200 Madison Avenue
New York, NY 10016

ISBN-13: 978-0-7394-7913-1

*Printed in the United States of America*

DEDICATED TO
EARL BETTINGER, THE HUSBAND WHO . . .

# The Cat Who Came to Breakfast

# One

It was a weekend in June—glorious weather for boating. A small cabin cruiser with *Double-Six* freshly painted on the sternboard chugged across the lake at a cautious speed. Stowed on the aft deck were suitcases, cartons, a turkey roaster without handles, and a small wire-mesh cage with a jacket thrown over the top.

"They're quiet!" the pilot yelled above the motor noise.

The passenger, a man with a large moustache, shouted back, "They like the vibration!"

"Yeah. They can smell the lake, too!"

"How long does it take to cross?"

"The ferry makes it in thirty minutes! I'm going slow so they don't get seasick!"

The passenger lifted a sleeve of the jacket for a surreptitious peek. "They seem to be okay!"

Pointing across the water to a thin black line on the horizon, the pilot announced loudly. "That's our destination! . . . Breakfast Island, ahoy!"

"YOW!" came a piercing baritone from the cage.

"That's Koko!" the passenger yelled. "He knows what 'breakfast' means!"

"N-n-NOW!" came a shrill soprano echo.

"That's Yum Yum! They're both hungry!"

The cabin cruiser picked up speed. For all of them it was a voyage to another world.

Breakfast Island, several miles from the Moose County mainland, was not on the navigation chart. The pear-shaped blip of land—broad at the south end and elongated at the northern tip—had been named Pear Island by nineteenth-century cartographers. Less printable names were invented by lake captains who lost ships and cargo on the treacherous rocks at the stem end of the pear.

The southern shore was more hospitable. For many years, fishermen from the mainland, rowing out at dawn to try their luck, would beach their dinghies on the sand and fry up some of their catch for breakfast. No one knew exactly when or how Breakfast Island earned its affectionate nickname, but it was a long time before the economic blessing known as tourism.

Moose County itself, 400 miles north of everywhere, had recently been discovered as a vacation paradise; its popularity was developing gradually by word of mouth. Breakfast Island, on the other hand, blossomed suddenly—the result of a seed planted by a real-estate entrepreneur, nurtured by a financial institution, and watered by the careful hand of national publicity.

Two days before the voyage of the *Double-Six*, the flowering of Breakfast Island was the subject of debate on the mainland, where two couples were having dinner at the Old Stone Mill.

"Let's drink a toast to the new Pear Island resort," said Arch Riker, publisher of the local newspaper. "Best thing that ever happened to Moose County!"

"I can hardly wait to see it," said Polly Duncan, head of the Pickax Public Library.

Mildred Riker suggested, "Let's all four of us go over for a weekend and stay at a bed-and-breakfast!"

The fourth member of the party sat in moody silence, tamping his luxuriant moustache.

"How about it, Qwill?" asked Riker. "Will you drink to that?"

"No!" said Jim Qwilleran. "I don't like what they've done to Breakfast Island; I see no reason for changing its name; and I have no desire to go there!"

"Well!" said Polly in surprise.

"Really!" said Mildred in protest.

The two men were old friends—journalists from "Down Below," as Moose County natives called the population centers of the United States. Now Riker was realizing his dream of publishing a country newspaper, and Qwilleran, having inherited money, was living a comfortable bachelor life in Pickax City (population 3,000) and writing a column for the *Moose County Something*. Despite the droop of his pepper-and-salt moustache and the melancholy look in his heavy-lidded eyes, he had found middle-aged contentment here. He walked and biked and filled his lungs with country air. He met new people and confronted new challenges. He had a fulfilling friendship with Polly Duncan. He lived in a spectacular converted apple barn. And he shared the routine of everyday living with two Siamese cats.

"Let me tell you," he went on to his dinner partners, "why I'm opposed to the Pear Island resort. When I first came up here from Down Below, some boaters took me out to the island, and we tied up at an old wooden pier. The silence was absolute, except for the scream of a gull or the splash of a fish jumping out of the water. God! It was peaceful! No cars, no paved roads, no telephone poles, no people, and only a few nondescript shacks on the edge of the forest!" He paused and noted the effect he was having on his listeners. "What is on that lonely shore now? A three-story hotel, a marina with fifty boat slips, a pizza parlor, a T-shirt studio, and *two fudge shops!*"

"How do you know?" Riker challenged him. "You haven't even been over there to see the resort, let alone count the fudge shops."

"I read the publicity releases. That was enough to turn me off."

"If you had attended the press preview, you'd have a proper perspective." Riker had the ruddy face and paunchy figure of an editor who had attended too many press previews.

"If I ate their free lunch," Qwilleran shot back, "they'd expect all kinds of puffery in my column . . . No, it was enough, Arch, that you gave them the lead story on page one, three pictures inside, and an editorial!"

The publisher's new wife, Mildred, spoke up. "Qwill, I went to the preview with Arch and thought XYZ Enterprises did a very tasteful job with the hotel. It's rustic and blends in nicely. There's a shopping strip on either side of the hotel—also rustic—and the signage is standardized and not at all junky." This was high praise coming from someone who taught art in the public schools. "I must admit, though, that you can smell fudge all over the island."

"And horses," said her husband. "It's a heady combination, let me tell you! Since motor vehicles are prohibited, visitors hire carriages or hail horse cabs or rent bicycles or walk."

"Can you picture the traffic jam when that little island is cluttered with hordes of bicycles and strollers and sightseeing carriages?" Qwilleran asked with a hint of belligerence.

Polly Duncan laid a hand softly on his arm. "Qwill, dear, should we attribute your negative attitude to guilt? If so, banish the thought!"

Qwilleran winced. There was some painful truth in her well-intended statement. It was his own money that had financed, to a great degree, the development of the island. Having inherited the enormous Klingenschoen fortune based in Moose County, he had established the Klingenschoen Foundation to distribute megamillions for the betterment of the community, thus relieving himself of responsibility. A host of changes had resulted, some of which he questioned. Nevertheless, he adhered to his policy of hands-off.

Polly continued, with sincere enthusiasm. "Think how much the K Foundation has done for the schools, health care, and literacy! If it weren't for Klingenschoen backing, we wouldn't have a good newspaper and plans for a community college!"

Riker said, "The Pear Island Hotel alone will provide three hundred jobs, many of them much-needed summer work for young people. We pointed that out on our editorial page. Also, the influx of tourists will pour millions into the local economy over a period of time. At the press preview, I met the editor of the *Lockmaster Ledger,* and he told me that Lockmaster County is green with envy. They say we have an offshore goldmine. One has to admire XYZ for undertaking such a herculean project. Everything had to be shipped over on barges: building materials, heavy equipment, furniture! Talk about giving yourself a few problems!"

The man with a prominent moustache huffed into it with annoyance.

"Why fight it, Qwill? Isn't the K Foundation a philanthropic institution? Isn't it mandated to do what's best for the community?"

Qwilleran shifted uncomfortably in his chair. "I've kept my nose out of the operation because I know nothing about business and finance—and care even less—but if I had offered more input, the directors might have balanced economic improvement with environmental foresight. More and more I'm concerned about the future of our planet."

"Well, you have a point there," Riker admitted. "Let's drink to environmental conscience!" he said jovially, waving his empty glass at a tall serving person, who was hovering nearby. Derek Cuttlebrink was obviously listening to their conversation. "Another Scotch, Derek."

"No more for me," said Mildred.

Polly was still sipping her first glass of sherry.

Qwilleran shook his head, having downed two glasses of a local mineral water.

Everyone was ready to order, and Riker inquired if there were any specials.

"Chicken Florentine," said the server, making a disagreeable face.

The four diners glanced at each other, and Mildred said, "Oh, no!"

They consulted the menu, and the eventual choice was trout for Mildred, sweetbreads for Polly, and rack of lamb for the two men. Then Qwilleran returned to the subject: "Why did they change it to Pear Island? I say that Breakfast Island has a friendly and appetizing connotation."

"It won't do any good to complain," Riker told him. "XYZ Enterprises has spent a fortune on wining and dining travel editors, and every travel page in the country has hailed the discovery of Pear Island. Anyway, that's what it's called on the map, and it happens to be pear-shaped. Furthermore, surveys indicate that a sophisticated market Down Below finds 'Pear Island' more appealing than 'Breakfast Island,' according to Don Exbridge." He referred to the X in XYZ Enterprises.

"They like the pear's erotic shape," Qwilleran grumbled. "As a fruit it's either underripe or overripe, mealy or gritty, with a choice of mild flavor or no flavor."

Mildred protested. "I insist there's nothing to equal a beautiful russet-colored Bosc with a wedge of Roquefort!"

"Of course! A pear needs all the help it can get. It's delicious with chocolate sauce or fresh raspberries. What isn't?"

"Qwill's on his soapbox again," Riker observed.

"I agree with him on the name of the island," said Polly. "I think 'Breakfast Island' has a certain quaint charm. Names of islands on the map usually reflect a bureaucratic lack of imagination."

"Enough about pears!" Riker said, rolling his eyes in exasperation. "Let's eat."

Mildred asked Qwilleran, "Don't you have friends who've opened a bed-and-breakfast on the island?"

"I do indeed, and it disturbs me. Nick and Lori Bamba were about to convert one of the old fishing lodges there. Then the Pear Island resort hoopla started, and they got sucked into the general promotional scheme. They would have preferred leaving the island in its natural state as much as possible."

"Here comes the food," Arch Riker said with a sigh of relief.

Qwilleran turned to the young man who was serving the entrées.

"How come you're waiting on tables, Derek? I thought you'd been promoted to assistant chef."

"Yeah . . . well . . . I was in charge of French fries and garlic toast, but I can make more money out on the floor, what with tips, you know. Mr. Exbridge—he's one of the owners here—said he might give me a summer job at his new hotel. You can have a lot of fun, working at a resort. I'd like to be captain in the hotel dining room, where they slip you a ten for giving them a good table."

"As captain you'd be outstanding," Qwilleran said. Derek Cuttlebrink was six-feet-eight and still growing.

Polly asked him, "Now that Pickax is getting a community college, do you think you might further your education?"

"If they're gonna teach ecology, maybe I will. I've met this girl, you know, and she's into ecology pretty heavy."

Qwilleran asked, "Is she the girl who owns the blue nylon tent?"

"Yeah, we went camping last summer. I learned a lot . . . Anything else you guys want here?"

When Derek had ambled away, Riker muttered, "When will his consumption of French fries and hot dogs start nourishing his brain instead of his arms and legs?"

"Give him a break. He's smarter than you think," Qwilleran replied.

The meal was untainted by any further argument about Breakfast Island. The Rikers described the new addition to their beach house on the sand dune near Mooseville. Polly announced that her old college roommate had invited her to visit Oregon. Qwilleran, when pressed, said he might do some free-lance writing during the summer.

In pleased surprise, Polly asked, "Do you have something important in mind, dear?" As a librarian, she entertained a perennial hope that Qwilleran would write a literary masterpiece. Although the two of them had a warm and understanding relationship, this particular aspiration was hers, not his. Whenever she launched her favorite theme, he found a way to tease her.

"Yes . . . I'm thinking . . . of a project," he said soberly. "I may undertake to write . . . cat opera for TV. How's this for a scenario? . . . In the first episode we've left Fluffy and Ting Foy hissing at each other, after an unidentified male has approached her and caused Ting Foy to make a big tail. Today's episode starts with a long shot of Fluffy and Ting Foy at their feeding station, gobbling their food amicably. We zoom in on the empty plate and the wash-up ritual, frontal exposures only. Then . . . close-up of a cuckoo clock. (Sound of cuckooing.) Ting Foy leaves the scene. (Sound of scratching in litter box.) Cut to female, sitting on her brisket, meditating. She turns her head. She hears something! She reacts anxiously. Has her mysterious lover returned? Will Ting Foy come back from the litter box? Why is he taking so long? What will happen when the two males meet? . . . Tune in tomorrow, same time."

Riker guffawed. "This has great sponsorship potential, Qwill: catfood, cat litter, flea collars . . ."

Mildred giggled, and Polly smiled indulgently. "Very amusing, Qwill dear, but I wish you'd apply your talents to belles lettres."

"I know my limitations," he said. "I'm a hack journalist, but a *good* hack journalist: nosy, aggressive, suspicious, cynical—"

"Please, Qwill!" Polly remonstrated. "We appreciate a little nonsense, but let's not be totally absurd."

Across the table the newlyweds gazed at each other in middle-aged bliss. They were old enough to have grandchildren but young enough to hold hands under the tablecloth. Both had survived marital upheavals, but now the easygoing publisher had married the warm-hearted Mildred Hanstable, who taught art and homemaking skills in the public schools. She also wrote the food column for the *Moose County Something*. She was noticeably overweight, but so was her bridegroom.

For this occasion Mildred had baked a chocolate cake, and she suggested having dessert and coffee at their beach house. The new addition had doubled the size of the little yellow cottage, and an enlarged deck overlooked the lake. Somewhere out there was Breakfast and/or Pear Island.

The interior of the beach house had undergone some changes, too, since their marriage. The handmade quilts that previously muffled the walls and furniture had been removed, and the interior was light and airy with splashes of bright yellow. The focal point was a Japanese screen from the VanBrook estate, a wedding gift from Qwilleran.

Riker said, "It's hard to find a builder for a small job, but Don Exbridge sent one of his crackerjack construction crews, and they built our new wing in a jiffy. Charged only for labor and materials."

A black-and-white cat with rakish markings walked inquisitively into their midst and was introduced as Toulouse. He went directly to Qwilleran and had his ears scratched.

"We wanted a purebred," said Mildred, "but Toulouse came to our door one day and just moved in."

"His coloring is perfect with all the yellow in the house," Polly remarked.

"Do you think I've used too much? It's my favorite color, and I tend to overdo it."

"Not at all. It makes a very spirited and happy ambiance. It reflects your new lifestyle."

Riker said, "Toulouse is a nice cat, but he has one bad habit. He pounces on the kitchen counter when Mildred is cooking and steals a shrimp or a pork chop, right from under her nose. When I lived Down Below, we had a cat who was a counter-pouncer, and we cured his habit with a spray bottle of water. We had a damp pet for a couple of weeks (that's spelled d-a-m-p), but he got the message and was a model of propriety for the rest of his life—except when we weren't looking."

The evening ended earlier than usual, because Polly was working the next day. No one else had any Saturday commitments. Riker, following his recent marriage, no longer spent seven days a week at the office, and Qwilleran's life was unstructured, except for feeding and brushing the Siamese and servicing their commode. "My self-image," he liked to say, "was formerly that of a journalist; now I perceive myself as handservant to a pair of cats—also tailservant."

He and Polly drove back to Pickax, where she had an apartment on Goodwinter Boulevard, not far from his converted apple barn. As soon as they pulled away from the beach house he popped the question: "What's all this about going to Oregon? You never told me."

"I'm sorry, dear. My old roommate phoned just before you picked me up, and the invitation was so unexpected, I hardly knew how to decide. But I have two weeks more of vacation time, and I've never seen Oregon. They say it's a beautiful state."

"Hmmm," Qwilleran murmured as he considered all the aspects of this sudden decision. Once she had gone to England alone and had become quite ill. Once she had gone to Lockmaster for a weekend and had met another man. At length he asked, "Shall I feed Bootsie while you're away?"

"That's kind of you to offer, Qwill, but he really needs a live-in companion for that length of time. My sister-in-law will be happy to move in. When I return, we should think seriously about spending a weekend on the island at an interesting bed-and-breakfast."

"A weekend of inhaling fudge fumes could be hazardous to our health," he objected. "It would be safer to fly down to Minneapolis with the Rikers. You and Mildred could go shopping, and Arch and I could see a ballgame." He stroked his moustache in indecision, wondering how much to tell her. He had an uneasiness about the present situation that was rooted in the old days, when he and Riker worked for large newspapers Down Below. They kept a punctilious distance from advertisers, lobbyists, and politicians as a matter of policy. Now, Riker was getting too chummy with Don Exbridge. XYZ Enterprises was a heavy advertiser in the *Moose County Something;* Exbridge had lent the Rikers a cottage for their honeymoon; and he had expedited the building of an addition to their beach house.

To Qwilleran it looked bad. And yet, he tried to tell himself, this was a small town, and everything was different. There were fewer people, and they were constantly thrown together at churches, fraternal lodges, business organizations, and country clubs. They were all on first-name terms and mutually supportive. And there were times when they covered up for each other. He had met Don Exbridge socially and at the Pickax Boosters Club and found him a hearty, likable man, ever ready with a handshake and a compliment. His cheerful face always looked scrubbed and polished; so did the top of his head, having only a fringe of brown hair over his ears. Exbridge was the idea man for the XYZ firm, and he said his cranium could sprout either ideas or hair but not both.

Polly said, "You're quiet tonight. Did you have a good time? You look wonderful—ten years younger than your age." Under his blazer he was wearing her birthday gift—a boldly striped shirt with white collar and a patterned tie.

"Thanks. You're looking pretty spiffy yourself. I'm glad to see you wearing bright colors. I assume it means you're happy."

"You know I'm happy, dear—happier than I've ever been in my life! . . . What did you think of Mildred's decorating?"

"I'm glad she got rid of all those quilts. The yellow's okay, I guess."

They turned into Goodwinter Boulevard, an avenue of old stone mansions that would soon be the campus of the new community college. The Klingenschoen Foundation had bought the property and donated it to the city. Currently there was some debate as to whether the institution should be named after the Goodwinters, who had founded the city, or after the original Klingenschoen, who was a rascally old saloonkeeper. Polly's apartment occupied a carriage house behind one of the mansions—within walking distance of the public library—and she was assured of a leasehold.

"Things will get lively here when the college opens," Qwilleran reminded her.

"That's all right. I like having young people around," she said, adding slyly, "Would you like to come upstairs and say goodnight to Boot-sie?"

Afterward, driving home to his barn, Qwilleran considered the hazards of letting Polly out of his sight for two weeks. She was a perfect companion for him, being a loving, attractive, intelligent woman of his own age, with a gentle voice that never ceased to thrill him.

Anything could happen in Oregon, he told himself as he turned on the car radio. After the usual Friday night rundown on the soccer game between Moose County and Lockmaster, the WPKX announcer said:

"Another serious incident has occurred at the Pear Island Hotel, the second in less than a week. An adult male was found drowned in the hotel pool at eleven-fifteen this evening. The name of the victim is being withheld, but police say he was not a resident of Moose County. This incident follows on the heels of the food poisoning that caused fifteen hotel guests to become ill, three of them critically. Authorities have given the cause as contaminated chicken."

As soon as Qwilleran reached the barn, he telephoned Riker. "Did you hear the midnight news?"

"Damn shame!" said the publisher. "The island's been getting so much national coverage that the media will pounce on these accidents with perverse glee! What concerns me is the effect the bad publicity will have on the hotel and other businesses. They've gambled a helluva lot of money on these projects."

"Do you really think the incidents are accidents?" Qwilleran asked pointedly.

"Here we go again! With your mind-set, everything's foul play," Riker retorted. "Wait a minute. Mildred's trying to tell me some-thing." After a pause he came back on the line. "She wishes you'd reconsider the idea of a weekend on the island—the four of us—when Polly returns from vacation. She thinks it would be fun."

"Well . . . you know, Arch . . . I don't go for resorts or cruises or anything like that."

"I know. You like working vacations. Well, sleep on the idea any-way. It would please the girls . . . and since you're such a worka-holic, how about writing three columns a week instead of two during the summer? Staff members will be taking vacations, and we'll be short-handed."

"Steer them away from Pear Island resort," Qwilleran said. "I have a hunch the ancient gods of the island are frowning."

# Two

The morning after the drowning in the hotel pool, Qwilleran was roused from sleep at an early hour by the ringing of the telephone. After a glance at his watch, he answered gruffly.

"Sorry to call so early," said a familiar voice, "but I need to see you about something."

"Where are you?"

"In Mooseville, but I can be in Pickax in half an hour."

"Come on down," Qwilleran said curtly. Then, grumbling to himself, he pressed the button on the computerized coffeemaker, threw on some clothes, and ran a wet comb through his hair. There was no sound from the loft, where the Siamese had their private quarters, so he decided to let sleeping cats lie. His mind was on Nick Bamba, who had phoned so urgently.

In Qwilleran's book, Nick and Lori were an admirable young couple. She had been postmaster in Mooseville until she retired to raise a family. Nick was head engineer at the state prison. It had been their dream to own and operate a bed-and-breakfast, in the hope that he could quit his well-paying but demoralizing job. Thanks to a low-interest loan from the Klingenschoen Foundation, they had bought an old fishing lodge on Breakfast Island. Before they could open their inn, however, they found themselves involved in the wholesale commercialization of the primitive island.

As Qwilleran understood its history, the island had been populated for generations by the descendents of shipwrecked sailors and travelers. According to popular legend, some of the early castaways on this deserted shore turned to piracy in order to survive, luring other ships onto the rocks to be looted. That was only hearsay, however; historians had found no proof. One fact was known: Subsequent generations lived in privation, hauling nets in summer and living on salt-dried fish and wild rabbits in winter, eked out by goat's milk and whatever would grow in the rocky, sandy terrain. Through the years, many islanders had moved to the mainland, but those who remained were independent and fiercely proud of their heritage. This much Qwilleran had learned from Homer Tibbitt, the Moose County historian.

In the 1920s, according to Tibbitt, affluent families from Down Below discovered the island. Railroad czars, mercantile kings, beer barons, and meat-packing tycoons were attracted by the sport fishing, healthful atmosphere, and utter seclusion. They built fishing lodges on the west beach—rustic pavilions large enough to accommodate their families, guests, and servants. Native islanders did the menial work for them, and for a while local goat cheese was all the rage at parties on the west beach. Then came the 1929 Stock Market Crash, and suddenly there were no more yachts moored offshore, no gin and badminton parties on the terraces. Not until after World War II did descendents of the czars and tycoons return to the family lodges to escape allergies and the stress of high-tech life Down Below.

Meanwhile, the islanders clung to their simple pioneer lifestyle. Once, when Qwilleran had visited the south end of the island with boating friends, it appeared deserted except for two gaunt old men who materialized out of the woods and stared at them with brooding hostility. That was several years before XYZ Enterprises moved in with their planners and promoters.

Nick Bamba's pickup truck pulled into the barnyard exactly on schedule, and a young man with a boat captain's cap on his curly black hair walked into the barn. With his flashing black eyes roving about the interior, he said what he always said: "Man! What a B-and-B you could make out of this baby!"

It was an octagonal apple barn, well over a hundred years old, with fieldstone foundation, shingled siding, and windows of various shapes and sizes. The interior was open to the roof, four stories overhead, and a ramp spiraled around the walls, connecting the rooms on three upper levels. On the main floor a large white fireplace cube in dead center divided the open space into areas for lounging, dining, and food preparation. In Qwilleran's case this meant opening cans, thawing frozen dinners, and pressing the button on the coffeemaker.

He poured mugs of coffee and ushered his guest into the lounge. Ordinarily Nick radiated vitality; today he looked tired, overworked, and dispirited. To open the conversation on a comfortable note Qwilleran asked him, "Is your entire family on the island?"

The young man recited in a monotone: "Jason is staying with my mother in Mooseville until school's out. I take him to the island for weekends. The two young ones are with Lori at the inn. So are the cats. We have five now, one pregnant. The island is overrun with feral cats, so ours don't go out, but they have the run of the inn. We also have a rent-a-cat service for guests who'd like a cat in their room overnight—just a gimmick—no extra charge."

"Can Lori manage the inn and take care of two youngsters?"

"She employs island women to help."

"I hope you're charging enough to make your venture worthwhile."

"Well, Don Exbridge advised us on rates. We're not cheap, but we're competitive."

"How many rooms?"

"Seven rooms, two suites, and five housekeeping cottages."

Nick's terse replies reflected his nervousness, so Qwilleran said, "You wanted to see me about something urgent."

"Did you hear about the drowning last night?"

"Only briefly, on the air. What were the circumstances? Do you know?"

"He'd been drinking in the hotel bar. They'll have to lock the pool gates after a certain hour or provide better security. But the worst thing was the food poisoning! Contaminated chicken brought in from the mainland! All food has to come by boat."

"Did the first incident affect business?" Qwilleran asked.

"Sure did! Sunday papers around the country had carried all kinds of publicity, so it was hot news when fifteen guests were struck down. Rotten timing! The hotel had wholesale cancellations right away. We had a honeymoon couple booked for the bridal suite in July, and they canceled."

"Sorry to hear that."

Nick lapsed into rueful silence while Qwilleran refilled the mugs. Then he said, "We had a bummer ourselves last Tuesday."

"What happened? I didn't hear about it."

"One of our front steps caved in, and a guest fell and broke a rib.

An old man. He was airlifted to the hospital on the mainland. It wasn't a big enough disaster to make the headlines, but I worry just the same."

"Are you afraid of being sued? Who was the victim?"

"A retired clergyman from Indiana. We're not worried about a lawsuit. He's not the type who'd take advantage of our insurance company. We're paying his medical expenses and giving him free rent, but . . . Qwill, there was nothing wrong with those steps! I swear! The building was thoroughly inspected before they gave us a license!"

Qwilleran patted his moustache in self-congratulation; it was just as he had guessed. "Are you suggesting sabotage, Nick?"

"Well, you know how my mind works, after eight years of working at the prison. I can't help suspecting dirty tricks. Three incidents right after the grand opening of the resort! It looks fishy to me! How about you?"

Qwilleran was inclined to agree. A tingling on his upper lip, which was the source of all his hunches, suggested an organized plot to embarrass, discredit, and possibly ruin the Pear Island resort. "Do you have any clues?" he asked.

"Well, this may sound crazy, and I wouldn't tell anyone but you." Nick leaned forward in his chair. "The island is getting a bunch of day-trippers from Lockmaster—dudes swaggering up and down the waterfront in high-heeled boots. They wear Lockmaster T-shirts and baseball caps with six-inch bills and raunchy slogans. They're just looking for trouble."

The enmity between Moose County and the relatively rich county to the south was well known. Violence often broke out at soccer games. Troublemakers periodically invented rumors of border incidents and then took vigilante revenge. Even mature citizens of Lockmaster took pleasure in vaunting their superiority, boasting about their rich horse farms, good schools, winning athletic teams, and fine restaurants. That was before Qwilleran's fluke inheritance. After that, the Klingenschoen millions began improving the quality of life in Moose County. Besides building a better airport and giving the high school an Olympic-size swimming pool, Klingenschoen money was luring the best teachers, physicians, barbers, and TV repairmen from Lockmaster. And now . . . Moose County had the Pear Island resort —an economic plum pudding, sauced with the sweet taste of national publicity.

Nick went on with his story: "Last Sunday three of these goons were actually sitting on our porch swings at the inn, smoking God-knows-what. I pointed to the No Smoking sign and asked if they were taught to read in Lockmaster. They gave me the finger and went on puffing, so I called Island Security. The county doesn't supply much police protection—Don Exbridge is lobbying for more—so we hire our own weekend security guys. They're uniformed like Canadian Mounties and look pretty impressive when they ride up on horses. So the hoods took off without any more trouble, but . . . it makes me wonder, you know?"

"Have you mentioned your suspicions to Exbridge?"

"Well, he's not on the island weekends, and I can't be there during the week. Besides, I'd feel stupid talking to him when I don't have anything but a gut feeling. What I wish, Qwill, is that you'd go to the island and snoop around. You're good at that kind of thing. You might come up with some evidence, or at least a clue. You could stay in one of our cottages. Bring the cats."

Qwilleran had an unbridled curiosity and a natural urge to find answers to questions. Also, he had spent years as a crime reporter Down Below. "Hmmm," he mused, tempted by the prospect of snooping.

Nick said, "It's really nice on the island, and you'd like the food. Lori's breakfasts are super; everybody says so. And the hotel has a chef from New Orleans."

"New Orleans?" Qwilleran repeated with growing interest. Food often figured in his decision making. "If I were to go over there, when would you suggest—?"

"Soon as possible. I have to bring Jason back here tomorrow afternoon, and I could ferry you to the island after that. I have my own boat now. If you meet me at the dock in Mooseville around four o'clock, we'll reach the island in plenty of time for you to get settled and go to the hotel for a good dinner."

"But no chicken!" Qwilleran quipped.

When Nick said goodbye and jumped into his pickup, there was more buoyancy in his attitude than when he arrived. It was still early, but Qwilleran climbed the ramp to release the Siamese from their loft apartment. Surprised at the early reveille, they staggered out of the room, yawning and stretching and looking glassy-eyed.

"Breakfast!" he announced, and they hightailed it into the kitchen, bumping into each other in their eagerness. "What would you two carnivores like to eat this morning? I can offer you a succulent rack of lamb from the famous kitchen of the Old Stone Mill, minced by hand

and finished with a delicate sauce of meat juices." He liked to talk to them in a declamatory voice when he was in a good mood, and the louder his voice, the more excited they became, prancing in circles and figure eights and yowling with ever-increasing volume. The noise stopped abruptly when he placed the plate on the floor, and they attacked it with quivering intensity.

They were seal-point Siamese with blue eyes, sleek bodies, and light fawn fur shading into dark brown. Yum Yum was a dainty minx with a piquant expression and winning ways. Koko, whose real name was Kao K'o Kung, was the noble male with imperial manner and inscrutable gaze. He was the quintessential Siamese—with some additional talents that were not in the breeders' manual.

Qwilleran watched them devour their breakfast, while pondering his next step: how to break the news to Arch Riker without losing face. After blasting the Pear Island resort all evening, he was now joining the enemy for two weeks, that being the length of Polly's vacation.

He waited until eight o'clock and then telephoned the Rikers' beach house. "Great party last night, Arch! Did I make myself a bore?"

"What do you mean?"

"My tirade against the Pear Island resort must have been somewhat tiresome. Anyway, I'd like to make amends."

"Uh-oh! What's the catch?" asked the man who had known Qwilleran since kindergarten. Their friendship had survived almost half a century of confiding, bantering, arguing, leg-pulling, rib-poking, and caring. "I suspect you have devious intentions."

"Well, to tell the truth, Arch, I'm still ticked off about the commercial rape of Breakfast Island, but—without playing politics—I'm willing to go there for a couple of weeks and write about island history, customs, and legends. I'd call it 'The Other Side of the Island.' How does it sound?"

"I'll tell you how it sounds, you dirty rat! It sounds as if Polly is going out of town for two weeks, and you're desperate for something to occupy your time! I can always read your hand; I've known you too long to fall for a fast shuffle."

"Will you okay my expense account?" Qwilleran asked to taunt him.

There was a moment of silence on the line. Riker was editor and publisher of the *Moose County Something,* but the Klingenschoen Foundation owned it. "Okay, go ahead," Riker said. "But it had better be good."

"I'll be staying at the Bambas' B-and-B. I don't know the phone number, but they call it the Domino Inn."

After that hurdle was cleared, the rest was easy. Qwilleran called his janitor, Mr. O'Dell, who said, "Faith an" you'll not catch me settin' foot on that island no more! What they're doin' is ag'in Auld Mither Nature, it is. Nothin' good'll come of it, I'm thinkin'."

Qwilleran also gave instructions to his secretarial service to forward mail in care of General Delivery at Pear Island—but only letters postmarked Oregon.

Finally, he phoned Andrew Brodie at home on Saturday evening. Brodie was chief of police in Pickax—a towering, swaggering Scot who played the bagpipe at weddings and funerals. When Mrs. Brodie answered, the inevitable television audio could be heard blatting in the background, and the chief came on the line with the gruffness of a televiewer whose program has been interrupted.

Amiably, Qwilleran opened with, "Sorry to snatch you away from your favorite cop series."

"Are you kidding? I'm watching a nature program. Terrible what's happening to the rain forest! Last week it was black bears, and before that, oil spills! What's on your mind? Want me to pipe at your wedding to Polly? For you two I'll do it for free."

"Polly's going to Oregon and may never return, and I'm going to so-called Pear Island and may never return. They say the fudge fumes are potentially lethal."

"What d'you want to go there for? You won't like what they've done to our Breakfast Island," Brodie predicted.

"Mainly I'm going to write about island life for the 'Qwill Pen' column," Qwilleran explained glibly, "but I might do a little amateur sleuthing on the side. They've had some incidents that raise questions —three in a little over a week."

"I only heard about two—the food poisoning and the drowning. The island is the sheriff's jurisdiction, and he's welcome to it. He'll have his hands full this summer, mark my word. All those tourists from Down Below—no good! No good!"

"How come we never hear any results of the sheriff's investigations, Andy?"

"If it's a big case, he calls in the troopers. If it isn't . . . well . . . no comment. Are you taking your smart cat with you? He'll show the sheriff's department a thing or two."

"I'm taking both cats. My barn will be unoccupied for two weeks, but Mr. O'Dell has the key and will check it regularly."

"We'll keep an eye on it, too," said the chief.

Brodie was one of the few persons who knew about Koko's investigative abilities. All cats are inquisitive; all cats are endowed with six senses, but Kao K'o Kung had more than the usual feline quota. His unique sensory perception told him when something was wrong. In many cases he knew what had happened, and in some cases he knew what was going to happen. The black nose quivered, the brown ears twitched, the blue eyes stared into space, and the whiskers curled when Koko was getting vibrations.

It was the whisker factor that tuned into the unknowable, Qwilleran had decided. In fact, his own moustache bristled and his upper lip tingled when he suspected malfeasance. These hunches, coupled with his innate curiosity, often led Qwilleran into situations that were none of his business. The fate of Breakfast Island was none of his business, yet he felt irresistibly drawn to the island, and he patted his moustache frequently.

Qwilleran's usual Saturday night dinnerdate with Polly was canceled, because she had to pack for her trip, but he drove her to the airport Sunday morning, without mentioning his own forthcoming excursion; he wanted to avoid explaining. "I'll miss you," he said, a declaration that was true and required no dissembling. "I suppose you're taking your binoculars and birdbook."

"They were the first things I packed," she said joyously. "It would be a thrill to add some Pacific species to my lifelist. I'd love to see a puffin bird. My college roommate lives on the shore and is quite knowledgeable about waterfowl."

"Is she—or he—also a librarian?"

Polly patted his knee affectionately. "There were no coed dormitories when I went to the university, dear. She's a residential architect, and I'm going to show her the snapshots of your barn renovation. She'll be greatly impressed. And what will you do while I'm away? Perhaps I shouldn't ask," she said coyly.

"I'll think of something," he said, "but life will be dull and devoid of pleasure and excitement."

"Oh, Qwill! Am I supposed to cry? Or laugh?"

After Polly had boarded the shuttle plane to Minneapolis, he went home to pack his own luggage. It was June, and the temperature was ideal in Moose County, but an island in the middle of the lake could have unpredictable weather. He packed sweaters and a light jacket as well as shorts and sandals. Not knowing how formal the hotel dining room might be, he packed good shirts and a summer blazer as well as knockabout clothing. He packed his typewriter, radio, tape recorder, and a couple of books from his secondhand collection of classics: Thoreau's *Walden* and Anatole France's *Penguin Island.* They seemed appropriate.

The Siamese watched with concern as a bag of cat litter and some canned delicacies went into a carton. Then the cagelike carrier was brought from the broom closet, and Yum Yum took flight. Qwilleran made a grab for her, but she slithered out of his grasp and escaped between his legs. The chase led up the ramp and across the balconies until he trapped her in the guestroom shower. "Come on, sweetheart," he said, lifting her gently, and she went limp.

Back on the main floor he put her in the carrier and announced, "All aboard for Breakfast Island!"

"Yow!" said Koko, and he jumped into the carrier. That was unusual. Ordinarily he disliked a change of address. Qwilleran thought, Does he know there's sabotage on the island? Or does he recognize the word 'breakfast'?

With the luggage stowed in the trunk of his sedan, and with the cat carrier on the backseat, Qwilleran drove north to Mooseville—past landmarks that had figured prominently in his recent life: the Dimsdale Diner, Ittibittiwassee Road, the turkey farm (under new management), the extensive grounds of the federal prison, and the significant letter K on a post.

Nick Bamba was waiting for him at the municipal pier, where a boat named *Double-Six* was bobbing lazily in the dock, but the young man's glum expression caused Qwilleran to ask, "Is everything all right?"

"Another incident!" Nick said. "Just this afternoon! A cabin cruiser blew up at the Pear Island marina. Owner killed."

"Any idea what caused it?"

"Well, he'd just bought this boat—a neat craft only three years old —and filled up at the marina gas pump. The manager thinks he didn't blow out the fumes before starting the engine."

"Inexperienced boater?" Qwilleran asked.

"Looks like it. When I bought this boat, I took a course in marine safety, but the majority of boaters don't bother. It's a bad mistake."

"Who owns the marina?"

"XYZ owns everything on the south beach. There was some damage to the pier and nearby craft, but luckily most boaters were out in the lake, fishing. What depresses me, Qwill, is that the guy was a family man. He came over on the ferry to close the deal on the boat. He paid cash for it and was going back to the mainland to pick up his wife and kids."

"A sad situation," Qwilleran said.

"What makes me sick," Nick said, "is the thought that . . . maybe it wasn't an accident!"

# Three

As they stowed the luggage and the cat carrier on the deck of the *Double-Six,* Nick Bamba said, "It's great of you to do this, Qwill. How long can you stay?"

"A couple of weeks. Officially I'll be researching fresh material for the "Qwill Pen" column."

"You're our guest, you know. Stay as long as you want."

"I appreciate the invitation, but let the newspaper foot the bill. It'll look better, and they can afford it."

As the pilot carried aboard the turkey roaster that had no handles, he said, "What's this for? Are you gonna do some serious cooking? I know the cats are crazy about turkey, but the cottage has all the pots and pans you'll need—or you can borrow from Lori's kitchen."

"That's the cats' commode," Qwilleran said in an offhand way.

"Well, I've gotta say I've never seen one like it, and I've seen a lot of cat potties."

"It's practical."

"I hope Koko and Yum Yum are good sailors."

"They've never had a boat ride, as I recall," said Qwilleran. "I'll throw my jacket over their coop in case there's too much breeze or spray from the wake. The water looks fairly choppy. I hope it won't be a bumpy ride. I don't worry about Koko, but the little one has a delicate stomach."

There was no need to worry about either of them. For the rest of the journey the Siamese were beguiled by the pleasures of the nose, raising their heads like beached seals and sniffing eagerly. During the voyage they registered the assorted smells of lake air, marine life, aquatic weeds, seagulls, and petroleum fumes. Arriving at the island they detected pails of bait, crates of fish, horses, fudge, and newness everywhere: new piers, new hotel, new shops selling new merchandise, new black-top paving, and new bicycles. Also assaulting their inquiring noses was a heady bouquet emanating from the milling mass of tourists—young and old, teen and preteen, washed and unwashed, healthy and unhealthy, tipsy and sober. Perhaps Koko's personal radar picked up friendly and unfriendly, as well, or even innocent and guilty.

As for Qwilleran, he found the island disturbingly different from the primitive scene he remembered. He had seen the photographs in the newspaper, but experiencing the altered environment was entirely unreal. The lakefront was fringed with the masts of sailboats and the superstructures of deepwater trolling vessels. A ferryboat, halfway between a tug and a barge, was unloading vacationers with luggage, and another was returning to the mainland carrying day-trippers with sunburn. Overlooking the marina was the rustic facade of the new Pear Island Hotel, artfully stained to look fifty years old. It was three stories high and a city-block long, with a porch running the entire length. Much had been said in the national publicity about the long porch and its fifty rocking chairs. Behind the hotel, making a dark-green backdrop, were tall firs and giant oaks that had been there before the first castaways were stranded on the shore.

Qwilleran thought, This is the forest primeval, and the pines and the hemlocks are murmuring "Ye gods! Wha' happened?"

The hotel was flanked by rows of rustic storefronts, each with a hitching post. Window-shoppers strolled along wooden sidewalks called "the boardwalk" in the publicity releases.

Nick said, "This is what the XYZ people call downtown."

"It resembles a movie set," Qwilleran remarked. "At least they had the good taste not to paint yellow lines on the black-top."

"Right! Don Exbridge wants to keep everything as natural as possible. The only motor vehicles permitted are police, ambulance, and fire, and they can't use sirens because of the horses. They use beepers."

There was indeed a unique hush along the waterfront, resulting from the absence of combustion engines—just a murmur of voices, the

clop-clop of hooves, and the screams of seagulls and excited youngsters.

Nick hailed a horse-drawn conveyance, loaded the luggage, and said
"Domino Inn" to the old man hunched sullenly over the reins. Without answering, he shook the reins, and the horse moved forward.

"What prompted the name of your inn?" Qwilleran asked.

"Well, it was a private lodge in the Twenties, and the family that
owned it was nuts about dominoes. We bought it completely fur-
nished, including a couple-dozen sets of dominoes. My name is really
Dominic, you know, so Lori thought we were destined to own the
place and call it the Domino Inn. It's different, anyway."

The downtown pavement and boardwalk ended, and the road became a dusty mix of sand, gravel, and weeds. "This is called West
Beach Road," Nick went on. "It should be sprayed with oil, but the
county is tight-fisted. They're getting all the new tax money, but they
don't want to supply any services." He waved to a mounted security
officer in red coat and stiff-brimmed hat. "We get spectacular sunsets
on the west beach. Farther up the road is the exclusive Grand Island
Club, where the rich folks have always had their clubhouse, private
marina, and big summer estates. Where we are, the lodges are outside
the Golden Curtain, as it's called, and they've been rezoned commercial. There are three B-and-Bs. We get a nice class of people at our
inn— quiet—very friendly. Do you play dominoes?"

"No!" Qwilleran replied promptly and with resolve.

"I know you like exercise. We have a sandy beach for walking, or
you can rent a bike and pedal up to Lighthouse Point. It's all uphill,
but is it great coasting down! Try it! There's also a nature trail through
the woods. If you like hunting for agates, go to the public beach on the
other side of the island. It's all pebbles, no sand."

"Can you keep the public off this beach? I thought the law had been
changed in this state."

"The public-access ordinance applies only to new owners like us,"
Nick explained. "Members of the Grand Island Club come under a
grandfather clause, or so they say. I don't know how legal it is, but
they get away with it."

"Where do the natives live?"

"In Piratetown, back in the woods, very isolated. Tourists are discouraged from going there."

There were fewer vehicles, cyclists, and joggers on West Beach
Road than Qwilleran expected, leading him to ask, "How's business?"

"Well, it started off with a bang, but it's slowing down. Lori says people are busy with weddings and graduations in June. It'll pick up in July. We hope. We don't know, yet, how harmful the negative publicity is going to be."

They passed six hikers with oversize backpacks, trudging single-file on their way to the ferry, and Nick said they had been hang gliding on the sand dune near the lighthouse.

The Siamese had been quiet in their carrier, which was on the floor of the wagon, close by Qwilleran's feet, but now there was a rumble of discontent. Before he could give them any soothing reassurances, a two-wheeled horse cab passed them, headed for downtown, and the passenger—a woman in a floppy-brimmed sunhat—waved and gave him a roguish smile. Taken by surprise, he only nodded in her direction.

"Who was that woman?" he asked Nick, although he thought he recognized the white makeup and red hair.

"Who? Where? I didn't notice. I was looking at the backpackers. They've got some healthy-looking girls in that group. I'm not good at names and faces, anyway. Lori says I've got to work on that if I'm gonna be an innkeeper. In my job, people are just numbers."

Qwilleran was hardly listening to the rambling discourse. The red-head was one person whom he actively disliked, and Polly shared his sentiments. Fortunately she was going in the opposite direction, and there was luggage piled in the cab. He allowed himself to wonder what she had been doing at Pear Island; it was hardly her kind of resort. Perhaps she had been a guest behind the Golden Curtain; that was more likely.

They had been ascending gradually after leaving downtown, and now the beach was below them, reached by steps, and the woods loomed on the other side. The road curved in and out along the natural shoreline, and when the wagon rounded a bend and stopped, Qwilleran let out a yelp. "Is that yours, Nick? I don't believe it! Why didn't you tell me?"

"Wanted to surprise you. It's the only one on the island—maybe the only one in the world!"

Domino Inn was a large ungainly building with small windows, completely sided with a patchwork of white birchbark. Qwilleran thought, Why would anyone strip a whole forest of white birches to produce such an eyesore? How could they get away with it? He answered his own question: Because no one cared, back in the Twenties. Then he asked himself, Why would they buy such a thing? Why would the K Foundation finance it?

Misconstruing his silence for awe, Nick said proudly, "I thought you'd be impressed. It was written up in most of the out-of-state publicity."

To Qwilleran it looked vaguely illegal. It looked like a firetrap. It could be, or should be, riddled with termites. Mentally he renamed it the Little Inn of Horrors.

The wagon turned into the driveway and stopped at a flight of wooden steps that led up to a long porch. There were no rocking chairs, but there were porch swings hanging from chains. Immediately the front door flew open, and Lori came bounding down the steps to give Qwilleran a welcoming hug. His former secretary was now an innkeeper and mother of three, but she still wore her long golden hair in girlish braids tied with blue ribbons.

"I could barely wait for you to see it!" she cried with excitement. "Wait till you see the inside! Come on in!"

"If you don't mind," he said, "I'd like to unload the cats first. They might express their emotions in some unacceptable way, if they don't de-coop soon. I'll feed them and then come in to register."

"Do you need catfood? Do you need litter?"

"No, thank you. We're well equipped."

Nick instructed the driver to continue around to the rear and then down the lane to the fourth cottage. The sandy lane was marked with a rustic street sign: PIP COURT. It reminded Qwilleran of a poultry disease and other illnesses, and he inquired about it. The spots on dominoes are called pips, he was told.

The five cottages, hardly larger than garages, were stained a somber brown, and the door of each was painted black with white pips. The fourth cottage was identified with a double-two.

"Yours is called 'Four Pips,' and it's deeper in the woods than the first three. The cats can watch birds and rabbits from the screened porch in back. Here's the key. You go in, and I'll offload everything."

The doorstep was hardly large enough to accommodate a size-twelve shoe, and when Qwilleran unlocked the giant domino, he stepped into the smallest living quarters he had experienced since an army tent. He was a big man, accustomed to living in a four-story barn, and here he was faced with a tiny sitting room, snug bedroom, mini-kitchen, and pocket-size bathroom. True, there was a screened porch, but it was minuscule and rather like a cage. How could he exist in these cramped quarters for two weeks with a pair of active animals?

There was more. Someone had painted the walls white and dressed them up with travel posters. Then someone had gone berserk and camouflaged furniture, bed, and windows with countless yards of fabric in a splashy pattern of giant roses, irises, and ferns.

"How do you like everything?" Nick asked as he looked for places to put the luggage. "Not much extra floor space," he admitted, "and the place gets a little musty when it's closed up." He rushed around opening windows. The kitchenette was new, he said, and the plumbing was new, although it took a while for the water to run hot. The cottages had originally been built for servants.

"Did I hear a gunshot?" Qwilleran asked.

"Just rabbit hunters in the woods. From Piratetown . . . If there's anything else you want, just whistle."

Qwilleran switched on two lamps and mentioned that he could use a higher wattage for reading.

"Will do. And now I've got to take Jason back to the mainland. I'll see you next weekend . . . G'bye, kids," he said to the occupants of the portable cage.

They emerged from the carrier with wary whiskers, their bodies close to the floor and their tails drooping. They sniffed the green indoor-outdoor carpeting. They sniffed the slipcovers critically and backed away. Qwilleran sniffed, too; "musty" was not quite the word for the pervading aroma. He thought it might be the dye in the gaudy slipcovers. They really belonged in the grand ballroom of a hotel in South America, he thought.

Before unpacking, he stripped the rooms of the homey touches that Lori had supplied and put them in drawers: doilies, dried flowers, figurines, and other knickknacks. The Siamese watched him until a knock on the door sent them scuttling under the bed. A small boy stood on the doorstep, holding out a brown paper bag.

"Thank you," Qwilleran said. "Are these my light bulbs?"

The messenger made a long speech that was unintelligible to a middle-aged, childless bachelor. Nevertheless, he made an effort to be sociable. "What's your name, son?"

The boy said something in an alien tongue and then ran back to the inn. In closing the door Qwilleran saw a notice nailed to an inside panel, along with a large No Smoking sign:

WELCOME TO DOMINO INN
For your pleasure, convenience, and
safety we provide the following:

*At the Inn*
Breakfast in the sunroom, 7 to 10 A.M.
Games, puzzles, books, magazines, and newspapers
in the Domino Lounge
Public telephone on the balcony landing
Television in the playroom
Fruit basket in the lounge. Help yourself

*In Your Cottage*
Set of dominoes
Two flashlights
Oil lamps and matches
Umbrella
Mosquito spray
Fire extinguisher
Ear plugs

The notice was signed by the innkeepers, Nick and Lori Bamba, with an exhortation to "have a nice stay."

Sure, Qwilleran thought, cynically anticipating rain, mosquitoes, forest fires, power outages, stray bullets from the woods, and whatever required ear plugs—all this in a rustic strait-jacket with slipcovers like horticultural nightmares. He located the emergency items listed on the door. Then he found the dominoes in a box covered with faded maroon velvet and put them in a desk drawer, out of sight. The drawers were hard to open, possibly because of island dampness; Yum Yum, who had the instincts of a safecracker and a shoplifter, would be frustrated. When she was frustrated, she screamed like a cockatoo; the ear plugs might be useful, after all. Koko was already eying a wall calendar with malice; it had a large photograph of a basset hound and a tear-off page for each month. It was a giveaway from a maker of dogfood.

Before dressing for dinner or even feeding the cats, Qwilleran went to the inn to register. On the way he noted that the five cottages were about fifty feet apart. Five Pips had the window shades drawn. Beyond it, at the end of Pip Court, was the start of a woodland trail that looked inviting. In the front window of Three Pips he could see an elderly couple playing a table game. A pair of state-of-the-art bicycles with helmets hanging from the handlebars were parked in front of Two Pips. One Pip appeared to be empty. At the head of the lane, a large cast-iron farm bell was mounted on a post with a dangling rope and a sign: FOR EMERGENCY ONLY. Three stray cats were scrounging around trash cans at the back door of the inn.

And then Qwilleran mounted the front steps of the inn, entered the lobby, and gazed upward in amazement. The Domino Lounge had a skylight about thirty feet overhead and balcony rooms on all four sides, and the entire structure was supported by four enormous tree trunks. They were almost a yard in diameter. The bark on these monoliths was intact, and the stubby ends of sawed-off branches protruded at intervals.

There were no guests in evidence at that hour, but the same boy who had delivered the light bulbs was sitting on the floor and playing with building blocks of architectural complexity. As soon as he caught sight of the man with a large moustache, he scrambled to his feet and ran to the door marked OFFICE.

A moment later, Lori came hurrying into the lounge. "What do you think of it, Qwill? How do you like it?" She waved both arms at the gigantic tree trunks.

"Words fail me," he said truthfully. "Are you sure they're not cast concrete?"

"They're the real thing—one of the wonders of the world, I think. And I hope you're impressed by the slipcovers." All the furniture in the lounge was covered in the same overscale pattern of roses and irises, but with the three-foot tree trunks, they looked good. "I made them all myself. It took six months. I bought an entire factory closeout for practically nothing."

They were glad to get rid of it, Qwilleran thought.

The boy who had summoned his mother was back again, and he said something to Qwilleran in the same mystifying language.

Lori came to the rescue. "Mitchell wants you to know he saw a flying saucer over the lake last week."

"Good for you, son!"

"Mitchell is four years old, and he's in charge of deliveries and communications. He's very enthusiastic about his job," she said. They went into the office to register. "I hope you like your cottage, Qwill. We also have a bridal suite upstairs, in case you and Polly ever make up your minds."

"We've made up our minds. Polly and I are happily unmarried until death do us part," he said gruffly. Then, pleasantly, he asked, "Who painted the cottage doors like dominoes?"

She raised her right hand. "Guilty! They needed refinishing, so I thought it would be fun to paint them black with white pips. Nick thought I was crazy, but Don Exbridge is pushing the fun ethic. What do you think, Qwill?"

"I think it's crazy . . . and fun. And what is the purpose of the big bell?"

"Oh, that! That's to alert everyone in case of fire. There's a volunteer fire department—Nick's on call weekends—but so far, there's been no alarm—knock on wood."

"Nick mentioned that one of your elderly guests took a tumble on the front steps."

Lori nodded contritely. "I feel terrible about that! Mr. Harding in Three Pips. He was vicar of a small church in Indiana before he retired. He and Mrs. Harding are such a sweet couple. He's back from the hospital now and insists he'll heal faster here than Down Below."

"Who repaired the step?" Qwilleran asked.

"Well, that was last Tuesday. Nick wasn't here, so I had to find an islander to fix it—an old man. He looked a hundred years old, but he did a good job and didn't charge too much."

"Did he say what had happened to the step?"

"They're not very communicative—these islanders—but he said the nails were rusty. He reinforced the whole flight with new nails and braces of some kind."

"And yet, the county inspector okayed the building before you opened for business," Qwilleran said.

"That's right. It makes you wonder how good the inspection was. The county commissioners, you know, were pushing to get the resort open by mid-May, because they wanted those tax dollars. I'll bet they told the inspectors not to be too fussy."

Qwilleran glanced at his watch. "Do I need a reservation for dinner at the hotel? Should I wear a coat and tie?"

"Heavens, no! Everything's informal, but I'll call the hotel and tell them you're coming. They'll put out the red carpet for the popular columnist from the *Moose County Something.*"

"No! Not that!" he protested. "I'm keeping a low profile during this visit."

"Okay. Shall I call a horse cab?"

"I think not. I'd like to walk. But thanks just the same."

"Walk on the edge of the road," Lori advised. "The horses, you know."

On the way back to the cottage to feed the cats and change into a fresh club shirt, Qwilleran met the elderly couple from Three Pips. "Don't miss the sunset tonight," said the man, who wore a black French beret at a jaunty angle. "We always order a special performance for a new guest."

Qwilleran could see the Siamese on the back porch, and he walked around to talk to them through the screen. "Are you fellow travelers ready for a can of boned chicken imported from Pickax?"

There were two chairs on the porch, one more comfortable than the other, and with catly instinct they had chosen the better of the two. They were sitting there calmly—too calmly. It meant that one or both had committed some small misdemeanor of which they were proud. He knew them so well!

Unlocking the front door, he walked into the scene of the crime. The desktop was littered with scraps of paper, and other bits were strewn about the floor. One said: Tuesday. Others were blank squares with numbers in the upper left-hand corner. Someone had attacked the wall calendar hanging above the desk. The glossy, full-color photo of a basset hound and the name of the dogfood manufacturer were still intact, but the month of June had been ripped off piece by piece, or day by day. It was now July in Four Pips.

"Which one of you incorrigible miscreants vandalized this calendar?" he shouted toward the porch. They paid no attention, being occupied with woodland sights and sounds.

He knew the culprit; Koko was the paper shredder in the family, but only when he had a reason. Did he think he could accelerate the passage of time by canceling the month of June? Did he want to get out of this Domino Dump and go home? "Clever thinking," Qwilleran called out to him, "but unfortunately it doesn't work that way."

# Four

Days were long in June and even longer in the north country. The sun was still high in the sky as Qwilleran walked downtown for his first dinner at the Pear Island Hotel. On the way, he passed the row of rustic shops on the boardwalk. Their standardized signs were computer-carved from weathered wood. A single generic label identified each establishment: SOUVENIRS, TEA ROOM, ANTIQUES, PIZZA, T-SHIRTS and, of course, FUDGE. He saw something in the window of the antique shop that he liked, but the door was locked, even though the sign in the window said Open. The T-shirt studio offered tie-dyes in garish colors, sweats and tees with slogans printed to order, and the official resort T-shirt with a large blushing pear, the size of a watermelon. Boaters, teens, retirees, couples walking hand in hand, and parents with their broods wandered aimlessly up and down the boardwalk or stood in line at the fudge shop. On the hotel porch they rocked in the fifty rocking chairs, and a few were eating take-outs from the pizza parlor.

The hotel lobby burst upon the senses as a celebration of piracy. A mural depicted swashbuckling pirates with chests of gold. Banners hanging from the ceiling had the skull-and-crossbones on a field of black. The reservation clerks wore striped shirts, red head bandanas, and a gold hoop in one ear. Qwilleran consulted the directory. There was a bar named the Buccaneer Den. The two dining areas were the Corsair Room and Smugglers' Cove. Glass doors led to the Pirates'

Hole, a large swimming pool rimmed with sun lounges and umbrella tables. Youngsters splashed and squealed at the shallow end of the pool, while adults sipped drinks around the rim. The latter kept the barhops busy—young men and women wearing black T-shirts with the pirate insigne.

Qwilleran ambled into the Buccaneer Den and sat at the bar. Spotlighted on the backbar was a chest of gold coins and the words of a sea chantey: *Fifteen men on a dead man's chest! Yo ho ho and a bottle of rum!* He was comfortable on a bar stool. Before circumstances had changed his habits and hobbies, he had leaned on press club bars all around the country and had developed a barfly's savoir faire that was instantly recognized by the professionals pouring drinks. There were three of them behind the bar in the Buccaneer Den, all wearing the skull-and-crossbones.

He signaled the one who appeared to be in charge and asked, "Is it against the law to order a Bloody Mary without any booze?"

"How hot?" asked the man with expressionless face and voice. He reached for a glass.

"Three-alarm fire." Qwilleran counted the dashes of hot sauce going into the tomato juice, took a critical sip, and nodded his approval. The bartender leaned against the backbar with arms folded, and that was Qwilleran's cue to say, "You run a smooth operation here."

"Keeps us stepping, all right. We service two dining rooms and the pool, as well as this bar and lounge. We've got twenty-five stools here, and on Friday and Saturday night they're double-parked." He had the eyes of a supervisor, roving around the room as he talked.

"I know what it takes," Qwilleran said sympathetically. "I've tended bar myself." He was referring to a Saturday night gig during senior year in college. "Are you from Washington? I seem to remember you at the Mayflower."

"Nope. Wasn't me."

"The Shoreham! That's where I've seen you."

The man shook his head. "Chicago. I worked the Loop for eighteen years. Poured enough booze to flood Commiskey Park."

"You get a different class of customer at a place like this."

"You tellin' me? Big crowds, small tabs, smaller tips." He looked hastily up and down the bar before saying, "The cola crowd—they're the worst! Order a soft drink, spike it with their own flask, and fill up on free peanuts." His busy eyes spotted an empty glass, and he signaled to a barhop.

Qwilleran asked, "What's the Pirate Gold drink that you're pushing?"

"All fresh, all natural. Fruit juice with two kinds of rum and a secret ingredient. The health nuts go for it."

Qwilleran gulped the rest of his tomato juice and slid off the stool. "Thanks. What's your name?"

"Bert."

"You mix a helluva good drink, Bert. Wish I'd known you when I was on the hard stuff. I'll be back." He left a tip large enough to be remembered.

In the lobby, a fierce character in pirate garb presided at a reservation desk. Qwilleran asked him, "Do you have a no-smoking section?"

"There's no smoking anywhere in the hotel, sir—orders of the fire department."

"Good! Do you have a no-kids section?" The lobby was teeming with vacationing small-fry, whooping and jumping with excitement.

"Yes, sir! The captain in the Corsair Room will seat you."

At that moment a friendly voice boomed across the lobby. "Qwill, you dirty P.O.B.! What are you doing here?" A young man grabbed his arm. Dwight Somers was employed as director of community services for XYZ Enterprises. They had met on a trip to Scotland and had developed an instant camaraderie. Jovially Dwight called Qwilleran a print-oriented bum and was called, in turn, a Ph.D., or doctor of publicity hackery.

"If the piracy doesn't extend to the prices," Qwilleran said, "I intend to take my life in my hands and have dinner here. Want to join me?"

It was quiet in the Corsair Room. The tables, most of them unoccupied, gleamed with white tablecloths, wine glasses, and flowers in crystal vases. "We're making some changes," Dwight said. "This class act intimidates your average tourist. We're down-scaling to vinyl tablecovers and ketchup bottles. Only tank tops will be a no-no. If you look around, you'll see we're the only dudes in club shirts."

A server in the official black-and-bones T-shirt took their order for drinks, and Qwilleran remarked to his dinner partner, "Don't you think you're working the pirate theme overtime?"

The XYZ publicity man shrugged apologetically. "The kids like it, and Don Exbridge says it's a historical reference. The island was a base of operations for lake pirates at one time. They lured ships onto the rocks so they could loot their cargo."

"You should change the name of this place to the Blackbeard Hotel. I hear one of your guests walked the plank last week. And that sea chantey on the backbar is right on target, with fifteen guests poisoned and one guest dead. Who was the guy? Do you know?"

"Just some lush from Down Below, looking for girls, or whatever."

"I'd question the secret ingredient in your Pirate Gold," Qwilleran advised.

The drinks came to the table, and Dwight said, "Where've you been? Don asked me why you didn't attend the press preview."

"I prefer to sneak around incognito and dig up my own stories. I'll be here a couple of weeks."

"Where are you staying? I know you're not on the hotel register, unless you're using an alias. I check daily arrivals."

"I'm at the Domino Inn."

"How come? There's a posh bed-and-breakfast on the west beach—called the Island Experience. It's run by two widows. Expensive, of course, but a lot better than where you're staying."

"Well, you see, I had to bring my cats," Qwilleran explained. "The Bambas are letting me have a catproof cottage."

"That makes sense, but isn't the Domino Inn the most godawful dump you ever saw? Still, it gets mentioned in all the national publicity, so maybe the Bambas knew what they were doing . . . I'm hungry. What are you going to eat?"

"Not chicken! Where has the hotel been getting its poultry?"

"From a chicken factory in Lockmaster. It's being investigated by the board of health. The hotel is absolved of blame. Don Exbridge has been in Pickax, smoothing things over. In the matter of the drowning, our head bartender is being fined for serving the guy too much liquor."

Qwilleran nodded and thought, The hotel pays his fine, and Exbridge gives him a bonus for keeping quiet. The menu featured Creole and Cajun specialties, and he ordered a gumbo described as "an incredibly delicious mélange of shrimp, turkey, rice, okra, and the essence of young sassafras leaves." "Turkey" was inked in where a previous ingredient had been inked out.

"You'll like it," said the enthusiastic waitress. "Everyone in the kitchen is giving it raves!" The waitstaff consisted of college men and women, who breezed around the dining room in a festive mood—all smiles, quips, and fast service.

Dwight, who had ordered a steak, said, "Okra! How can you eat that mucilaginous goo?"

"Are you aware that gumbo is the African word for okra?" Qwilleran asked with the lifted eyebrows of a connoisseur.

"By any other name it's still slimy." The two men concentrated on chomping their salads for a while, and then Dwight said, "How do you like the generic signs on the strip mall? There's a big turnover in resort businesses, and if Luigi's pizza parlor doesn't make a profit this summer, he can be replaced by Giuseppe next summer."

"Sounds like Exbridge's idea."

"Yeah, he comes up with some good ones, and others not so good—like his helicopter stunt. There's a landing pad behind the rescue station, and Don wants to rent a chopper and offer sightseeing trips over the island."

"If he does that," Qwilleran said with a threatening scowl, "the islanders will shoot it down with their rabbit guns; the private club will take him to court; and I'll personally crucify XYZ in my column! I don't care how much advertising revenue they pour into our coffers."

"I don't like it either," said Dwight, "but my boss is a hard guy to reason with, and now he's in a bad mood because of the boat explosion and the pickets that were parading in front of the hotel this weekend."

"Who were they?"

"Just kids from the mainland, protesting the name change from Breakfast Island, but it ruined the view for guests sitting in the porch rockers, and the chanting drowned out the seagulls and frightened the horses."

Qwilleran said, "Downtown isn't the only target. Did you hear about the accident at the Domino Inn?"

Dwight snapped to attention. "What kind of accident?" He listened to Qwilleran's description of the broken step and the injury to the elderly guest. "If you ask me, Qwill, that whole building will collapse one day like the One Hoss Shay."

"Does the island have a voice on the board of commissioners? Or is it a case of exploitation without representation?"

"Well, there's a so-called Island Commissioner, but he lives in Pickax and has never been to the island. He gets seasick on the lake. He's very cooperative, though, and Don has a good rapport with him."

The waitress interrupted with the entrées and a flutter of bonhomie: "The gumbo looks so good, and the cornbread is right out of the oven! . . . And look at this steak! Yum! Yum!"

When she was out of earshot, Qwilleran asked Dwight, "Do you write her script? Or is she a graduate of the Exbridge Charm School?"

After a few moments of serious eating, Dwight said, "The initial response to the resort has been largely motivated by curiosity, we can assume, so my job is to keep interest alive—bike races, kite-flying contests, prizes for the biggest fish, and all that hoopla, but we also need some indoor programs for the rocking chair crowd—and for rainy days, heaven forbid! The conservation guys will show videos on wildlife and boat safety. How would you like to give a talk on our trip to Scotland?"

"I wouldn't. Get Lyle Compton. He tells hair-raising tales about Scottish history."

"Good idea!" Dwight scribbled in a pocket notebook. "Any more suggestions? We can offer an overnight and dinner for two, plus a small honorarium."

"How about Fran Brodie? She gives a talk on interior design that's entertaining as well as informative, and she's attractive."

Dwight made another note. "That'll be something for the wives while their husbands are out fishing."

"Or vice versa."

"You're really clicking tonight, Qwill. Does okra stimulate the brain cells? It might be worth the yucky experience."

"Then there's Mildred Hanstable Riker," Qwilleran suggested. "She gives talks about cats and shows a video."

"Scratch that one. My boss hates cats. There are wild ones hanging around the hotel all the time."

For dessert Qwilleran ordered sweet potato pecan pie, which the waitress delivered with a rah-rah flourish, and he asked Dwight, "Where do you get these cheerleaders to wait on tables? When I was in college, I didn't have half that much bounce. Does your boss put steroids in their gumbo?"

"Aren't they great kids? We're planning to use them for a Saturday night cabaret show. All they have to do is sing loud and kick high. Vacation audiences aren't too critical of the entertainment at a resort. You said you used to write stuff for college revues. Would you like to write a skit for us?"

Qwilleran said he could write a song parody, such as, *Fudge, your magic smell is everywhere.* "But Riker wants me to bear down on writing more copy for the paper."

"I see . . . Well, you're welcome to use the hotel fax machine for filing your copy, Qwill."

"Thanks. I'll remember that."

Then Dwight made a startling announcement. "Don has hired Dr. Halliburton as our summer director of music and entertainment."

"Dr. who?"

"June Halliburton, head of music for the Moose County schools."

"Yes, I know," Qwilleran said impatiently. "I didn't realize she had a doctorate."

"Oh, sure! She has lots of degrees and lots of talent, as well as sexy good looks. She'll be here all summer after school's out. Right now she's spending only weekends and getting the feel of the resort."

Qwilleran cleared his throat. "I believe I saw her driving to the ferry today, when I was arriving."

"Then you know her! That's great! You'll be neighbors, in case you want to collaborate on something for the cabaret. She'll be staying at the Domino Inn."

Qwilleran huffed into his moustache. "Why not the hotel?"

"She wants housekeeping facilities and a studio; we're sending a small piano to her cottage. But I think the real reason is that she likes her cigarettes, and Don has outlawed smoking anywhere on the hotel grounds."

On this sour musical note the dinner ended. Leaving the hotel, Qwilleran was in a bad humor, contemplating two weeks in confined space plus a next-door neighbor he actively disliked. There was nothing to improve his mood when he explored the strip mall on the far side of the hotel: VIDEO, DELI, CRAFTS, POST OFFICE, FUDGE again, and GENERAL. The general store sold chiefly fishing tackle, beach balls, and paperback romances. He turned around and headed for home—or what he was to consider home for the next two painful weeks.

At the antique shop he had another look at the display window. There it was—something he had always wanted—the classic pair of theater masks called Tragedy and Comedy. They had a mellow gilded finish and could be, he thought, ceramic, metal, or carved wood. Also in the window were pieces of glass, china, brass, and copper, plus a tasteful sign on a small easel:

ANTIQUES BY NOISETTE

PARIS . . . PALM BEACH

The sign piqued his curiosity. Why would a dealer with Paris and Palm Beach credentials choose Pear Island as a summer venue?

There were other signs that interested him. The one in the window that had said Open when the shop was closed had now been turned around to read Closed when the shop was open. Taped on the glass panel of the door was another piece of information:

*No Children Allowable If Not
in Chargement of an Adult*

There were no customers in the store, and he could understand why. Noisette sold only antiques—no postcards, fudge, or T-shirts. He sauntered into the shop in slow motion to disguise his eagerness about the masks; that was the first rule of standard antiquing procedure, he had been told. First he examined the bottom of a plate and held a piece of crystal to the light as if he knew what he was doing.

From the corner of his eye he saw a woman sitting at a desk and reading a French magazine. She was hardly the friendly, folksy dealer one would expect on an island 400 miles north of everywhere. She had the effortless chic that he associated with Parisian women: dark hair brushed back to emphasize a handsomely boned face; lustrous eyes of an unusual brown; tiny diamond earrings.

"Good evening," he said in the mellifluous voice he reserved for women he wanted to impress.

"Oh! Pardon!" she said. "I did not see you enter." Her precise speech said "Paris," and when she stood up and came forward, her jade silk shirt and perfectly cut white trousers said "Florida."

"You have some interesting things here," he said, mentally comparing them with the plastic pears and bawdy bumper stickers in the shop next door.

"Ah! What is it that you collect?"

"Nothing in particular. I walked past earlier and your door was locked."

"I was taking some sustainment, I regret." She walked to a locked vitrine that had small figures behind glass. "Are you interested in pre-Columbian? I take them out of the case."

"No, thanks. Don't bother. I'm just looking." He did some more aimless wandering before saying, "Those masks in the window—what are they made of?"

"They are fabrications of leather, a very old Venetian craft, requiring great precisement. I have them from the collection of a famous French film actor, but I have not the liberty to use his name, I regret."

"Hmmm," said Qwilleran without any overt enthusiasm. He then picked up an ordinary-looking piece of green glass. "And what is this?"

"It is what one calls Depression glass."

The rectangular tray of green glass was stirring vague memories. His mother used to have one on her dresser when he was young. She would say, "Jamesy, please bring my reading glasses from the pin tray on my bureau—that's a good boy." He had never seen any pins on the pin tray, but he definitely remembered the pattern pressed into the glass.

"How much are you asking for this?" he asked.

"Twenty-five dollars. I have a luncheon set in the same pattern—sixteen pieces—and I make you a very good price if you take the entirement."

"And how much are you asking for the masks?"

"Three hundred. Are you a theater activist?"

"I'm a journalist, but I have an interest in drama. I'm here to write some features about the island. How's business?"

"Many persons come in for browsement, but it is too early. The connoisseurs, they are not yet arrived."

With studied nonchalance Qwilleran suggested, "You might let me have a closer look at the masks."

She brought Comedy from the window display, and he was surprised to find it lightweight (when it looked heavy) and soft to the touch (when it looked hard). He avoided making any comment or altering his expression.

"If you really like them," the dealer said, "I make you a little reducement."

"Well . . . let me think about it. May I ask what brought you to the island?"

"Ah, yes. I have a shop in Florida. My customers fly north in the summer, so I fly north."

"Makes good sense," he said agreeably. After a measured moment he asked, "What is the very best you can do on the masks?"

"For you, two seventy-five, because I think you appreciate."

He hesitated. "What will you take for the piece of green glass?"

"Fifteen."

He hesitated.

Then Noisette said, "If you take the masks, I give you the piece of glass."

"That's a tempting offer," he said.

"Then in probability you will come back and take the luncheon set."

"Well . . ." he said reluctantly. "Will you take a personal check?"

"With the producement of a driver's license."

"To whom do I make the check payable?"

"Antiques by Noisette."

"Are you Noisette?"

"That is my name." She wrapped the masks and the tray in tissue and put them in an elegant, glossy paper totebag.

As he was leaving, he remarked, "You and your shop would make an interesting feature for my newspaper—the *Moose County Something* on the mainland. Might we arrange an interview?"

"Ah! I regret I do not like personal publicity. But thank you, with apologies."

"That's perfectly all right. I understand. Do you have a business card?"

"But no. I have ordered some cards, and they have not yet arrived. How to explain the delayment, I do not know."

As Qwilleran walked up West Beach Road with his totebag he frequently touched his moustache; his curiosity about Noisette was turning into suspicion. Any individual in the business world who declined free publicity in his column was suspect. Her stock was scant; customers were few, if any; she was out of place on Pear Island, where a flea market would be more appropriate; her prices seemed high, although . . . what did he know about prices? He knew what he liked, that was all, and he liked those masks.

On West Beach Road the sky was gearing up for a spectacular sunset. Even the Domino Inn looked less objectionable in the rosy glow, and all the porch swings were occupied by swingers waiting for the color show. The wooden two-seaters squeaked on their chains, musically but out of tune. As Qwilleran crossed the porch on the way to see Lori, two white-haired women smiled at him sweetly, and the Hardings waved.

"How was your dinner?" Lori asked.

"Excellent! I had shrimp gumbo, and I stopped in the antique shop and bought you a pencil tray for your desk—Depression glass, circa 1930."

"Oh, thank you! My grandmother used to collect this!"

"I also bought a couple of masks I'd like to hang on my sitting room wall, if it's permissible."

"Sure," she said. "Two more holes in those old walls won't hurt. I'll give you a hammer and some nails. How do the cats like the cottage?"

"I believe they're victims of culture shock." Gallantly he refrained from mentioning the slipcovers that discomforted all three of them with their pattern if not their odor.

"Cats sense when they are surrounded by water," Lori said with assurance. "But in three days they can get used to anything."

Qwilleran said, "Koko has vandalized your wall calendar, but I'll buy you a new one and take it out of his allowance. He tore off the month of June, and now . . ." He stopped abruptly as the roots of his moustache tingled. "By the way, who are my next-door neighbors on Pip Court?"

"In Three Pips we have Mr. and Mrs. Harding, a darling elderly couple. Five Pips is rented for the season to June Halliburton from the mainland. I'm sure you know her."

"I do indeed," he said crisply. "Did anyone occupy Four Pips before we arrived?"

"As a matter of fact, she used it the first two weekends but asked to move to the end of the row. She was afraid her music would disturb the Hardings. It was very thoughtful of her . . . Are you going to watch the sunset from the porch, Qwill?"

"I have something to do first," he said as he hurried from the office.

# Five

When Qwilleran returned from dinner at the hotel, the
Siamese were still boycotting the slipcovers. Instead of lounging on
seat cushions or bed, they crouched in awkward positions on the desk,
kitchen counter, dresser, or snack table.

"Okay, you guys!" he ordered. "Clear out! We're trying an experi-
ment." He chased them onto the porch while he stripped the premises
of slipcovers, draperies, and bedcover. He also opened all the windows
to dispel the haunting memory of June Halliburton, which blended
her musky perfume with stale cigarette smoke. Did the Bambas know
she was an inveterate smoker? Probably not. He stuffed the offending
slipcovers into the bedroom closet temporarily.

What remained—when the roses and irises were gone—was as grim
as the previous decor was flashy: roller blinds on the windows, a no-
color blanket on the bed, and well-worn leatherette upholstery on sofa
and chairs. He felt guilty about leaving the Siamese cooped up in this
stark environment.

"How about a read?" he asked them. He stretched out in a lounge
chair that was comfortable except for one broken spring in the seat.
Yum Yum piled into his lap, and Koko perched on the arm of the
chair as he read to them from *Walden*. He read about the wild mice
around Walden Pond, the battle of the ants, and the cat who grew
wings every winter. Soon his soothing voice put them to sleep, their
furry bellies heaving in a gentle rhythm.

It was their first night on the island, and it was deadly quiet. Even in rural Moose County one could hear the hum of tires on a distant highway. On the island there was breathless silence. The wind was calm; there was no rustling of leaves in the nearby woods; the lake lapped the shore without even a whisper.

Suddenly—at the blackest hour of the night—Qwilleran was frightened out of slumber by a frenzy of demonic screams and howls. He sat up, not knowing where he was. As he groped for a bedside table, he regained his senses. The cats! Where were they? He stumbled out of the bedroom, found a light switch, and discovered the Siamese awake and ready for battle—arching their backs, bushing their tails, snarling and growling at the threat outside.

He rushed to the porch with a flashlight and turned it on a whirl-wind of savage creatures uttering unearthly screeches. He ran back to the kitchen, filled a cookpot with water, and threw it out the back door. There was a burst of profanity, and then the demons disappeared into the night. The Siamese were unnerved, and he left the bedroom door open, spending the rest of the night as a human sandwich between two warm bodies.

While dressing for breakfast the next morning, he thought, Dammit! Why should we stay here? I'll make some excuse. We'll go back on the ferry.

"Ik ik ik" came a rasping retort from the next room, as if Koko knew what Qwilleran was thinking.

"Is that vote an aye or a nay, young man?"

"Ik ik ik!" The connotation was definitely negative.

"Well, if you can stand it, I can stand it, I suppose." Avoiding the closet, with its aromatic bundle of slipcovers and whatnot, Qwilleran dressed in shorts and a tee from the dresser drawer and went to the inn for breakfast, carrying a hammer. He had hung the two gilded masks over the sofa, between two travel posters, and their elegance made the sturdy, practical furnishings look even bleaker by comparison.

In the sunroom he nodded courteously to a few other guests and took a small table in a corner, where he found a card in Lori's handwriting:

GOOD MORNING
*Monday, June 9*
*Pecan Pancakes With Maple Syrup*
*and Turkey-apple Sausages*

*or*
*Tarragon-chive Omelette*
*With Sautéed Chicken Livers*
*Help yourself to fruit juices, muffins, biscuits,*
*homemade preserves, and coffee or milk*

"These pancakes are delicious," Qwilleran said to the plain-faced waitress, who shuffled about the sunroom. "Did Mrs. Bamba make these herself?"

"Ay-uh," she said without change of expression.

When the serving hours ended, he stopped drinking coffee and went to the office, where he found Lori slumped in a chair, looking frazzled. "That was a sumptuous breakfast," he said. "My compliments to the chef."

"Today I had to do it all myself," she replied wearily. "My cook didn't show up, and the waitress was late. Two of the guests volunteered to wait on tables until she came. I believe in hiring island women, but they can be annoyingly casual. Perhaps that's why the hotel hires college kids. Anyway, I'm glad you liked your first breakfast. Did you have the pancakes or the omelette?"

"To be perfectly honest, I had both."

Lori shrieked with delight. "Did you sleep well? Did you find the bed comfortable?"

"Everything was fine except for the catfight outside our back door."

"Oh, dear! I'm sorry. Did it disturb you? It only happens when strays from the other inns come over in our territory. We have three nice strays that we take care of: Billy, Spots, and Susie. They were here before we were, so we adopted them. You'll notice a lot of feral cats around the island."

Qwilleran asked, "What do the islanders think about the resort's invasion of their privacy?"

"The old-timers are dead-set against it, but they can use the jobs. My cook is an older woman. Mr. Beadle, who fixed our steps, is a great-grandfather; he's grumpy but willing to work. And the old men who drive the cabs are as grumpy as their horses. The young islanders are glad to get jobs, of course; they're not exactly grumpy, but they sure don't have any personality. They're good workers—when and if they report—but I wish they'd take their commitments more seriously."

"I'd like to talk with some of them about life on the island before the resort opened. Would they cooperate?"

"Well, they're inclined to be shy and suspicious of strangers, but there's one woman who'd have a wider perspective. She grew up here, attended high school on the mainland, and worked in restaurants over there. Now she's back on the island, operating a café for tourists—with financial aid from the K Foundation, of course. You probably know about Harriet's Family Café."

"The K Foundation never tells me anything about anything," he said. "Where is she located?"

"Up the beach a little way, in one of the old lodges. She serves lunch and dinner—plain food at moderate prices. Most of our guests go there. She also rents out the upper floors as dorm rooms for the summer help at the hotel. It's a neat arrangement. Don Exbridge masterminded this whole project, and he thought of everything."

"What is Harriet's last name?"

"Beadle. The island is full of Beadles. It was her grandfather who fixed our steps. She got him for me when I was desperate. Harriet's a nice person. She's even a volunteer firefighter!"

Before leaving the inn, Qwilleran was introduced to the Bamba brood. Shoo-Shoo, Sheba, Trish, Natasha, and Sherman were the resident cats.

"Didn't you have a Pushkin?" Qwilleran asked.

"Pushkin passed away. Old age. Sherman is pregnant."

Then there were the children. The eldest, Jason, was in first grade on the mainland; a photo of him showed a lively six-year-old with his mother's blond hair. The talkative Mitchell, age four, had his father's dark coloring and serious mien, and he spoke so earnestly that Qwilleran tried his best to understand him.

"He wants to know," his mother translated, "if you'll play dominoes with him."

"I don't know how," Qwilleran said. Actually, he had played dominoes with his mother while growing up as the only child in a single-parent household. The game had been his boyhood bête noir, along with practicing the piano and drying the dishes.

"Mitchell says he'll teach you how to play," Lori said. "And this is Lovey, our youngest. She's very smart, and we think she'll be president of the United States some day . . . Lovey, tell Mr. Qwilleran how old you are."

"Two in April," said the tot in a clear voice. She was a beautiful little girl, with a winning smile.

"That was last year, Lovey," her mother corrected her. "Now you're three in April."

"I'll tell you one thing," Qwilleran said, "you'd better change her name, or she'll never get past the New Hampshire primary. The media will have a picnic with a name like Lovey." Then he asked Lori if she had a place to store the slipcovers from Four Pips, as he seemed to be allergic to the dye. "I tried stripping the rooms last night," he said, "and haven't had any bronchitis or asthma today."

"I never knew you had allergies, Qwill! That's too bad! The housekeeper will get them out of your way as soon as possible."

"They're all in the bedroom closet," he said. "Tell her not to let the cats out."

At the bike rack downtown Qwilleran rented an all-terrain bicycle for his first island adventure, a trip to Lighthouse Point. West Beach Road was uphill all the way. As he passed the Domino Inn, guests waved to him from the porch, and Mitchell chased him like a friendly, barking dog. Next came three other B-and-Bs, Harriet's Family Café, and a unique service operation called Vacation Helpers. According to the sign in front of the converted lodge, they would "sit with the baby, wash your shirt, bake a birthday cake, sew a button on, cater a picnic, address your postcards, mail your fudge, clean your fish."

Qwilleran stopped to read it and thought it a good idea. The upper floors were apparently dormitories for hotel employees, because a group of them were leaving for work, wearing the skull-and-cross-bones. One of them waved to him—the waitress from the night before.

At that point the commercial aspect of the beach road ended, and a forbidding sense of privacy began. First there was the exclusive Grand Island Club with tennis courts, a long row of stables, and a private marina, docking small yachts and tall-masted sailboats. Beyond were the summer estates, with large, rustic lodges set well back behind broad lawns. On the other side of the road, flights of wooden steps led down to private beaches with white sand. There were no bathers; the lake was notoriously cold, even in summer, and the lodge owners would undoubtedly have heated swimming pools.

Driveways were marked with discreet, rustic signs identifying the estates as RED OAKS or WHITE SANDS or CEDAR GABLES. The last and largest was THE PINES, protected by a high iron fence similar to that in front of Buckingham Palace.

How, Qwilleran wondered, were these elite vacationers reacting to the increased traffic on the beach road? On weekends there would be a continual parade of cyclists pedaling to the lighthouse. Carriageloads of gawking sightseers would stop in front of the grandest lodges to take pictures and listen to the guides spieling about family scandals.

By the same token, how would the reclusive islanders react to the noisy strangers, the aroma of fudge polluting their lake-washed air, and brash cityfolk wearing clown colors and trespassing on their sacred privacy? Would these rugged natives resent the intrusion strongly enough to retaliate? They might be an underground army of little Davids aiming slingshots at a well-capitalized Goliath who was getting a tax break.

After The Pines, the lush woods dwindled to stunted, windswept vegetation atop a mountain of sand. Beyond could be seen the lighthouse, a pristine white against a blue sky. For the last few hundred yards the road was steep, but Qwilleran bore down on the pedals resolutely. He was breathing hard when he reached the summit, but he was in better shape than he had realized.

Lighthouse Point was a desolate promontory overlooking an endless expanse of water to the north, east, and west. The tower itself was dazzlingly white in the strong sunlight, and adjacent buildings were equally well maintained. There was no sign of life, however. Such romantic figures as the lighthousekeeper and the lighthousekeeper's daughter had been made obsolete by automation. A high, steel fence surrounded the complex. Inside the fence, but visible to visitors, a bronze plaque was a reminder of the old days:

IN MEMORY OF THREE LOYAL LIGHTKEEPERS
WHO SAVED HUNDREDS OF LIVES BY
KEEPING THE BEACON BURNING BUT
LOST THEIR OWN IN THE LINE OF DUTY

There followed the names of the three men—typical north-country names that could be found in the old cemeteries of Moose County: Trevelyan . . . Schmidt . . . Mayfus. Yet, for some reason they were considered heroes. Qwilleran asked himself: What did they do to earn this recognition? Were there three isolated incidents over a period of years? Or were they swept off the rock in a storm? Why is none of this in the county history? He made a mental note to discuss the oversight with Homer Tibbitt.

On the public side of the fence the ground was a plateau of stones and weeds that showed evidence of unauthorized picnicking. There were no picnic tables or rubbish containers provided. Empty bottles were scattered about the site of a campfire, and food wrappers had blown against the fence and over the edge of the cliff. Down below were the treacherous rocks, where old wooden sailing ships had been dashed to pieces in the days before the lighthouse was built.

Moose County, in its nineteenth-century boom years, had been the richest in the state. Every month hundreds of vessels passed the island, transporting lumber, ore, gold coins, and rum, according to Mr. Tibbitt. Hundreds of wrecks now lay submerged and half buried in sand under those deep waters.

Today the lake could only gurgle and splash among the boulders, but the wind was chill on top of the cliff, and Qwilleran soon coasted back down the hill. He gripped the handlebars and clenched his jaw in concentration as the bike loped recklessly over rocks and ruts. Two young athletes in helmets and stretch pants were pedaling their thirty-speed bikes easily up the slope that had caused him so much effort. They even had breath enough to shout "Hi, neighbor! Nice goin' " as they passed.

After returning his own bike to the rental rack, he bought a supply of snacks and beverages at the deli—for himself and possible visitors. There were two large shopping bags, and he hailed a horse cab to carry them home. Without even greeting the Siamese, he checked the bedroom closet. The slipcovers had been removed, as Lori had promised, but the same odor rushed out to meet his offended nose; it had permeated his clothing.

"That woman!" Qwilleran bellowed. "May her piano always be out of tune!" Without a word to the bewildered cats, he stuffed his belongings into the two shopping bags and hiked up the beach road to Vacation Helpers.

The enterprise occupied the main floor of the former fishing lodge. In one large, open space there were work tables and such equipment as washer, dryer, ironing board, sewing machine, word processor, and child's playpen.

When Qwilleran dumped the contents of his shopping bags on one of the tables, the young woman in charge sniffed and said, "Mmm! Someone lovely has been hanging around you!"

"That's what *you* think," he said grouchily. "How fast can you do this stuff? I need some of it to wear to dinner."

"One shirt is silk, and it'll need special care, but most of it's wash-and-wear. I can have everything ready by . . . six o'clock?"

"Make it five-thirty. I'll pick it up." Without any of his usual pleasantries he started for the door.

"Sir! Shall I give your bundle to anyone with a big moustache?" she asked playfully. "Or do you want to leave your name?"

"Sorry," he said. "I had something on my mind. The name's Qwilleran. That's spelled with a QW."

"I'm Shelley, and my partners are Mary and Midge."

"How's business?" he asked, noticing that none of the roomful of equipment was in use.

"We're just getting organized. The rush won't start till July. Our picnic lunches are the most popular so far. Want to try one?"

He was going out to dinner, but it appeared that they needed the business, so he paid his money and took home a box that proved to contain a meatloaf sandwich, coleslaw, cookies, and . . . a pear! He put it in the refrigerator and dropped into his lounge chair. Oops! He had forgotten the broken spring. He seated himself again, this time with circumspection.

Then: What are those cats doing? he asked himself.

Koko was on the porch, trying to catch mosquitoes on the screen, the problem being that they were all on the outside.

"And you're supposed to be a smart cat," Qwilleran said.

Yum Yum was in the tiny kitchen area, fussing. When Yum Yum fussed, she could work industriously and stubbornly for an hour without any apparent purpose and without results. In Qwilleran's present mood he found the unexplained noises nerve-wracking—the bumping, clicking, thudding, and skittering.

"What on God's green earth are you doing?" he finally said in exasperation.

She had found a rusty nail in a crevice and, having worked and worked and worked to get it out, she pushed it back into another crevice.

"Cats!" he said, throwing up his hands.

Nevertheless, the rusty nail brought to mind the front steps of the Domino Inn. The aged carpenter blamed the collapse of the steps on rusty nails. Lori blamed a careless inspection. Nick wanted to blame the troublemakers from Lockmaster. Qwilleran favored the David-and-Goliath theory. Meanwhile, it was advisable to return to the Buccaneer Den while the bartender still remembered him and his magnanimous tip.

The bartender's craggy face—hardened after eighteen years in Chicago's Loop—brightened when Qwilleran slid onto a bar stool. "Have a good day?" he asked jovially as he toweled the bartop.

"Not bad. Has the bar been busy?"

"Typical Monday." Bert waggled a double old-fashioned glass. "Same?"

"Make it a four-alarm this time. Gotta rev up for one of those Cajun specials in the Corsair Room."

"Yep, pretty good cook we've got. I send a Sazerac to the kitchen several times a day." He placed the blood-red glassful on the bar and waited for Qwilleran's approval. "How long y'here for?"

"Coupla weeks."

"Staying in the hotel?"

"No. At the Domino Inn. Friend of mine owns it."

"Sure, I know him. Short fella, curly black hair. Nice guy. Family man."

"What do you think of his inn?"

"Sensational!" said Bert. "That treebark siding has acid in it that keeps insects out. That's why it's lasted. Besides that, it looks terrific!"

"Have you been to the lighthouse?" Qwilleran asked.

"Sure. A bunch of us went up there in a wagon before the hotel opened. Mr. Exbridge arranged it. He's a good boss. Very human. Owns a third of XYZ, but you'd never know it from his attitude. Pleasure to work for him."

"I've heard he's a good guy. Too bad about the food poisoning and the drowning. Were they accidents? Or did someone have it in for XYZ?"

Bert paused before answering. "Accidents." Then he became suddenly busy with bottles and glasses.

Qwilleran persisted. "The guy that drowned—do you remember serving him?"

"Nope."

"Was he drinking in the lounge or by the pool?"

The bartender shrugged.

"Do any of the poolside waiters remember him?"

Bert shook his head. He was looking nervously up and down the bar.

"Was he a boater or a guest at the hotel? It would be interesting to know who was drinking with him."

Bert moved away and went into a huddle with his two assistants, who turned and looked anxiously at the customer with a sizable moustache. Then all three of them stayed at the far end of the bar.

So Exbridge had imposed the gag rule. Qwilleran had guessed as much when having dinner with Dwight Somers. Finishing his drink, he went to the Corsair Room for jambalaya, a savory blend of shrimp, ham, and sausage. He had been on the island twenty-four hours, although it seemed like a week. There was something about an island that distorted time. There was also something about jambalaya that made one heady.

He hailed a cab for the ride home—a spidery vehicle with a small body slung between two large spoked wheels that looked astonishingly delicate. He climbed in beside the lumpish old man holding the reins and said, "Do you know the Domino Inn on the west beach?"

"Ay-uh," said the cabbie. He was wearing the shapeless, colorless clothes of the islanders. "Giddap." The gig moved slowly behind a plodding horse with a swayback.

"Nice horse," Qwilleran said amiably.

"Ay-uh."

"What's his name?"

"Bob."

"How old is he?"

"Pretty old."

"Does he belong to you?"

"Ay-uh."

"Where do you keep him?"

"Yonder."

"How do you like this weather?" Qwilleran wished he had brought his tape recorder.

"Pretty fair."

"Is business good?"

"Pretty much."

"Have you always lived on the island?"

"Ay-uh."

"Do you get a lot of snow in winter?"

"Enough."

"Where is Piratetown?"

"Ain't none."

Eventually the cab reached the Domino Inn, and Qwilleran paid his fare plus a sizable tip. "What's your name?" he asked.

"John."

"Thanks, John. See you around."

The old man shook the reins, and the horse moved on.

# Six

.:.

It was sunset time. Guests filled the porch swings as Qwilleran walked up the front steps of the inn.

"Beautiful evening," said the man who wore a French beret indoors and out. He spoke with a pleasant voice and a warmly benign expression on his wrinkled face.

"Yes, indeed," Qwilleran replied with a special brand of courtesy that he reserved for his elders.

"I'm Arledge Harding, and this is my wife, Dorothy."

"My pleasure. My name is Qwilleran—Jim Qwilleran."

The retired vicar moved with a physical stiffness that added to his dignity. "We're quite familiar with your name, Mr. Qwilleran, being privileged to read your column in the Moose County newspaper. It's most refreshing! You write extremely well."

"Thank you. I was sorry to hear about your accident. Which was the faulty step?"

"The third from the top, alas."

"Were you walking down or coming up?"

"He was going down," said Mrs. Harding. "Fortunately he had hold of the railing. I always remind him to grip the handrail. It's strange, though. Arledge weighs like a feather, and that husky young man who rides a bicycle runs up and down the steps all the time—"

"But in the middle, my dear. I stepped on the end of the step, and the other end flew up in a seesaw effect. The carpenter blamed it on rusty nails, and I do believe the nails in this building are even older than I am."

His wife squirmed to get out of the wooden swing. "Do sit here, Mr. Qwilleran."

"Don't let me disturb you," he protested.

"Not at all. I have things to do indoors, and I'll leave my husband in your good hands . . . Arledge, come inside if you feel the slightest chill."

When she had bustled away, Qwilleran said, "A charming lady. I didn't mean to chase her away."

"Have no compunction. My dear wife will be glad of a moment's respite. Since my accident she feels an uxorial obligation to attend me twenty-four hours a day—and this for a single fractured rib. I tremble to think of her ceaseless attention if I were to break a leg. Such is the price of marital devotion. Are you married, Mr. Qwilleran?"

"Not any more, and not likely to try it again," said Qwilleran, taking the vacant seat in the creaking swing. "I understand you have visited the island in the past."

"Yes, Mrs. Harding and I are fond of islands, which is not to imply that we're insular in our thinking—just a little odd. Individuals who are attracted to islands, I have observed, are all a little odd, and if they spend enough of their lives completely surrounded by water, they become completely odd."

"I daresay you've noted many changes here."

"Quite! We were frequently guests of an Indianapolis family by the name of Ritchie—in the decades B.C. Before commercialization, I might add. The Ritchies would have deplored the current development. They were a mercantile family, good to their friends and employees and generous to the church, rest their souls."

Qwilleran said, "The name of Ritchie is connected with the Mackintosh clan. My mother was a Mackintosh."

"I recognized a certain sly Scottish wit in your writing, Mr. Qwilleran. I mentioned it to Mrs. Harding, and she agreed with me."

"What was this island like in the years B.C.?"

Mr. Harding paused to reflect. "Quiet . . . in tune with nature . . . and eminently restorative."

"Did the Ritchies have the lodge behind the high iron fence?"

"Gracious me! No!" the vicar exclaimed. "They were not at all pretentious, and they found delight in poking fun at those who were."

"Then who is the owner of The Pines? It looks like quite a compound."

"It belongs to the Appelhardts, who founded the private club and were the first to build in the 1920s. The Ritchies called them the royal family and their estate, Buckingham Palace . . . What brings you to the island, Mr. Qwilleran?"

"A working vacation. I'm staying in one of the cottages because my cats are with me, a pair of Siamese."

"Indeed! We once had a Siamese in the vicarage. His name was Holy Terror."

Mrs. Harding suddenly appeared. "A breeze has sprung up, and I'm afraid it's too chilly for you, Arledge."

"Yes, a storm is brewing. I feel it in my bones, and one bone in particular." The three of them went into the lounge and found comfortable seating in an alcove, whereupon the vicar asked his wife, "Should I tell Mr. Qwilleran the story about Holy Terror and the bishop?"

"Do you think it would be entirely suitable, Arledge?"

"The bishop has been entertaining the civilized world with the story for twenty years."

"Well . . . you wouldn't put it in the paper, would you, Mr. Qwilleran?"

"Of course not. I never mention cats and clergymen in the same column."

"Very well, then," she agreed and sat nervously clutching her handbag as her husband proceeded:

"It was a very special occasion," Mr. Harding said with a twinkle in his left eye. "The bishop was coming to luncheon at the vicarage, and we discovered that he enjoyed a Bloody Mary at that time of day. This required much planning and research, I assure you. After consulting all available experts, we settled upon the perfect recipe and took pains to assemble the correct ingredients. On the appointed day our distinguished guest arrived and was duly welcomed, and then I repaired to the kitchen to mix the concoction myself. As I carried the tray into the living room, Holy Terror went into one of his Siamese tizzies, flying up and down stairs and around the house at great speed until he swooped over my shoulder and landed in the tray. Glasses catapulted into space, and the Bloody Mary flew in all directions, spraying tomato juice over the walls, furniture, carpet, ceiling, and the august person of the bishop."

The gentle Mr. Harding rocked back and forth with unholy mirth until his wife said, "Do try to control yourself, Arledge. You're putting a strain on your rib." Then she turned to Qwilleran and asked the inevitable question: "Do you play dominoes?"

"I'm afraid I have to say no, and I suppose I should go home and see what profane terrors my two companions have devised."

Gasping a little, Mr. Harding said, "I would deem it . . . a privilege and a pleasure . . . to introduce you to a game that promotes tranquility."

Sooner or later, Qwilleran knew, he would have to play dominoes with *someone,* and he could use a little tranquility after the events of the day. He followed the Hardings to a card table under a bridge lamp. When the old man was properly seated, his wife excused herself, saying the best game was two-handed.

The vicar opened a box of dominoes and explained that there were twenty-eight pieces in the set, having pips similar to the spots on dice. "Why the one game is considered nice and the other is considered naughty, I am unable to fathom, especially since the naughty game is so often played on one's knees with certain prayerful exhortations. Or so I am told," he added with a twinkle in his good eye. "You might address that weighty question in your column some day. As a clue, let me mention that a domino was originally a hood worn by a canon in a cathedral."

The two men began matching pips in geometric formations, and Qwilleran began thinking longingly about a chocolate sundae, a symptom of boredom in his case. When the game ended, and the Hardings retired to their cottage, he found Lori and asked if Harriet's Family Café would be open at that hour.

"She'll be open, but she may not be serving the regular menu. If you're starving, though, she'll scramble some eggs for you."

"All I want is some ice cream."

Before walking to the restaurant, Qwilleran picked up his tape recorder and a flashlight at the cottage, moving quietly to avoid waking the Siamese. They were sleeping blissfully in the bowl-shaped leatherette cushion of the lounge chair. Groggy heads raised indifferently, with eyes open to slits, and then fell heavily back to sleep.

The café occupied one of the more modest lodges, built when the west beach was being invaded by the *lower* upperclass and even the upper *middleclass.* Whatever residential refinements had been there were now superseded by a bleak practicality: fluorescent lights that made it easy to clean the floor; dark, varnished paneling that would not show grease spots; tables with stainproof, plastic tops and kick-proof, metal legs. It had been a busy evening, judging by the number of highchairs scattered among the tables. The last customer stood at the cash register, counting his change, and the cashier was clearing tables and sweeping up jettisoned food.

"Sorry to bother you," Qwilleran said. "Am I too late for an ice cream sundae?"

"You can sit down," she said in a flat voice. "What kind?"

"Can you rustle up some chocolate ice cream with chocolate sauce?"

She left the dining room and returned, saying, "Vanilla is all."

"That'll do, if you have chocolate sauce." He sat at a table near the kitchen to save the weary employee a long trek. To his surprise, another woman burst through the kitchen door, carrying his sundae. She was a husky woman of about forty, wearing a chef's hat (unstarched) and a large canvas apron (streaked with tomato sauce). She had the lean face and stony expression typical of island women, and she walked with a lumbering gait.

Plunking the dish down in front of the customer, she said, "I know you—from Pickax. You came into the Old Stone Mill to eat. I worked in the kitchen. Derek would come back and say, 'He's here with his girlfriend.' Or he'd say, 'He's here with a strange woman, much younger.' Then we'd peek through the kitchen door, and we'd put an extra slice of pork or turkey on your plate. We always had a doggie bag ready for you . . . Eat your ice cream before it melts."

"Thank you," he said, plunging his spoon into the puddle of chocolate sauce.

"How come you didn't ask for hot fudge? I can cook some up if you want. I know you like it."

"This is fine," he said, "and it's late, and you must be tired."

"I'm not tired. When you have your own business, you don't get tired. Funny, isn't it?"

"You must be Harriet Beadle. I'm staying at the Domino Inn, and Lori told me you helped her find a carpenter when she was in trouble."

"Lori's nice. I like her . . . Want some coffee?"

"I'll take a cup, if you'll have one with me."

Harriet sent her helper home, saying she'd finish the cleanup herself. Then she brought two cups of coffee and sat down, having removed her soiled apron and limp headgear. Her straight, colorless hair had been cut in the kitchen, Qwilleran guessed, with poultry shears and a mixing bowl. "I know you like it strong," she said. "This is island coffee. We don't make it like this for customers."

He could understand why; he winced at the first sip. "What brought you back to the island?"

"There's something about the island—always makes you want to come back. I always wanted to run my own restaurant and do all the cooking. Then Mr. Exbridge told me about this and told me how to go about it—borrow the money, buy secondhand kitchen equipment, and all that. He's a nice man. I s'pose you know him. What are you doing here? Writing for the paper?"

"If I can find anything to write about. Perhaps you could tell me something about island life."

"You bet I could!"

He placed his recorder on the table. "I'd like to tape our conversation. Don't pay any attention to it. Just talk."

"What about?"

"Breakfast Island when you were growing up."

"It was hard. No electricity. No bathrooms. No clocks. No phones. No money. We don't call it Breakfast Island over here. It's Providence Island."

"Who gave it that name?"

"The first settlers. A divine providence cast 'em up on the beach after their ship was wrecked."

"You say you had no money. How did you live?"

"On fish. Wild rabbit. Goat's milk." She said it proudly.

"What about necessities like shoes and flour and ammunition for hunting rabbits?"

"They used traps, back then. Other things they needed, they got by trading on the mainland. They traded fish, mostly, and stuff that washed up on the beach. My pa built a boat with wood that washed up."

"Is he still living?" Qwilleran asked, thinking he might be one of the unsociable cab drivers.

"He drowned, trying to haul his nets before a storm." She said it without emotion.

"And your mother?"

"Ma's still here. Still using oil lamps. Never left the island—not even for a day. She'd just as soon go to the moon."

"But surely electricity is now available to islanders. The resort has it. The summer estates have had it a long time."

"Ay-uh, but a lot of people here can't afford it. A lot of 'em still make their own medicines from wild plants. My ma remembers when there was no school. Now we have a one-room schoolhouse. I went through eight grades there—everybody in one room with one teacher." She said it boastfully.

"How did you arrange to go to high school?"

"Stayed with a family on the mainland."

"Did you have any trouble adapting to a different kind of school?"

"Ay-uh. Sure did. It was hard. I was ahead of the mainland kids in some things, the teachers said, but islanders were supposed to be dumb, and we got called all kinds of names."

"How did you feel about that?" Qwilleran asked sympathetically.

"Made me mad! Had to beat up on 'em a coupla times." Harriet clenched a capable fist.

He regarded this Amazon with astonishment and grudging admiration. "You must be very strong."

"Gotta be strong to live here."

"Where do the islanders live? I don't see any houses."

"In Providence Village, back in the woods."

"Is that what the mainlanders call Piratetown?"

"Ay-uh. Makes me mad!" The clenched fist hit the tabletop and made the dishes dance.

"How do your people feel about the new resort?"

"They're afraid. They think they'll be chased off the island, like they were chased off the west beach when the rich folks came."

"What do they think about the tourists?"

"They don't like 'em. Some of the tourists are cocky . . . rowdy . . . half-naked. Last coupla weekends, a bunch of 'em camped near the lighthouse and flew kites big enough to ride in."

"Hang gliders," Qwilleran said, nodding. "Was that considered objectionable?"

"Well . . . they sat around with *no clothes on,* drinking beer and playing the radio loud."

"How do you know?"

"Some rabbit hunters saw 'em . . . Want more coffee?"

For the first time in his life Qwilleran declined a second cup; he could feel drums beating in his head. "What's your personal opinion of the Pear Island Hotel?" he asked her.

"Too much stuff about pirates. Makes me mad!"

"Are you saying that there were no pirates in the history of the island? Maybe they were here before your ancestors came."

Harriet looked fierce and banged the table. "It's all lies! Made-up lies!"

He thought it a good idea to change the subject. "There's a plaque at the lighthouse, honoring three lightkeepers. Do you know what happened to them?"

"Nobody knows," she said mysteriously. "I could tell you the story if you want to hear it."

The drums stopped beating in Qwilleran's head, and he snapped to attention. "I'd like to hear it, but you've had a long hard day. You probably want to go home."

"I don't go home. I have a bed upstairs."

"Then let me take you to lunch on your day off. We'll eat in the Corsair Room."

"I don't take a day off. I work seven days a week. Wait'll I get another cup of coffee. Sure you don't want some?"

Qwilleran had a feeling that he had just found buried treasure. The lighthouse mystery had never been mentioned by Homer Tibbitt.

Harriet returned. "My grampa told this story over and over again, so I practically know it by heart. My great-grampa was mixed up in it."

"Is that so? Was he a lightkeeper himself?"

"No, the guv'ment never hired islanders. That made 'em mad! It was like saying they were too dumb, or couldn't be trusted. The guv'ment hired three men from the mainland to live on the rock and keep the light burning. It was an oil lamp in those days, you know. Every so often a guv'ment boat delivered oil for the beacon and food for the keepers, and it was all hauled up the cliff by rope. There were some zigzag steps chiseled in the side of the cliff—you can see 'em from the lake—but they were slippery and dangerous. Still are! When the guv'ment boat brought a relief man, he was hauled up like the groceries, by rope."

"How did your great-grandfather become involved, Harriet?"

"Well, he was kind of a leader, because he could read and write."

"Was that unusual?"

"Ay-uh. They didn't have a school. The settlers were kind of a forgotten colony—not only forgotten but *looked down on.*"

"Where did your great-grandfather get his learning, then?"

"His pa taught him. His pa was kind of a preacher, but that's another whole story."

Qwilleran said impatiently, "Don't keep me in suspense, Harriet. What happened?"

"Well, one dark night my great-grampa woke up suddenly and

didn't know why. It was like a message from the Lord. Wake up! Wake up! He got out of bed and looked around outside, and he saw that the beacon wasn't burning. That was bad! He put on his boots and took a lantern and went to the lighthouse, to see what was wrong. It was about a mile off. When he got there, there weren't any men around, and then he shouted—no answers! The fence gate was locked, so he climbed over. The door on the keepers' cottage was standing open, but there was nobody there. He thought of trying to light the beacon himself, but the door to the tower was locked. He didn't know what to do."

"There was no wireless at that time?" Qwilleran asked.

"No wireless—no radio—no telephone. That was a long time ago, Mr. Q. So . . . my great-grampa went home. Passing ships must've reported the beacon being out, because . . . pretty soon the island was swarming with constables and soldiers, arresting people, searching houses, and even digging up backyard graves. They didn't have regular cemeteries then."

"Did they think the islanders had murdered the men? What would be the motive?"

"The guv'ment thought the islanders really wanted ships to be wrecked so they could rob them. They believed the old lie about pirate blood. That was a hundred years ago, and people still believe it! Makes me boiling mad!"

"Old legends never die," Qwilleran said. (They only get made into movies, he thought.) "Were the bodies ever found?"

"Never. The police suspected my great-grampa and took him to the mainland for questioning."

"Why? Because he climbed over the fence?"

"Because he could read and write. They thought he was dangerous."

"Incredible! Are you sure this story is true, Harriet?"

She nodded soberly. "He kept a diary and wrote everything down. My ma has it hidden away."

Qwilleran said, "I'd give a lot to see that diary!" He was thinking, What a story this will make! . . . Homer Tibbitt, eat your heart out!

"Ma won't show the diary *to anybody,*" Harriet said. "She's afraid it'll be stolen."

"Haven't you ever seen it?"

"Only once, when I was in seventh grade. I had to be in a program for Heritage Day, so my ma let me see it. It had some weird things."

"Like what?" he asked.

"I remember one page, because I had to memorize it for the program. *August 7. Fine day. Lake calm. Light wind from southeast. Hauled nets all day. Mary died in childbirth. Baby is fine, thank the Lord . . . August 8. Cool. Some clouds. Wind shifting to northeast. Three rabbits in traps. Buried Mary after supper. Baby colicky.* A few days after, the light burned out," Harriet concluded, "and the soldiers dug up the grave."

"Ghastly!" Qwilleran said. "How could your great-grandfather write about such things without emotion?"

"Islanders don't cry. They just do what they have to do," said Harriet, "and it doesn't matter how hard it is."

Qwilleran thought, They never laugh either. He asked her, "Had the islanders been on friendly terms with the lightkeepers?"

"Ay-uh. They celebrated feast days together, and Grampa took them fresh fish sometimes. They'd give him some hardtack. The islanders couldn't go inside the fence, but the keepers could come out."

"Were there any changes in the system after the disappearance?"

"Well, the guv'ment kept on sending three men from the mainland to do the job, but they had big dogs."

"Congratulations, Harriet. You report the facts as if you were actually there."

"I've heard it so many times," she said modestly.

"It'll make a sensational piece for the 'Qwill Pen' column. Is it okay to quote you?"

Her pleasure at being complimented turned to sudden alarm. "Which do you mean? Not the lighthouse story!"

"Especially the lighthouse mystery," he corrected her. "This is the first I've heard of such an incident, and I've read a lot of county history."

Harriet put her hands to her face in chagrin. "No! No! You can't write anything about that! I just told you because I thought you'd be personally interested. I didn't know . . ."

Why, Qwilleran wondered, do people give journalists sensational information or personal secrets that they don't want published? And why are they so surprised when it appears in print? What would happen if I ran this story anyway? *Historical data obtained from an anonymous source . . .* And then he thought, The lighthouse story might be a hoax. Does she know it's not true? It might be a family fiction invented to go with the ambiguous bronze plaque in the lighthouse compound. As for the diary, that's probably a myth, too. To Harriet he said, "Give me one good reason why I shouldn't publish the lighthouse story. Your reason will be confidential."

"It'll make trouble. It'll make trouble in the village." She moistened her lips anxiously.

"What kind of trouble?"

"Don't you know what happened Memorial weekend? I think Mr. Exbridge stopped it from getting in the paper. Some men from the mainland—from Lockmaster—came to the village with shovels and started digging for buried pirate treasure. They dug big holes in front of Ma's house and near the school. They had a map that they'd bought for fifty dollars from some man in a bar."

Qwilleran suppressed an urge to chuckle. "How did the villagers get rid of them?"

"Some rabbit hunters chased them out. The diggers complained to the sheriff's deputy about harassment, but he laughed and told them to go home and say nothing about it, or they'd look like fools. He reported it to Mr. Exbridge, though, and Mr. Exbridge said he'd done right."

Qwilleran said, "I'm sure it was annoying to the villagers, but I don't blame the deputy for laughing. The question is: What does this have to do with my running the lighthouse mystery?"

"Don't you see?" she said angrily. "Someone would sell maps, and the men would be back, digging for bones!"

# Seven

On the way home from Harriet's Family Café, Qwilleran's mind was busy filming mental images: Harriet built like a Mack truck, working like a Trojan, and apparently happy as a lark . . . Harriet in her drooping chef's hat . . . Young Harriet piling into a bunch of kids with her fists flying. Was she honest? Were any of the islanders honest? They never cry, she had said; they do what they have to do. Were they capable of committing the perfect crime a hundred years ago? Generations of hardship would make them crafty. They could lure the lightkeepers to their deaths under the pretext of friendship. (A few cups of island coffee would do it!) But what was their motive? And where were the bodies?

Mist was rising from the lake and shrouding the dark beach road. Darting lights in the distance, like a swarm of fireflies, were the flashlights of hotel employees returning to their dormitories. Yelling, laughing, singing, they were a different breed from the shy, tongue-tied, sober-faced islanders.

A storm was on its way, no doubt about it. Mr. Harding could feel it in his bones; Koko and Yum Yum could feel it in their fur. As soon as Qwilleran, arriving at the cottage, slid cautiously into his lounge chair, both cats clomped to his side, looking heavy; then they landed in his lap like two sacks of cement. Even Koko, not normally a lap sitter, felt the need for propinquity. As barometers, the Siamese could predict "too wet" and "too windy." A heavy cat meant a muggy downpour; a crazy cat meant an approaching hurricane.

Now they sank ponderously into his lap, and he sank into the seat cushion with his feet up and his head back, thinking great thoughts: What would Lori serve for breakfast on Tuesday? When would he hear from Polly? Who won the ballgame in Minneapolis? . . . From there he progressed to deeper speculation: Why was the classy Noisette doing business in this backwoods resort? More to the point, what kind of business was she doing? Was the boat explosion really an accident? Who had been drinking with the hotel guest found floating in the pool? How could contaminated chicken sneak past the nose of a good chef? Wouldn't it smell? Where could one find an informant—an insider—who could ask gossipy questions without being suspected?

Before he could think of answers, he dozed off and slept soundly until shocked awake by a terrifying roar, as if a locomotive were crashing through the house! It was followed by a hollow silence. Had it been an audio dream? The cats had heard it, too. Both were on top of the wallcabinet in the kitchenette. Then the empty silence was broken by another bellowing blast. It was the Breakfast Island foghorn on Lighthouse Point. It could be heard thirty miles out in the lake, and on Pip Court it sounded as if it were in the backyard. Now Qwilleran understood the ear plugs on the emergency list. The Siamese came down from their perch and slept peacefully throughout the booming night. Lori, in her infinite wisdom about cats, explained to Qwilleran the next day that they associated the regular bleating of the horn with their mother's heartbeat when they were in the womb.

Reporting for breakfast, he appreciated the green-and-white golf umbrella that came with the cottage. Two others were dripping on the front porch of the inn, and his neighbors from Pip Court were seated at a large, round table.

"Please honor us with your company," said Mr. Harding, his dignified stiffness aggravated by the dampness. He introduced the other couple as the newlyweds in Two Pips.

"We're checking out today," they said. "We have to bike back to Ohio before the weekend."

"In this weather?" Qwilleran questioned.

"We have raingear. No problem."

"Can you tell me anything about the nature trail at the end of the lane?"

"Super!" said the young woman. "It goes all the way to the sand dune, and there's a hidden pond with a beaver dam and all kinds of wildflowers."

"It's really a swamp with all kinds of mosquitoes," said the young man, a realist.

"Is the trail well marked?" Qwilleran asked. "Last year I lost my way on a mountain and would still be wandering in circles if it weren't for a rescue dog."

"Stay on the main path; you can't go wrong. Just be alert for snakes, wood ticks, and bush shooters. The rabbit hunters shoot at anything that moves, so wear bright colors." The bikers stood up. "We've got to catch the ten o'clock ferry. Have a nice day, you guys." This was said with a humorous nod at the rain-drenched windows.

"Deck thyself in gladness," Mr. Harding said with ecclesiastical pomp and a twinkle in his good eye.

"Charming young people," Mrs. Harding muttered when they had loped with athletic grace from the breakfast room. "There should be more like them on Pear Island."

Qwilleran said, "Are you aware that this island has three names? It's Pear Island on the map, Breakfast Island to mainlanders, and Providence Island to the natives."

"There is yet another name," said the vicar. "When the millionaires built their stately mansions—for their souls and their social prestige, we presume—they considered 'Pear Island' incompatible with their delusions of grandeur, so they renamed it. Perhaps you've seen the sign: GRAND ISLAND CLUB."

Qwilleran ate slowly and prolonged his first breakfast, hoping the elderly couple would leave and allow him to order a second breakfast without embarrassment.

They lingered, however. "Good day for a friendly game of dominoes, if you feel so inclined," the vicar said.

"Unfortunately I have a deadline to meet," Qwilleran replied, and he excused himself from the table, having had the souffléed ham and eggs with fresh pineapple, but not the waffles with ricotta cheese and strawberries. He felt deprived.

On the way out he was selecting a couple of apples from the communal fruit basket when a sweet voice at his elbow said, "You should take a banana." She was one of the two white-haired women who always smiled at him in unison when he crossed the porch or entered the lounge.

"An apple a day keeps the rain away," he said.

"But bananas, you know, are an excellent source of potassium."

"The banana," he declaimed facetiously, "was invented as a base for three scoops of ice cream, three sundae toppings, two dollops of whipped cream, a sprinkling of nuts, and a maraschino cherry. Other uses are marginal."

"Oh, Mr. Qwilleran," she said with a delighted smile, "you sound just like your column! We've been reading it in the local paper. You should be syndicated. It's so trenchant!"

"Thank you," he said with a gracious bow. He liked compliments on his writing.

"I'm Edna Moseley, and I'm here with my sister Edith. We're retired teachers."

"A pleasure to meet you. I hope you're enjoying your stay. Let's hope the weather clears shortly." Taking two apples and a banana, he edged away. She and her sister were domino players, as were the Hardings. He had classified most of the guests. The newlyweds had been jigsaw puzzlers. Two older men played chess; probably retired teachers. A young couple with a well-behaved child played Scrabble.

Then there was an attractive young woman who read magazines or talked to two men who were traveling together. None of them looked like a vacationer or showed any interest in dominoes, puzzles, sunsets, or the fruit basket. Qwilleran suspected they were a detective team from the state police. All three left the next day.

Back at Four Pips Qwilleran tried to write a trenchant column, but the pelting rain and fretting Siamese disturbed him. He empathized with the cats. They had no room to practice their fifty-meter dash or their hurdles or broad jumps. For a while he amused Yum Yum by flipping a belt around for her to chase and grab. Floor space was limited, however. The sport entertained her briefly; Koko, not at all. He watched the performance as if they were both numbskulls. Koko preferred pastimes that challenged his sentience. It was that understanding that gave Qwilleran his next idea—one that would prove more significant than he expected.

"Okay, old boy, how about a friendly game of dominoes?" he proposed. He remembered Koko's interest in Scrabble and his fascination with a dictionary game they had invented Down Below. "Cats," he had written in his column, "are ingenious inventors of pastimes. Even a kitten with a ball of yarn can play an exciting game of solitaire with original rules." That column had brought him a bushel basket full of fan mail.

On that rainy day in June he and Koko collaborated on a new version of dominoes, predicated ostensibly on blind chance. First, the contents of the maroon velvet box were emptied onto the small oak table in the front window, where they were spread at random, facedown. Then Qwilleran pulled up two oak chairs facing each other. Koko enjoyed moving any small object around with his paw, whether bottlecap or wristwatch, and there were twenty-eight small objects. He stood on his hind legs on the chair, placed his forepaws on the table, and studied the black rectangles with eyes that were wide, intensely blue, and concentrated. A faltering paw reached out, touching first one domino and then another until, with a swift movement, he knocked one off the table.

"Interesting," said Qwilleran as he picked it up and found it to be 6-6. The name painted on Nick's boat was *Double-Six,* and it happened to be the highest scoring piece in the set. "That was only a test. Now we start to play." He found paper and pen for scoring and shuffled the dominoes facedown. "Your draw."

Koko looked down at the jumbled mass in his studious way, then swiped one off the table. It was 6-6 again.

"Amazing!" Qwilleran said. "That's twelve points for you. You're entitled to four draws, then it's my turn. It's not necessary or desirable to knock everything on the floor. Just *draw,* like this."

Nevertheless, Koko enjoyed shoving a small object from a high place, peering over the edge to see it land. His second draw was also high-scoring, 5-6, but the next to land on the floor were 2-3 and 0-1, reassuring Qwilleran that it was the luck of the draw. When all the pieces had been drawn, the fourteen on the floor totaled 90 pips; Qwilleran's score was 78. The game proved only one thing: Cats like to knock things down.

The game had been stimulating enough to satisfy Koko's needs, and he joined Yum Yum in her leatherette nest, while Qwilleran set up his typewriter on the oak table. The thousand words he wrote for his "Qwill Pen" column were about the island with four names and four cultures: the natives, who had lived on Providence Island for generations; the mainlanders who knew Breakfast Island as a haunt for fishermen; the summer residents from Down Below, pursuing their affluent lifestyle on Grand Island; and now the tourists, bent on having a good time on Pear Island, as it was named on the map. He called the demographic situation "a heady mix on a few square miles of floating real estate."

When he finished his column, it was still raining, and he rode downtown in a horse cab to fax his copy. In the hotel lobby, bored tourists were milling aimlessly, or they were slumped in lobby chairs, reading comic books. From adjacent rooms came electronic sounds mingling in jarring dissonance: television, video games, and bar music.

Qwilleran spotted a conservation officer in a Boat Patrol uniform, and he asked him. "Shouldn't you be out on the lake, protecting the fish from the fishermen?"

The officer acknowledged the quip with a dour grimace. "In this weather, who's crazy enough to be out fishing? I'm showing educational videos in the TV room."

"Has the influx of boaters increased your work?"

"You can bet it has! We chug around the lake counting poles and writing up violations. The law allows two poles per licensed fisherman, you know. Coupla days ago we saw a sport-fishing craft with eight poles and only three men visible on deck. We stopped them and asked to see their fishing licenses. When they could show us only two, they explained that the third guy wasn't fishing; he just came along for the ride. That was a big laugh. Now they had eight poles and only two fishermen! But that wasn't the end of it. We did a safety check, and their fire extinguisher wasn't charged! We sent 'em back to shore to get it recharged and face a hefty fine for illegal lines."

"How about the sport divers?" Qwilleran asked. "Are they giving you any trouble?"

"They're the sheriff's responsibility. He has divers and patrol boats that keep tabs on them. Divers aren't supposed to take artifacts from wrecks, but they're crazy about those brass portholes!"

Qwilleran asked, "Do you know what caused the explosion at the marina last weekend?"

"Sure. The usual. Carelessness and ignorance. Landlubbers know they have to take a road test and written exam to drive a car, but they buy a $25,000 boat and think it's just a toy." He looked at his watch. "Gotta grab something to eat, then do another video for this captive audience. When it rains, they're so bored, they'll watch anything!"

While Qwilleran was waiting for the dining room to open, he looked at the Tuesday edition of the *Moose County Something*. On the editorial page there were several letters from readers regarding Pear Island.

To the Editor:

My family and I just spent a wonderful weekend at Pear Island. We are so fortunate to have such an exciting playground, just a short ferry ride away. We rode bikes, swam in the hotel pool, and hunted for agates on the beach. It was super fun!

—Cassie Murdoch
Pickax

Qwilleran assumed that Cassie was Exbridge's secretary or sister or mother-in-law.

To the Editor:

Pear Island is okay for people who have money to spend, but what it needs is a campground for tents and cookouts. I'd like to see a tent city where you could meet people. All they'd have to do is cut down some trees in the center of the island.

—Joe Ormaster
North Kennebeck

Qwilleran thought, No one's going to love you, Joe. Not XYZ. Not the environmentalists. Not the islanders.

To the Editor:

I took my elderly mother to Pear Island for the day, and she was shocked by some of the distasteful slogans on shirts and caps worn by some of the other visitors. Also, the restrooms are too far from the ferry dock, and the smell of fudge everywhere made her sick, but we had a good time. She enjoyed the ferry ride, although all the benches were taken, and no one offered her a seat. She is 84.

—Mrs. Alfred Melcher
Mooseville

To the Editor:

My husband and I had a lovely time on Pear Island. But why do they allow those people to march back and forth in front of the hotel, carrying signs and yelling? It spoils the happy vacation mood for the rest of us who pay good money to sit in the rocking chairs and enjoy the view.

—Mrs. Graham MacWhattie
Toronto, Canada

When it was time for the dining room to open, Qwilleran reported to the reservation desk in the lobby. To his surprise, the new captain was seven feet tall, if one included the black pirate tricorne. "Derek! Glad to see you got the job!" Qwilleran greeted him.

"How d'you like my costume?" Derek asked. "I think I should have one gold earring." As a member of the Pickax Theater Club, Derek liked roles that required spectacular costumes.

"You're perfect. Don't change a thing."

"Are you staying at the hotel?"

"No, I merely came for dinner. I'm lodging at the Domino Inn."

"I get a room at the Vacation Helpers, rent paid. That's one of the perks. The job only pays minimum wage, but it'll look good on a resumé, and I get to meet a lot of girls," Derek said.

In a lower voice Qwilleran asked, "Would you be interested in doing some undercover work for an investigative reporter—as a side job?"

"Who? You?"

"I'm the go-between."

"Any risks? How much does it pay?"

A line was beginning to form behind Qwilleran, and he said loudly, "I'd like a table for one in the Corsair Room." In a conspiratorial whisper he added, "Stop at Domino Inn on your way home tonight. We'll talk."

Qwilleran hurried through dinner and was ordering a horse cab for the ride home when Dwight Somers hailed him. "Are you here for dinner, Qwill?"

"Just finished."

"Come into the lounge and have a drink."

"I can stand another cup of coffee and some dessert."

They sat in a booth to assure conversational privacy, and Dwight said, "Just got some good news. Don Exbridge has been in Pickax lobbying to get the island sprayed for mosquitoes, and the county's going to do it."

"That's good news for tourists," Qwilleran said, "but the ecologists will hit the ozone layer."

"By the way, Qwill, we don't call them tourists any more; it has a negative connotation. They're *vacationers,* by decree from the boss. He's also twisting some political arms to get the beach road paved all around the island, with a strip for bikers and joggers."

"I hate to be a wet blanket, Dwight, but the summer people will fight it to the last drop of their blue blood. The natives won't be so hot for it, either."

"The natives are against any kind of progress. They almost rioted when the post office was moved downtown. It had been in some woman's kitchen in Piratetown for years."

"We don't call it Piratetown any more, Dwight; it has a negative connotation. It's Providence Village."

Dwight ordered a burger and beer. Their booth was within sight of the bar, and Qwilleran noticed the head bartender eying him strangely as he talked with the hotel's publicity chief. "What do you think of this rain?" Dwight asked. "It wasn't predicted."

"The ancient gods of the island are not only frowning, they're weeping. Maybe your boss is lobbying the wrong hierarchy. In less than two weeks you've had two deaths, one broken rib, a wrecked boat, fifteen stomach aches, and unscheduled rain. Someone is trying to tell you something."

"Well, those are the bugs you have to expect in new operations. Did you see the letters to the editor today? We're batting about .200."

"What kind of response are the merchants getting? I never see any customers in the antique shop."

"Her stuff is too good for this place. A flea market would be more in line."

"Why would someone like Noisette choose to come here? Or did Exbridge party in Palm Beach last winter and invite her?"

"Don't ask *me.*"

"Not only are her prices high, but she has a very limited inventory. I recall a similar instance Down Below; it was a front for something else. Maybe that's the situation here."

"Please! Not that!" Dwight pleaded. "We've got problems enough! The latest is bird droppings. The—uh—vacationers sit on the porch and throw bread to the seagulls. Then the stray cats come around for the crumbs. The birds make a mess. The cats fight . . . Honestly and confidentially, Qwill, how do you size up this whole project?"

"I think you've got a tiger by the tail. A resort should be a happy place. XYZ has created a rat's nest of conflict, culture clash, and—if you'll pardon my frank opinion—sabotage."

"You're not serious," Dwight said.

"I'm serious. It's easy to second-guess, of course, but it now becomes clear to me that XYZ should have done a feasibility study before launching this project. They might have discovered that the pirate legend has no historical verification and that the islanders resent the implication. It's my belief that the hotel's celebration of the pirate myth is creating hostility."

"It's all in fun. It's just fantasy."

"The islanders have no sense of humor. Neither would you, if you lived in Providence Village."

"But what harm can it do?"

"Do you realize a con artist was selling Pear Island treasure-hunting maps for fifty dollars in bars on the mainland? Dunderheads are coming over on the ferry with shovels."

"That's a cheap racket."

"Your promotional theme is responsible. Why not taper off a little?"

Dwight said, "XYZ has invested a bundle in the pirate gimmick."

"My heart bleeds for XYZ," Qwilleran said.

"Well, shed a few drops for me, too. Don's a great boss as long as things are going right, but when something backfires, he goes berserk, and I get hell!"

With a surge of sympathy for his friend, Qwilleran said, "Are you still looking for material for your cabaret? I have an idea for a humorous skit, although it might not appeal to your literal-minded boss."

"Write it anyway," Dwight said. "Write it!"

As Qwilleran rode home to domino headquarters in a cab, he congratulated himself on lining up Derek Cuttlebrink as an undercover agent. There were those who thought the young man scatter-brained, but Qwilleran was confident that he had promise. Inside that lanky, goofy kid there was a short, serious young man trying to find himself.

Derek had muttered a cryptic "Ten-fifteen" as Qwilleran passed the reservation desk on the way out. Shortly before that hour Qwilleran took the green-and-white golf umbrella and walked to the wet and deserted porch to meet him. The wooden swings were covered with plastic, and the chairs were leaning against the back wall. Soon a babble of young voices could be heard coming up the beach road. When the troupe reached the Domino Inn, the tallest one peeled off and approached the porch steps, flapping his arms with a surplus of youthful energy. In his yellow slicker, nor'easter rainhat, and muddy boots, Derek looked like a scarecrow.

Qwilleran raised his hand for silence and put an index finger to his lips. "Say nothing," he whispered. "Follow me. This meeting is confidential." He led the way to the dark end of the porch. "Sorry it's too wet to sit down."

"I never sit down," Derek said. "What's it all about?"

"I'll make this brief. Some suspicious incidents have occurred on the island. No doubt you know about the food poisoning."

"Yeah, they crack a lot of chicken jokes in the kitchen."

"Good! I want you to listen to the scuttlebutt and report to me what you hear." He knew that would come naturally for Derek. As a native of Moose County, he had been weaned on gossip. "Another incident was a drowning in the hotel pool. The victim was a guest who had been drinking on the premises. Employees have obviously been instructed not to talk to outsiders, but we can be sure they gossip among themselves. As a newcomer to the staff, you can show a healthy curiosity about the case. Right?"

"Check!" said Derek.

"What was he drinking? Pirate's Gold? How much did he consume? Did he drink in the bar or on the edge of the pool? Who found the body? Was he dressed for a swim or fully clothed? Did anyone see him dive in or fall in?"

"Maybe he was pushed."

"You're getting the idea, Derek," said Qwilleran as he patted his moustache. "I have a hunch there's more to the story than anyone wants to admit. Who was the guy? Why was he there? Was he a registered guest or a drop-in? Was he drinking alone? If not, who was with him? Male or female? One or more companions? I've heard that he was hunting."

"Yeah," said Derek, "it's kind of a singles bar. If we're caught hanging out there, we get fired . . . What about the food poisoning?"

"It would be interesting to know who was working in the kitchen that night. Islanders or mainlanders? What was their background? How did they get their jobs? Was anyone fired after the poisoning? Was anyone fired shortly *before the poisoning?*"

"Yeah, that's a good question."

"You're a good actor, Derek. You can carry this off without blowing your cover, and you make friends easily; people will talk to you. If they know anything, they'll be only too glad to spill it in a safe ear. What hours do you work?"

"Split shift, lunch and dinner. It's a good deal—gives me time to play volleyball, ride a bike, meet girls. How do you want me to report?"

"I'll be in for dinner frequently. Slip me a note."

"Check!"

# Eight

It rained again on Wednesday. One day of rain at a resort is an adventure, of sorts. Two successive days of rain are a bore. The Siamese were bored and still heavy from the hundred percent humidity. Qwilleran was equally bored and felt heavy mentally and physically.

First he gave the cats their breakfast and their daily grooming. Waving the walnut-handled brush that Polly had given them for Christmas, he announced, "Brush! Brush! Who wants to go first?" Koko always went first, despite efforts to introduce him to precepts of chivalry. Both of them had their ideas about the grooming process. Koko liked to be brushed while walking away, forcing his human valet to follow on his knees. Yum Yum missed the point entirely; she fought the brush, grabbing it, biting the bristles, and kicking the handle. The daily ritual was a farce, but it was an expected prelude to their morning nap.

Qwilleran reported to the inn for his own breakfast with *Penguin Island* in one pocket of his waterproof jacket; in another pocket he had the pear from his box lunch of the day before. The walk up the lane was surprisingly unmuddy; the sandy island drained like a sieve. Parking his green-and-white umbrella on the porch, he went directly to the sunless sunroom. There were no other guests, and he was able to order both breakfasts without embarrassment: eggs Benedict with Hollandaise sauce and johnnycakes with sausages and apple sauce. On the way out he avoided the domino players but stopped at the fruit basket, where he exchanged his pear for two apples, one red and one green. So far, so good.

At Four Pips the boredom descended more heavily with every bucket of rain. He tried to read; he paced the floor; he ate an apple; he took a nap; he made a cup of instant coffee; he tried to write something trenchant. All his typewriter could produce was "The rain in the lane goes mainly to the brain." It was still only one o'clock, and out of sheer boredom he ate his box lunch from the Vacation Helpers. It was not bad for day-old food. The meatloaf, in fact, was very well flavored. When the Siamese finally struggled out of their somnolence, he offered them a morsel, but they were not interested.

"Good! All the more for me!" he said. "How about a stimulating game of dominoes?"

They recognized the maroon velvet box and took their places: Yum Yum crouching on the table as referee; Koko standing on the chair, ready to push dominoes onto the floor.

In the interest of scientific research and the hope that it might make a trenchant subject for his column, Qwilleran was keeping a daily record of Koko's selections. Strangely, one of his draws duplicated the first one of the day before, although in a different order: 5-6, 0-1, 6-6, 2-3.

Also, the cat won again. Did he sense that certain black rectangles had more white pips than others? If so, what did he know—or care—about winning? Was he trying to convey a message? Double-six! Double-five! There was usually a message in his madness. Or was he making a contribution to parapsychology? In some ways, Qwilleran was convinced, Koko knew more than he did.

When the game was over and Qwilleran was boxing the dominoes, he felt a pang of loneliness. There was no one with whom he could discuss these abstruse theories seriously. Polly listened politely; Riker kidded him; even the police chief talked about Koko's proven exploits with tongue in cheek. Perhaps one had to be a trifle odd to believe in the cat's ESP. Perhaps the Hardings—

His ruminations were interrupted by an urgent hammering on the door. Opening it, he found himself looking down on an open umbrella, from under which a small hand extended, holding a note.

"Thank you," Qwilleran said. "Are you Mitchell, vice president in charge of communications?"

The messenger jabbered something and ran back to the inn.

The note was a message from Lori: "Arch Riker phoned. Call him at the office. Urgent."

Qwilleran huffed into his moustache. What could be so urgent? He had faxed his copy yesterday, and it was already past the Wednesday deadline. Furthermore, it was still raining hard. He would have to change his shoes and put on his waterproof jacket . . . Then it occurred to him that the apple barn might have been damaged by the storm. There had been flashes of lightning over the mainland. He pulled on his duck boots and grabbed his umbrella.

Most of the guests were in the lounge, playing dominoes or snoozing in their chairs; even Koko and Yum Yum went to sleep after a domino session. Qwilleran strode purposefully up the stairs to the phone booth on the landing and called the newspaper office, collect.

An annoyingly cheerful voice came on the line. "How're things on the island with four names?"

"Wet!" Qwilleran answered curtly. "What's on your mind, Arch?"

"I like your column in today's paper. No one but you can write a thousand words about nothing and make it sound interesting."

"Some of my readers consider my stuff trenchant and not just interesting."

"So be it. When can we expect your next copy?"

"Is that all you called about? I risked drowning to get to this blasted phone! . . . But to answer your question: I've talked to an island woman who dismisses the pirate myth completely."

"Soft-pedal that aspect," the editor advised. "It's the main theme of the hotel."

"I know Don Exbridge has invested his life savings in black T-shirts, but the natives object. I don't see why we should support a commercial gimmick and reinforce a spurious legend because of an advertiser's ignorant whim."

"Cool it, Qwill. Isn't the native community called Piratetown?"

"Only by ignorant outsiders. Officially it's Providence Village, and trespassers are not welcome. In fact, I suspect a covert hostility that may explain the so-called accidents. The boat explosion was the fourth, and the people in charge of the waterfront are doing a lot of fast talking, so no one will get the idea it was a bomb. I'll tell you more when I see you."

"Which is why I called, Qwill," said the editor. "Mildred and I want to spend a weekend at a bed-and-breakfast before the resort gets crowded—this weekend, if it isn't too short a notice. The weather's due to clear up tomorrow and stay nice for a while. Would you make a reservation for us? Mildred wants you to pick out a B-and-B with a little class."

That eliminates the Domino Inn, Qwilleran thought. "Do you trust my judgment?"

"No, but Mildred apparently does. We plan to arrive late Friday, and we hope you'll have dinner with us Saturday night."

"I'll see what I can find. I'll call you tomorrow."

"Great! How are the mosquitoes?"

"Not too bad if you stay out of the woods. In the tourist area, they're automatically gassed by the fudge fumes."

Qwilleran walked slowly downstairs from the phone booth, regretting that he had mentioned the pirate controversy prematurely. Harriet may have been lying. She might not know the real truth about her heritage. The island might very well have been a pirate stronghold in prehistoric times. (Prehistoric in Moose County was anything before the War of 1812.) There was a hotel owner on the mainland who boasted of his pirate ancestry; why were the islanders so sensitive about the possibility?

He was intercepted at the foot of the stairs by Lori. "Is everything all right, Qwill?"

"Just a misplaced comma in my copy," he said archly. He opened his mouth to mention the Rikers' impending visit but closed it again; he could hardly ask the owner of the Domino Inn to recommend a B-and-B with more class!

Later, he remembered seeing a bed-and-breakfast brochure near the cash register at Harriet's café. He went there for dinner and ordered vegetable soup, two hot dogs with everything, and apple pie with ice cream. He could hear Harriet shouting orders in the kitchen like a drill sergeant. While eating, he read the advertising blurbs in the brochure: The Domino Inn was described as "Absolutely unique, with hearty, delicious breakfasts lovingly prepared. Newly redecorated with original 1920s furniture." The Seagull Inn featured brass beds and a billiard room. The B-and-B called Yesteryear-by-the-Lake had a cobblestone fireplace and a collection of toy trains. None of these would thrill the Rikers.

Then he read about the Island Experience: "Charming ambiance and gracious hospitality, with antique furnishings and gourmet breakfasts! Canopied beds have eyelet-embroidered bedlinens and handmade quilts. Complimentary champagne in the gazebo every afternoon."

Mildred would swoon over such amenities. Arch would prefer complimentary Scotch in the gazebo but would appreciate the antiques; he and his first wife Down Below had been experienced collectors. It was the bottom line that interested Qwilleran personally: *Innkeepers Carla Helmuth and Trudy Feathering are former members of the Grand Island Club.* With no motive other than curiosity about the private estates, he determined to check out the Island Experience the next day, rain or shine. He went home and trimmed his moustache.

The sun was shining Thursday morning. Before going to breakfast, Qwilleran laid out his clothing for the visit with the former members of the Grand Island Club: a brushed silk shirt that Polly had given him for Sweetest Day, his new khaki twill trousers, and his British tan loafers.

The Hardings were leaving the breakfast room as he arrived. "Lovely day for the nature trail!" Mrs. Harding told him. "The wild-flowers will be at their best, but don't forget the mosquito repellent. Spray and pray, as Arledge says."

"With emphasis on the latter," said her husband. "After a heavy rain, their buzzing sounds like a pondful of bullfrogs."

"By the way," Qwilleran asked them, "when you used to visit the Ritchies, did you meet any clubmembers named Feathering or Helmuth?"

The couple searched each other's eyes for answers, then admitted that the names were only vaguely familiar. "We didn't know any of the clubmembers well. The Ritchies were not what you would call clubby."

"It's not important," he said. "I merely heard that their widows were running a bed-and-breakfast here."

"How interesting," murmured Mrs. Harding, although it was clear that she was not interested at all.

After smoked salmon and scrambled eggs, followed by ham-and-potato cakes with chutney, Qwilleran returned to Four Pips to dress for his visit with the widows. As he unlocked the door he heard sounds of commotion; when he walked in, he saw a scene of disaster: table lamp on the floor, chair knocked over, desk papers scattered. He stepped on something; it was a domino. He kicked something; it was his green apple. Koko was circling the room wildly, jumping over furniture, ricocheting off the walls, and yowling with pain—or glee. He was having a catfit.

"Stop! Stop!" Qwilleran yelled.

Koko made a few more turns about the room before stopping and licking his battered body. Yum Yum came crawling out from under the sofa.

"You ruffian! What's the matter with you?" Qwilleran scolded. Patiently he put the room in order. Nothing was broken. The lamp shade had flown off, and the harp was bent, but there was no harm done. The dominoes scattered about the floor were found; only the cover of the maroon velvet box was missing. It would show up somewhere. He put the dominoes in a desk drawer. Then he went into the bedroom to change clothes.

First he noticed a sock on the floor. Next he saw his trousers crumpled on the floor behind the bedside table. And where was his silk shirt? Hunting for it on hands and knees, he found it wadded up under the dresser.

"You fiend!" Qwilleran exploded. "I just had this washed and pressed! I can't wear any of this now."

Koko stood in the doorway, looking impudent—with legs splayed, tail stiffly curled, and ears pointed in two directions.

Qwilleran sat down abruptly on the bed. Could it be that Koko did not want him to visit the Island Experience? The cat knew nothing about the inn, or the women who ran it, or the reason for going there! Or did he? Something was going on in that little cat brain!

Qwilleran shrugged in resignation. No one would believe that a man of his size, intelligence, education, and *wealth* could be tyrannized by a ten-pound animal. Now he had lost the wherewithal and the incentive to visit the Island Experience.

He brought a bottle of club soda from the refrigerator and took it to the porch to drink while he simmered down. It was calm on the porch. The woods were beautiful after the rain. He saw some yellow flowers outside the screens that had not been there before. When a rabbit hopped out of the underbrush and came close to the porch, Qwilleran remained quiet and motionless. And then he witnessed the incredible. The Siamese came out of the house and ambled toward the rabbit. There was no stealth, no stalking, no hostile posturing. They looked at the visitor, and the rabbit looked at them with his nose twitching. Then he hopped away.

Qwilleran finished his drink and then changed clothes. He put on some lightweight jeans, a long-sleeved T-shirt, and his yellow baseball cap. "I'll be back after a while," he told the Siamese. He found the mosquito repellent and headed for the nature trail.

There was a wagon in front of Five Pips, delivering a small barroom piano. Lori had unlocked the door for the deliverymen, but the window shades were still drawn. "Hi, Qwill!" she said. "The hotel is lending her a piano. Isn't that nice? She'll be here starting this weekend."

"Have you ever taken the nature trail?" he asked.

"I haven't had time, but I hear it's lovely."

The approach to the trail was mysteriously inviting. The path was thick with pine needles and spongy after the rain. On either side there were tall, straight pines with lofty branches admitting shafts of sunlight, while oaks and graceful birches dappled the path with shade. At intervals, small paths led into the underbrush on the left, each marked by a name painted on a shingle or small boulder: SEAGULL INN . . . ISLAND EXPERIENCE. Farther along there was a larger marker: GRAND ISLAND CLUB—PRIVATE, followed by the elegantly simple names of summer estates like SEVEN OAKS and THE BIRCHES. Narrower trails, darkly forbidding, led into dense woods on the right; an occasional sign said KEEP OUT . . . or simply DOGS.

Qwilleran never attempted to identify flora and fauna. Through painful experience he knew poison ivy when he saw it, and he knew which small animals had long ears and which had bushy tails. Otherwise he was botanically and zoologically illiterate. He merely enjoyed being alone in the forest with his thoughts. No one else was abroad after the recent deluge. He was in a small, green, private world of sights and sounds, plus the occasional prick of a proboscis on the back of his neck. The trail went on and on. He climbed over hillocks and trotted down into bosky gullies. At one time he asked himself, Will I be able to write a thousand words about this?

Eventually the fresh, verdant aroma mingled with another—the dark muskiness of marshland. Once more he misted his clothing with mosquito spray. When he passed a boulder marked THE PINES, he knew he would soon reach the sand dune and the end of the trail. He would round one more bend and then turn back.

As he skirted a large shrub, however, he caught a glimpse of an apparition on the path ahead. He stepped back out of sight to assess the situation, then cautiously peered through the shrub's branches. It was a woman on the path ahead . . . with fluttering garments of pale green . . . and long, lank hair like a mermaid. In a flash of nonthink he imagined a lacustrine creature washed ashore in the recent rain. The notion soon vanished. This woman was real, and she was apparently studying the low-growing plant life. He found himself thinking, Watch out for poison ivy, lady! She would stoop to touch a leaf, rise to write in a book, then turn to the other side of the trail to examine another specimen. It was odd garb for a botanist, Qwilleran thought; when Polly went birding, she wore hiking boots and jeans. This woman's movements were graceful, and her apparel added to the enchantment. He felt like a mythic satyr spying on a woodland nymph.

A sudden scream brought him back to reality. She had been reaching into the ground cover when she shrieked and recoiled in horror!

Without thinking, he rushed forward, shouting inanely, "Hello! Hello!"

"Ricky! Ricky!" she screamed in panic.

"What's the trouble?" he called out as he ran toward her.

"A snake!" she cried hysterically. "I'm bitten! I think it was a cottonmouth! . . . Ricky! Ricky!"

"Where is he?"

She pointed vaguely with her left hand, dropping her book. "At home," she groaned between sobs.

"I'll help you. Where d'you live?"

"The Pines." Then she cried in a weaker voice, "Ricky! Ricky!"

"Take it easy! I'll get you there." Scooping her up in his arms, he started backtracking toward the boulder that marked the right path, keeping his pace fast but smooth. She was surprisingly lightweight; the voluminous garments covered an emaciated frame. She clutched her right wrist, which was swelling rapidly. "Let your arm hang down," he ordered.

"The pain!" she moaned. "My whole arm!"

He broke into a gliding trot. "You'll be okay . . . I'll get you home." They had reached the boulder and turned down the private path. "Won't be long now," he managed to say between heavy breathing. "We'll get a doctor."

"Ricky's a doctor . . . I feel sick!" Then she fell ominously silent, her thin face pale. The path was ending. He could see green grass ahead. Two men were standing on the grass.

"Ricky!" Qwilleran shouted with almost his last breath.

Startled, they looked up. One ran forward. "Elizabeth! What happened?"

"Snake bite," Qwilleran gasped.

"I'll take her!" The man named Ricky gathered her up and ran to a golf cart nearby. As the cart headed toward a clump of buildings in the distance, he was talking on a portable phone.

The other man calmly finished a maneuver with a croquet mallet. "Bonkers!" he announced with satisfaction. Turning to Qwilleran, he said, "I suppose I should thank you for rescuing my baby sister. She's been warned to stay out of the woods . . . I'm Jack Appelhardt. And you're . . . ?"

"Jim Qwilleran. Staying at the Domino Inn. I happened to be—"

"What?" the man interrupted with an unpleasant smile. "Does anyone actually stay at that place?" His remark was meant to be jocular.

Qwilleran was not amused. Gruffly he replied, "Hope she'll be all right." He turned away and walked up the access path as briskly as his lungs would permit. He could hear a motorized vehicle beeping in the languid atmosphere. It grew louder, then stopped. He could visualize the rescue squad running with a stretcher, loading the victim into the ambulance, radioing for the helicopter. "Ricky" would accompany the patient; it helped to have a doctor in the house. This was one island incident that Qwilleran could not attribute to foul play.

Reaching the main trail, he sat on the boulder to catch his breath before starting home. Then a prick on the back of his neck made him realize he had lost his mosquito spray. He returned to the scene of the rescue and retrieved not only the spray can but a silver pen and a leatherbound book stamped in gold: "E. C. Appelhardt." It contained lists of botanical names, along with dates and places. The latest entry was: *Dionaea muscipula (Venus's flytrap)*.

He returned home with the lost articles and a potpourri of thoughts: Strange woman . . . so thin . . . how old? . . . Could be young . . . face full of pain . . . why so thin? . . . who was the doctor? . . . strange brother . . . very strange woman . . . unusual clothing . . . hair like a mermaid . . .

As he reached the end of the trail and turned into Pip Court, he remembered the last-minute catfit that had raised havoc with a silk shirt and a good pair of pants. Otherwise, he would have been having refreshments in a gazebo with two widows instead of risking a heart attack to rescue a not-so-fair damsel in distress . . . And then he thought, Was the cat's tantrum just a coincidence? Or what?

He could never be sure whether Koko's catfits were the result of a stitch in the side, a twitch in a nerve end, or an itch in the tail. Sometimes the cat had an ulterior motive. Sometimes he was trying to communicate.

# Nine

When Qwilleran arrived at Four Pips following the episode on the nature trail, the Siamese were playing a cozy domestic
scene in the lounge chair, which they had commandeered as their
own. Koko was biting Yum Yum's neck, and she was slobbering in his
ear.

"Disgusting!" Qwilleran said to them.

He stripped off his clothes and took a shower. Despite the arduous
detour through the woods, he still had to check the Island Experience
and make a reservation for the Rikers. He took a rest and revived
himself with some packaged snacks before dressing in his second-best
shirt and pants. His crumpled duds he stuffed into a plastic bag for
another trip to the Vacation Helpers.

On the way he could not resist stopping at the inn to report his
adventure to the Hardings. They were sitting in their favorite swing,
close to the front door, where they could see everyone coming and
going.

"I've just met some members of the royal family," he told them as
he walked up the steps.

"The Appelhardts?" the vicar said in surprise. "Dare one inquire
how that came about?"

Qwilleran related the story without mentioning his aerobic feat with
an armful of hysterical botanist. "She said she lived at The Pines, and
I helped her get home. Two men were playing croquet, and one of

them happened to be a doctor. He took her away in a golf cart, and I would guess she was airlifted to the mainland."

"Well, well, well!" Mrs. Harding exclaimed.

"Three holes in the ground," her husband said mockingly.

"Oh, Arledge!" She slapped his wrist. "He always says that," she complained to Qwilleran fussily.

The vicar said, "We haven't seen the royal family since the Ritchies disposed of their property. As their house guests we were invited to garden parties at The Pines. The matriarch of the Appelhardts always presided like the dowager queen mother."

"The refreshments were sumptuous," Mrs. Harding recalled, "and there were peacocks strutting around the garden, spreading their tails and making horrendous noises when one least expected it."

"Alas, the Ritchies are gone, and the royal family is still with us," the vicar said in a grieving tone. "If you are interested in a little authentic history, Mr. Qwilleran—"

"I'm very interested!" He pulled up a chair.

"In the 1920s, the Appelhardts bought the western half of the island from the government and displaced the islanders, who had been tolerated as squatters. They established the Grand Island Club for millionaires who enjoy nature—if not too uncomfortably natural. According to widespread belief, they bought the land for ten dollars an acre and sold it to club members for ten dollars a square foot. I suspect it is now worth ten dollars a square inch." He finished with a chuckle that developed into a coughing spell.

Mrs. Harding rummaged in her handbag. "Here, Arledge, take this lozenge, and do be careful!"

Qwilleran said, "I had only a brief glimpse of their estate from the rear, but it seems extensive."

"Oh, yes!" she said. "Besides the main lodge there are smaller lodges for the married sons, cottages for the help, stables for the horses, a large swimming pool with pool house, tennis courts—"

"My dear, you sound like a real-estate agent," her husband chided.

She gave him a reproving glance and continued. "The married sons are professional men. The young woman you met is their only daughter. She never married. There's also a very handsome son—married several times, I believe. He appears to have no serious calling."

"The prodigal son," Mr. Harding explained. "Inevitable in every family of means."

His wife said, "The Moseley sisters will want to hear about this, Mr.

Qwilleran. The daughter was a student at the school where they taught. I'm sure you've met Edith and Edna, haven't you?"

"I met one of them at the fruit basket, but I don't know whether it was Edna or Edith. She was promoting bananas as a source of something-or-other."

"That was Edna. She's the taller of the two and wears glasses."

"It's Edith who wears glasses," her husband corrected her. "Edna wears corrective shoes and speaks with a soft voice. Edith taught dramatic arts and always projects from the diaphragm. Edna taught science, I believe. She's the prettier of the two—"

"Well, you must excuse me," Qwilleran said as Mr. Harding paused for breath. "I have an important errand to do. We'll continue this later."

His next stop was the Vacation Helpers service center, where he dropped off his clothes to be pressed. Shelley greeted the silk shirt like an old friend. "You're really hard on your clothes," she said.

"Don't blame me. My roommate flew off the handle."

"Do you let her get away with that?"

"My roommate is a male with four legs and a tail and sharp teeth," he explained.

"Oh, don't tell me! Let me guess! You have a German shepherd. . . . No? A Weimaraner?"

"You're not even warm. I'll give you a clue. He has a dark mask."

"A Boxer!"

"No. I'll tell you what," Qwilleran said. "I'll pick up my pressing in an hour or so, and you think about it in the meantime."

The Island Experience was the last in the row of commercial establishments on West Beach Road, and it was the most imposing. The rustic lodge was landscaped with taste and money. Instead of the traditional porch, a contemporary deck spanned the front elevation, overlooking the lake. There were tubs of salmon-pink geraniums to match the salmon-pink umbrella tables, but there were no guests in the salmon-pink canvas chairs.

Qwilleran assumed they were all in the gazebo, drinking the complimentary champagne. He rang the bell.

The woman who greeted him was a handsome, well-dressed, mature woman with a sparkling smile. "Welcome to Island Experience! I'm Carla, your merry innkeeper."

"I'm Jim Qwilleran, a bad-humored traveler from the mainland."

"Trudy!" she called over her shoulder. "Guess who just walked in! The Qwill Pen himself!"

Another woman with designer-style appearance and personality came briskly into the foyer, smiling and extending both hands in welcome. "We've been reading your column in the little newspaper here, and it's enchanting! We remember your by-line from Chicago, too. Are you looking for a place to stay? Be our guest!"

"To tell the truth, I've been on the island since Sunday," he said. "I'm traveling with pets, so I'm obliged to stay in one of the cottages at Domino Inn."

"Why don't you stay here and let the animals have the cottage? The Vacation Helpers will feed them and walk them for you."

"It's not so simple as that," he objected. "I appreciate the suggestion, but my purpose here at the moment is to find lodgings for a couple of friends. Arch Riker and his wife—he's publisher of the 'little newspaper'—want to spend this weekend on the island. I believe they'd enjoy your inn."

While standing in the foyer he had scanned the adjoining rooms and had noted the impressive antiques and impressive decor and also the lack of guests. Someone was hovering in the living room, but she wore a salmon-pink uniform and was dusting the bric-a-brac.

"Let us show you around," Carla offered. "It took nerve to paint the plank paneling white, but I think it enhances our country antiques, don't you?"

There were loungy sofas in the living room, foils for the expensively severe tables, desks and cupboards. In the dining room Windsor chairs surrounded a long trestle table; its pedigree was palpable even to Qwilleran. Upstairs, only one door was closed; open doors revealed perfectly appointed bedrooms and sitting rooms that seemed to be waiting for a magazine photographer.

"Do you think your friends would like a suite?" Trudy asked as she handed him a card listing the rates.

There were four bedrooms and two suites. The Garden Suite was twice the price of a bedroom, and the English Suite was the most expensive of all, having a Jacobean canopy bed with twisted posts.

"I think Mr. and Mrs. Riker would like the English Suite," he said, chuckling inwardly at the thought of his friend's indignation. Arch could afford it, but he always played the tightwad. Furthermore, he had been goading Qwilleran for his Scottish thrift for four decades. It was time for sweet revenge.

"We put fresh flowers in the English Suite," one of the women said. "Do you happen to know what the lady likes?"

"Yellow."

"Perfect! Yellow looks lovely with the dark oak. We'll phone the mainland and have them shipped over by ferry."

With the arrangements completed, Qwilleran was invited to have champagne in the gazebo. "Make mine a soft drink, and I'll accept with pleasure," he said.

The gazebo was screened, not only against mosquitoes but against wandering cats. Several healthy specimens, two of them pregnant, were prowling about the backyard, waiting for the hors d'oeuvres.

"Everyone feeds them," Trudy said. "The island is really overcat-ted."

They sat in white wicker chairs while a timorous young island woman in salmon pink brought the champagne bucket, glasses, and a flavored mineral water for Qwilleran. He proposed a toast to the two merry innkeepers and then asked the standard question: What had brought them to the island? The women looked at each other briefly for cues and then began an overlapping dialogue:

Carla: "Both our families have been members of the Grand Island Club since it began, so we've been summer neighbors all our lives, until—"

Trudy: "Our husbands died, and our children thought the Caymans were more exciting, so—"

Carla: "We sold our memberships and—"

Trudy: "Started traveling together, buying antiques and staying at country inns."

Carla: "We collected so much stuff, we had two options—"

Trudy: "To open an antique shop or start a bed-and-breakfast, so—"

Carla: "We decided we'd like an inn, because we love meeting people and playing the host."

Trudy: "And then we heard about the Pear Island opportunity. Imagine our surprise when—"

Carla: "We realized it was our own Grand Island with a different name."

Trudy: "Actually, we're delighted, because—"

Carla: "There's something about this island that gets into the blood."

As they stopped for breath, Qwilleran blinked his eyes and shook his head. Seated between them, he was turning rapidly from side to side to keep up with their dizzying recital. "May I change my seat in order to see both of you lovely ladies?" he asked. It was no exaggeration; he wondered how many hairdressers, masseuses, dressmakers, cosmetic surgeons, orthodontists, and voice coaches had labored to produce these perfect womanworks. Their well-modulated voices assumed a higher pitch, however, with each pouring from the bottle.

A tray of canapés was brought to the gazebo by the painfully awkward server, who was trying hard to do everything right. When she had gone, Qwilleran asked, "Do you staff your inn with islanders?"

"We debated that. Don Exbridge wanted us to hire students from the mainland, but our families always hired islanders, and we felt comfortable with them. They're part of the island experience, you know."

Another chilled bottle of champagne arrived, and another bottle of kiwi-flavored mineral water, and Qwilleran said, "You mentioned that you sold your *memberships*. Not your real estate?"

The women exchanged a glance that said, Shall we tell him? Then they succumbed to his sincere gaze and sympathetic manner. They were relaxing. They were eager to talk.

"Well," Trudy began, "when we decided to sell our property—which our families had held since the 1920s—we learned we had to sell it back to the club *at their price,*which was much less than market value. It was in the original contract. Nothing we could do about it."

Carla interrupted with belligerence, "If my husband had been alive, he'd have found a loophole, believe me!"

"The Grand Island Club is controlled by the Appelhardt family, who founded it, and Mrs. Appelhardt, the mother, is a hard woman," Trudy said.

Carla again: "I call her a Harpy! I always felt sorry for her kids. They grew up with our kids. None of them turned out the way she intended."

Trudy: "Poetic justice! She wanted the eldest to be a lawyer. He got through law school but could never pass the bar exam."

Carla: "The next was supposed to be a heart surgeon. And what is he? A perfectly wonderful vet! He always loved animals."

Trudy: "And what about the girl? She's a real flake!"

Carla: "And the youngest boy! She's bailed him out of three marriages already."

Trudy: "It would be funny if it wasn't so sad."

Carla: "Why does he bother to get married?"

Trudy: "He's just an easy mark who can't say no."

When the merry innkeepers signaled for a third bottle of champagne, Qwilleran stood up, thanked them for their hospitality, and explained that he had another appointment. Leaving them happily relaxed in the wicker chairs, he walked down West Beach Road, marveling at the intrigue behind the Golden Curtain. He picked up his pressed garments, then stopped at the Domino Inn to phone Riker's office. He left the information about the reservation with the secretary.

"He's here. Want to talk to him?" asked Wilfred.

"Haven't time. Late for an appointment." Qwilleran knew that his friend's first question would be "How much?"

On the way out of the building he was stopped by the Moseley sisters. "You're a hero!" they said. "The Hardings told us about the rescue."

"Just happened to be in the right place at the right time."

"We knew Elizabeth very well," said the one with glasses. "She was a student at our school in Connecticut. When we read about Pear Island resort in the Boston papers and made our reservation, we had no idea we were coming to her beloved Grand Island."

"Have you seen her since you've been here?"

"Oh, no! We wouldn't think of intruding," said the pretty one with a soft voice. "Is she looking well?"

"In the throes of a snake bite one is never at one's best."

"Very true." They nodded, smiling at his arch observation.

"But to answer your question seriously, she seems to be unhealthily thin."

One sister murmured to the other, "She's having problems again. She's not eating. Too bad she can't get away from that environment."

A profile of the rich little mermaid was forming in Qwilleran's mind. "Was she a good student?"

"Oh, yes," said Edith. "All her life she'd had private tutors and was a prodigious reader, but she was a nervous wreck when she came to us. We all worked hard to improve her diet and elevate her spirit and draw her into campus life."

"We succeeded to a degree, and she should have gone on to college, but . . . it didn't happen. The reason was never explained. We corresponded for a while, but gradually she slipped away into her small world. Poor Elizabeth!"

Qwilleran concealed his personal curiosity by inquiring, "And now that you've seen her beloved island, what do you think of it?"

"It's not the idyllic spot we expected," said Edna ruefully. "The Bambas are a lovely family, but we doubt that we'll stay our full two weeks."

"The island isn't even pear-shaped," Edith said. "We've taken carriage rides on both beaches, and it's an isosceles triangle!"

Edna said, "You should put that in your column, Mr. Qwilleran."

As he ambled back to Four Pips, he was painting a mental picture of the royal family, brushstroke by brushstroke: the daughter who wouldn't eat . . . the son who couldn't stop marrying . . . the law graduate who couldn't (or wouldn't) pass the bar exam . . . the doctor who preferred to treat animals . . . the autocratic mother who was said to be a Harpy.

Upon arriving home he immediately wrote a brief note to Mrs. Appelhardt: "Found these on the nature trail. Hope your daughter recovers swiftly." He signed it "J. Qwilleran." Then he set out for the Vacation Helpers once more, carrying the botany book and the silver pencil.

Shelley was at the counter. "Back again?" she said in surprise. "Was the pressing okay?"

"No complaint," he said, "except for the scorch marks on the back of the shirt."

Her look of horror melted quickly to a smile. "Oh, you're a male chauvinist comic! What can we do for you now?"

"Could you wrap these two articles and deliver them to an address on West Beach Road? Tomorrow will do."

"We'll be happy to. I have a nice box and some seagull giftwrap."

"This is not a gift," he said. "On the other hand, I don't want it to look like a homemade bomb. Here's the note to go with it, and here's the address." He looked over her shoulder to the rear of the room. "Is your cat supposed to be scratching himself in the baby's playpen?"

"No! No! Out! Out!" she screamed, chasing him and slamming a door. "Somebody left the door open. That's Hannibal, one of our resident strays."

"A 'resident stray' sounds like an oxymoron," he said.

"Hannibal is foxy, but he's no moron," she quipped. "He knows a good place to eat. How did you like your box lunch?"

"The meatloaf was excellent. Could you deliver a whole one to me, say, every other day? I'd pay in advance."

"Absolutely!" said Shelley. "We'll start tomorrow. Midge makes four-pounders for sandwiches and two-pounders for snacks."

"Two-pounders will be ample."

"Is it for your roommate?" she asked, looking him steadily in the eye. "Your roommate is a raccoon, isn't he?"

Shelley looked so triumphant, so pleased with herself, that he said mildly, "How did you guess?"

# Ten

On Friday morning Qwilleran opened a can of lobster for the cats' breakfast. "This is the last junk food you're going to get for a while. For the rest of our stay here, you'll have homemade meatloaf, delivered fresh, every other day, by bicycle. That's the good news. The bad news is that you are now raccoons."

Through long association with this pair of connoisseurs, he knew their favorites: freshly roasted turkey, homemade meatloaf, and canned red salmon, top grade. Nevertheless, they gobbled the lobster with rapturous slurping, waving of tails, and clicking of fangs on the plate. Yum Yum looked up after each swallow to confirm that Qwilleran was still there. Afterward, she jumped onto his lap while he drank his coffee, stroked her fur, and paid her extravagant compliments. He called it their après-breakfast schmooz.

Their dinner was served earlier than usual that evening, because Qwilleran wanted to check the post office before it closed. He cubed the meatloaf precisely—five-sixteenths of an inch, he estimated. "Don't say I never do anything for you," he said to the waiting cats. They were quieter than usual, and they were sitting a little farther away. After placing a generous plateful on the floor, he stepped back to enjoy their ecstasy. They approached it stealthily and backed away. He sampled a cube himself. There was nothing wrong with it; in fact, it might be described as . . . *tasty*. "Try it! You'll like it!" They walked away with heads lowered and tails drooping.

"Well, I'm not going to stand here and do catfood commercials for you brats!" He left the plate on the floor and dressed for his trip downtown.

The resort area was gearing up for what everyone hoped would be a busy weekend, although the atmosphere was more wishful than confident. Horse cabs lined up at the ferry dock. Cargo was being offloaded for the deli and general store—mostly beer. In an extra bid for business, the T-shirt studio was hanging choice designs on clotheslines strung across the front of the shop.

In the same spirit of hopeful doubt, Qwilleran checked the post office, but there was no news from Oregon. He assumed Polly was having a rollicking vacation—looking for puffin birds, giggling with her college roommate, and talking about *him.*

For a while he watched vacationers disembarking with bevies of children, their shouts punctuating the waterfront hush: "Junior, don't hang over the railing! . . . Mom, did you bring my rollerblades? . . . Lookit all the horses! What are they for? . . . Hey, Dad, could this island sink?"

Among the arrivals were six backpackers. The size of their gear suggested they were the crew who had been camping at the lighthouse on weekends and hang gliding on the dune. They were attractive young people, Qwilleran thought: the women, healthy; the men, athletic; and all exposed skin, enviably suntanned. Also arriving, with luggage to be loaded into a carriage, was Dr. June Halliburton with a limp-brimmed sunhat shading her white skin and red hair.

In the hotel lobby Qwilleran picked up a copy of Friday's *Moose County Something* and was surprised to find the following item on page one:

SNAKE-BITE VICTIM

AIRLIFTED FROM ISLAND

The sheriff's helicopter evacuated a victim of snake bite from Pear Island to the Pickax General Hospital Thursday. Elizabeth C. Appelhardt, 23, a summer resident of the Grand Island Club, was in good condition today after treatment, according to a hospital spokesperson. This is the third medical emergency handled by the sheriff's airborne division this month.

Only the sheriff would like the coverage, Qwilleran mused; he was always campaigning for re-election or lobbying for more funds to buy rescue equipment. The queen mother would dislike the publicity because it invaded her family's Olympian privacy. The victim would take umbrage at the mention of her age. Don Exbridge would explode because the report made the island sound hazardous to one's health.

There was already a commotion erupting in the manager's office, and Qwilleran caught sight of a bald head and waving arms as Exbridge shouted, "Get those damned T-shirts off the front of the store! What do they think this is? A Persian bazaar?"

As soon as the dining room opened, Qwilleran presented himself at the reservation desk.

"Hi, Mr. Q! You're early," said Derek Cuttlebrink, resplendent in pirate's tricorn and one gold earring. "Are you all alone tonight?"

"No, I've brought my friend, Anatole France." He held up his copy of *Penguin Island.* "I'd like a quiet table where I can read—also a reservation for tomorrow night at eight o'clock—three persons." In a lower voice he asked, "Any luck with your assignment?"

Derek nodded importantly. "Gotta contact," he mumbled while appearing to study his reservation chart. "How about Sunday night? I'm off early."

"Come to the fourth cottage behind the inn."

Over shrimp bisque and Cajun pork chops Qwilleran finished reading his book and was leaving the dining room when another blowup occurred in the manager's office. There was a torrent of invective, and Dwight Somers came rushing out. He caught sight of Qwilleran. "I need a drink! Come into the bar."

He led the way to a secluded booth and ordered a double martini. "That guy's a madman when things don't go the way he planned. And don't try to reason with him, or you'll get your head lopped off. If I'm still here by the Fourth of July, I'll be surprised. Either I'll be fired, or I'll be in jail for murder."

"What's happened now?" Qwilleran asked sympathetically.

"It's a funny thing, Qwill. The chicken incident didn't faze him because he could use his clout to squash the implications, but little things drive him bananas—like the pickets last weekend, and the critical letters to the editor, and the snake-bite item in today's paper. He says, 'Who cares if some snooty rich kid gets bitten by a snake?' He says it's not important news. He says it only tarnishes the image of the resort, which is a boon to the community. When the paper reported the county's decision to spray for mosquitoes by plane, he got all kinds of flak, and he blamed you guys for playing it up on page one."

"Are we running a newspaper or a publicity agency?" Qwilleran asked.

"He's not dumb; he knows he can't dictate to the press," said Dwight, "but he has these insane tantrums! If I play Devil's advocate, in the interest of public relations, I get dumped on. Wait'll you hear his latest brainstorm!" He gulped the rest of his drink and waved his glass at the waiter.

Qwilleran advised him to order some food, too. "I'll have coffee and a piece of pie . . . Okay, what's his latest noodle?"

"Well, he's afraid we're getting too many families with five kids and a picnic basket, instead of the sophisticated crowd he intended. So he wants to offer a Midsummer Night's Dream weekend package—everything first class and limited to thirty persons, adults only. It includes transportation from the mainland by private boat; flowers and champagne in the rooms; breakfast in bed; and a supper-dance on Midsummer's Eve."

"Sounds okay," Qwilleran said.

"He wants it outdoors, with white tablecloths, fresh flowers on the tables, three wine glasses at every place, hurricane candles, strolling musicians, and waiters in white coats with black bowties. No pirate shirts! That would be okay around the pool; if it rained, we could set up indoors. But here's the fly in the soup: He wants it at the lighthouse!" Dwight took a swig of his second double martini.

"Can you imagine the logistics?" he went on. "First you need a fleet of wagons to transport tables, chairs, portable dance floor, table settings, food warmers, chilled wine, and portable johns. There are no facilities up there. Then you need a fleet of carriages to transport the guests. The ground behind the lighthouse is uneven, and how do you keep the tables and chairs from wobbling? The wind is capable of whipping the tablecloths around, blowing the napkins away, putting out the candles, breaking the glass chimneys, and even blowing the food off the plates! And suppose it starts to rain!"

"Hasn't Don ever been to Lighthouse Point?"

"Of course he has, but he never lets reality and common sense get in the way of a fanciful idea."

Qwilleran said, "I see a great scenario for a comedy skit. You have all the guests on the rock, getting happily plastered, and it starts to rain. No shelter. No carriages; they've returned to the stables. Everyone's drenched. The steaks are swimming on the plates. Thunder is crashing; lightning is flashing. Then the fog horn starts blatting, fifty feet from everyone's eardrums. The guests riot. Two of them take refuge inside the portable potties and refuse to come out. I think it has infinite possibilities for laughs."

"Not funny," said Dwight, but he laughed just the same and applied himself to his steak. Finally he said to Qwilleran, "And what have you been doing all week?"

"Not much. I rescued a mermaid from certain death, that's all." He described the incident with more detail than he had wasted on other listeners.

"It figures," Dwight said with envy. "The guy who has an indecent fortune of his own is the lucky one who rescues an heiress. What's she like?"

"She has the svelte figure of a rainbow trout, the hair of a mermaid, and flowing garments that probably hide a tail. Want me to line her up for you? In case you get fired, it would be useful to have an heiress on the string."

"No, thanks. Finders keepers," said Dwight. "What do you hear from Polly?"

"She hasn't even sent a postcard, but I bet she phones Pickax every night and talks to Bootsie."

"I'm envious of your relationship with Polly, Qwill. You're comfortable friends, and you keep your independence. I've been in Moose County almost a year without any luck. I've bought dinner for every unattached female within fifty miles, except Amanda Goodwinter, and I may get around to her yet. So far, no one has passed the litmus test. Hixie Rice is my type, if you want to know, but she's tied up with that doctor."

"It won't last long," Qwilleran reassured him. "No one ever lasts long with Hixie, and that would go for you, too."

Dwight said sheepishly, "I even took June Halliburton to dinner at the Palomino Paddock and spent half a week's salary. It was a bust!"

"What happened?" Qwilleran asked, although he could guess.

"You know how she is! She has looks, talent, and credentials, but she says the damnedest things! We were drinking seventy-dollar champagne, and she looked at me with those suggestive eyes and said, "You're a handsome, intelligent man, Dwight, with a wonderful personality. Why don't you shave off that scruffy beard and invest in a good toupee?" That's typical of that woman. She pursues guys as if she likes them, and then stomps on 'em. How well do you know her?"

"Well enough to know I don't want to know her any better."

"I think of her as a predatory misanthrope."

"That'll do until a stronger word comes along," Qwilleran said. "At the Rikers' wedding she was coming on to every man at the reception, including the bridegroom. Polly can't stand her. When they meet, you could light a cigarette from the sparks."

"Did you ever write June up in your column?"

"Almost. I intended to interview her about music in the schools, but she wanted to make it a social occasion at her apartment. When I insisted on an office appointment, she proved impossible to interview. It was verbal football. She called the plays, carried the ball, straight-armed questions, and made end runs around the subject. The way it ended, she scored all the points, but I won the game. I never wrote the column."

"You media types always get the last word. I'm in the wrong business."

Qwilleran said, "Another time, I invited the Comptons over for a drink after the theater, and they brought June. She didn't stay long. She said the circular building and diagonal ramps gave her a headache. Actually it was Koko giving her the whammy. When he stares at someone's forehead, it's like a gimlet boring into the brain."

"What was his problem?" Dwight asked.

"Apparently he didn't like her scent."

"Starting this weekend, she'll be here for the whole summer."

"I know," Qwilleran said. "I saw her getting off the ferry with a lot of luggage—and an eye for the mounted security men in red coats. Was she another of Exbridge's bright ideas?"

"No, she approached him with the proposition."

"What is she doing in this remote part of the country anyway? With all her talents she belongs in a major city Down Below. I'll have to ask Lyle Compton how she landed in Moose County. He's the one who hired her."

"Lyle will be here Sunday night, doing his talk on Scotland. Do you have any big plans for the weekend?"

"Just dining with Arch and Mildred tomorrow night," Qwilleran said, "and avoiding my musical neighbor."

As Qwilleran walked back to the Domino Inn, he had to stand aside for emergency vehicles speeding up the beach road. He could imagine that a member of the Grand Island Club had a heart attack, or a carriageful of tourists overturned, or the kid who was leaning over the ferry railing fell over the cliff at the lighthouse. By the time he reached the inn, the vehicles were speeding back downtown, and the sheriff's helicopter could be heard.

The guests sitting in porch swings were all agog when Qwilleran walked up the driveway. Someone called out, "Mitchell, he came back!" The four-year-old rushed indoors and rushed out again to hand him an envelope with an important crest on the flap.

Mrs. Harding said, "It was delivered by a man in green livery, driving a very handsome buggy with a beautiful horse!"

At Four Pips the Siamese were allowed to sniff the envelope, and their noses registered excitement. The note read:

> Dear Mr. Qwilleran,
>     Please honor us by having tea at The Pines Sunday afternoon. We wish to thank you in person for coming to the rescue of our daughter Elizabeth after her unfortunate mishap. She is out of danger, we are glad to say, and returns to the island tomorrow. It will be our pleasure to send a carriage for you at four o'clock Sunday.

It was signed "Rowena Appelhardt." She was the queen mother, Qwilleran guessed, and this was to be a command appearance at Buckingham Palace. At least, he would see the peacocks, and Mrs. Harding said the refreshments were commendable.

The Siamese were prowling and yowling and looking lean and hungry. He checked their feeding station. The plate was empty, but the cubes of meatloaf had merely been scattered about the floor of the kitchenette. They looked dry and unappetizing.

"Shame on you!" he said. "There are homeless cats that would kill for a taste of this meatloaf! And it behooves you to get used to it, because we have another eight pounds coming."

He shoveled up the rejected delicacy and took it up the lane to the old glazed birdbath that served as a feeding station for the wild cats. Before he could even empty his bowl, three of them came from nowhere to fight for their share. Then he saw Nick Bamba, home for the weekend and hammering nails into a wooden contraption.

"What are you doing?" Qwilleran asked.

"Building a rack to keep the trash barrels off the ground. It's neater, and the strays can sleep underneath. Lori's idea."

"You never quit, do you, Nick?"

"Compared to my job at the prison, this is R-and-R. Did you have a good week? Did you find out anything?"

"So far I've been feeling my way and making contacts. Stop in tomorrow, and we'll talk."

Qwilleran went into the lounge for an apple and found that the
basket was filled with pears! While there he heard a radio newscast
coming from an alcove, where a family of three were playing dominoes. He walked over and said, "Mind if I listen? I'm interested in
tomorrow's weather."

"You've just missed it," said the father. He turned to his son. "Do
you remember what they said about the weather, Brad?"

The boy was about ten years old and looked too intelligent for his
age; he wore a T-shirt printed with the words: Ask Me. He said,
"Moderately high winds subsiding at midnight. Waves three to four
feet. Tomorrow sunny and warm with light winds from the southeast,
veering to southwest by afternoon. High tomorrow: seventy-five.
Low—"

"Hush," his father said, holding up a hand and inclining his head
toward the radio. The announcer was saying:

". . . police bulletin from Pear Island, where a shooting claimed
the life of a vacationer this evening. The victim, an adult male, was
hang gliding on the sand dune at the north end of the island when his
companions heard a gunshot and the kite fell into the shallow water of
the lake. Suffering from hypothermia as well as loss of blood, he was
given emergency aid at the scene by the volunteer rescue squad before
being airlifted by sheriff's helicopter to the mainland. He was pronounced dead on arrival at the Pickax General Hospital. Gunfire, not
unusual on the island, had been noted throughout the day and evening. The fatal bullet is thought to be a stray shot fired by a varmint
hunter, according to the sheriff's department. The victim's name has
not been released at this time, but police say he was not a resident of
Moose County."

"Nobody told us about gunfire on the island!" said the mother. "I
hate guns!"

As Qwilleran walked back to Four Pips, he thought, Another incident! . . . Nick will spend a sleepless night, worrying about the future of the inn . . . The woman who hates guns will convince her
husband to cut their visit short . . . The Moseley sisters will be glad
they're canceling . . . The two men who look like detectives, having
left, will come back.

He counted on his fingers: One, food poisoning. Two, drowning.
Three, bad fall. Four, explosion. Five, shooting . . . He was impressed by the diversity of the mishaps. There was no pattern, except

that they all targeted tourists at regularly spaced intervals. Qwilleran pictured a consortium of saboteurs, each performing his own specialty. The islanders were crafty, skilled, and knowledgeable as a result of the hard life they lived. What mystified him was Koko's lack of interest and cooperation. In the past he had sensed the presence of crime and sniffed for clues. Perhaps the island atmosphere dulled his senses. True, he had staged a catfit that caused Qwilleran to be the right person in the right place at the right time, but that had nothing to do with the five suspicious incidents.

At Four Pips the Siamese continued to look at Qwilleran reproachfully and hungrily, and it required great fortitude to hold out against their wiles. He would give them their crunchy bedtime snack, but that was all; for breakfast he would serve meatloaf again on a take-it-or-leave-it basis.

After dark the three of them liked to sit on the screened porch, listening to mysterious sounds in the trees and underbrush, but tonight there was competition from Five Pips: piano playing, voices, recorded music, laughter. Qwilleran sorted out the voices: two of them, one female, one male. Later, the music stopped and the voices were muffled. He went indoors, read for a while, gave the cats their treat, and then retired.

He fell asleep easily and had one of his fanciful dreams: The natives living on Pear Island were penguins, and the tourists were puffin birds. A great bald eagle appeared and attempted to tow the island to the mainland, but he was shot down by a rabbit hunter, and the island sank to the bottom of the lake.

"Whew!" Qwilleran gasped, waking and sitting up in bed. He could hear happy voices next door, saying good night. The male guest was leaving with a flashlight, and Qwilleran hoped it would illuminate the man's face when he passed Four Pips—not that it was any of Qwilleran's business, but he was observant by nature and by profession. His curiosity was aroused, however, when the visitor left by way of the nature trail.

# Eleven

Qwilleran may not have known it, but he was losing the Battle of the Meatloaf. Two hungry and indignant cats started yowling outside his bedroom door at six A.M. Saturday. He endured it for almost an hour and then—in bare feet and pajama bottoms—went to the kitchen to prepare another plate of meatloaf for the ungrateful wretches. They were quiet as he cut the food, mincing it this time instead of cubing it. They were quiet when he placed the plate on the floor. They looked at it in disbelief, as if to say, What is this stuff? . . . Are we supposed to eat this dog dinner? Just as they were shaking their paws exquisitely and walking away from the plate, there was a knock on the front door.

Qwilleran's watch said seven-fifteen. It must be Mitchell—who else? He might be bringing a message from the Rikers. Perhaps they had not arrived last night. Perhaps some emergency had arisen. He pulled the door open with anxiety.

To his embarrassment it was June Halliburton, fully clothed and squinting through the smoke of a cigarette that she held gracefully in one hand. She appraised his rumpled pajama bottoms and uncombed hair and grinned impishly. "Want to go to breakfast with me? Come as you are."

"Sorry," he said. "I won't be ready for food for another couple of hours. Go along without me. They serve an excellent breakfast."

"I'm aware of that," she said loftily. "I spent two weekends in this cottage, keeping your bed warm for you. Did anyone tell you I'm handling the entertainment for the hotel? While you're sitting around doing nothing, you might try writing some material for me. I can't guarantee I'll use it, but it should be good practice for you." These typically shabby remarks were made with the insolent smile that was her trademark.

Qwilleran had been writing college revues when she was still sucking teething rings. Before he could think of a retort within the bounds of civility, Koko came up behind and swooped to his shoulder, teetering there as if ready to spring and fixing the intruder with his laser stare.

"Well," she said, "come over to Five Pips for a drink, or some music, or anything—anytime." She flicked her cigarette, tossed her glistening red hair, and sauntered away.

Koko jumped to the floor, and Qwilleran said, "Thanks. You're a good egg! Tell you what I'm gonna do. I'll chop some smoked oysters and add them to the meatloaf."

Both cats went to work on the exotic hash and extracted the oyster while avoiding the meatloaf.

"Cats!" Qwilleran said. "You can't win!"

For his own breakfast he had ham biscuits with cheese sauce and then codfish cakes with scrambled eggs. It was late, and only one other table was taken. The family who had checked into Two Pips had an infant in a highchair and a tot who was attracted to Qwilleran's moustache. When he inadvertently made eye contact, she squirmed out of her chair and toddled to his table, offering him a piece of toast, partly masticated.

"Sandra, don't bother the man," her father said.

"She's very friendly," her mother explained.

Qwilleran groaned inwardly. He felt besieged by finicky cats, pushy piano players, and now gregarious youngsters. When he returned to Four Pips, the piano player was doing scales and finger exercises, a monotonous recital that made it difficult to concentrate on reading or writing. Eventually there was a pause. It felt good when she stopped! Then there was a knock on the front door. Irritably he yanked it open.

"Morning, Qwill," said Nick Bamba. He had two of his children by the hand. "Lovey wants to see your kitties, and this is Jason, who just graduated from first grade. He's our vice president in charge of waste baskets and litter boxes."

"We learned about Indians and squabs and cabooses," said the blond boy. "They lived in wigs with a hole for the smoke."

Qwilleran said, "And how is the future Madame President this morning?"

"Two in April," she said and lunged after Yum Yum, who slithered under the sofa. Koko looked on with haughty disapproval.

"The kitties are bashful," her father said, "but you've seen them now, and you can go home . . . Jason, take your sister back. Mr. Qwilleran and I have business to discuss."

"Okefenokee!" said Jason. He grabbed his sister's hand, and the two of them trudged up the lane, Lovey gazing back longingly.

Nick handed Qwilleran a plastic sack. "Here's some pears, Qwill. I bought a bushel on sale, but they have to be eaten right away."

"Thanks. Shall we sit on the porch?"

"Better sit indoors. The air is still this morning, and voices carry. Have you been downtown yet? The pickets came over on the first ferry, and they're marching again. They don't want the mosquitoes sprayed."

"What do you think about the hang-glider shooting?" Qwilleran asked.

"The sheriff blames a stray shot from a hunting gun. I say the sheriff is full of it! . . . So what's with you, Qwill?"

"I've lined up an undercover agent who can work from the inside. It's my contention that there's covert hostility among the natives. They don't come out punching, but they've infiltrated the resort as kitchen helpers, hack drivers, servants, busboys, dockworkers, handymen, and plenty we don't know about. They're silent. They're shadowy. I'm convinced your front steps were okay until one of these silent, shadowy islanders tampered with them—perhaps pulled a few nails under cover of darkness. Unfortunately I have no evidence . . . Is there any more news about the poultry farm in Lockmaster?"

"That investigation fizzled out," said Nick. "Nobody died. Everybody wants to forget it. Food poisoning is something that just happens."

"How will Exbridge react to the shooting last night?"

"This is not for publication, Qwill, but he's lobbying to get hunting banned on the island. The sound of gunfire makes tourists nervous, he says, especially those from big cities."

Qwilleran said, "The pickets will have a grand old time with that issue! Rabbit is a staple of the islanders' diet, and a mainstay of their economy."

"Want to hear something else, off the record? Don wants the county to pave the beach roads and cut through the sand dune to make it a ring road."

"The environmentalists are hypersensitive about sand dunes, you know, and the summer people will fight the paving project to the last drop of their blue blood. How do you and Lori feel about all these changes?"

"Well, it isn't the dream we had—not by a long shot—but now we're in it with both feet and every dollar we have, plus some we don't have."

"Nick, I hate to be a pessimist, but I bet Exbridge will want a golf course next. Then the ordinance against motor vehicles will be rescinded. There'll be RVs, motorcycles, bumper-to-bumper traffic and a gas station on Lighthouse Point. Emissions will kill the wildlife and defoliate the woods, and Piratetown will go condo. The island will be so honeycombed with wells and septic tanks that it'll sink like a sieve to the bottom of the lake."

"Qwill, I hope you're not gonna write anything crazy like that for your column. This was all confidential, you know." Nick stood up. "I've gotta go and do my chores . . . G'bye, kids," he said to the Siamese.

Qwilleran walked with him up the lane. The strays were hanging around the trash cans as usual. "They're all over," Nick said. "They're around restaurants, picnic tables, docks—wherever there's food. Exbridge wants the board of health to exterminate them."

"If he proposes that, he'll have another American Revolution on his hands."

"For God's sake, don't mention it!"

Qwilleran looked up sharply. "What's all that noise?"

"They're picnickers and day-trippers," Nick said. "They're supposed to use the public beach on the other side of the island, but they like our sand. You can't blame them."

Qwilleran left him and ambled across the road to the beach, where children were screaming and throwing sand and having a wonderful time; young adults were rocking to boom boxes; and volleyball players were yelling good-natured threats and insults. The scene gave him an idea for a satire on tourism, and he went back to Four Pips to set up his typewriter on the snack table. What he had in mind was a skit spoofing package weekends. It would require a cast of two: a tourist couple in shorts, sandals, and Pear Island T-shirts. The scene would be the hotel porch with rocking chairs. The tourists would be rocking, eating a box lunch, and reading aloud from an advertising flyer.

FANTASTIC FUN-FILLED WEEKEND
ON WONDERFUL PEAR ISLAND
ONLY $149.50
(Children under 12, 15% extra)

*Friday Afternoon* . . . You are met at the jetport by our friendly guide, who will give you a pear-shaped luggage tag (one per person) and a discount coupon for a T-shirt. Depart promptly for enchanting Moose County aboard a deluxe single-engine prop aircraft with seat belts and headrests. Peanuts will be served in flight, with only one scheduled stop for refueling, repairs, and use of facilities. Arrive at Moose County airport and proceed in the comfort of a converted school bus to an all-night restaurant famous for pirogi and boiled cabbage. After a delicious repast, continue to the historic Hotel Booze in the unspoiled lakeside town of Brrr, where you will spend your first exciting night.

*Saturday* . . . After a complimentary breakfast (choice of biscuit or muffin), you depart on a delightfully quaint coal-burning ferry for the voyage to the island. (Life preservers provided, but passengers are advised to use facilities before leaving hotel.) Enjoy the rare thrill of feeding the seagulls that follow the boat. (Bird bread not included.) Folding chairs available for passengers over 75. (Birth certificate required.)

On arrival at fabulous Pear Island, transfer to the spectacular Pear Island Hotel to register and receive your generous sample of mosquito spray. Your first day is entirely free—for walking around, splashing in the hotel pool, and rocking in the hotel's fifty rocking chairs. Watch the ferries unload; write postcards; shop for T-shirts; buy fudge; and thoroughly enjoy yourself. Feeling adventurous? Walk to the Riviera-type stone beach to hunt for agates. (Not included in the package: carriage rides, bike rentals, fishing parties, or lunch.)

Your exciting, fun-filled evening begins with a memorable dinner featuring the hotel's Very Special Chicken and a choice of sinfully delicious desserts: pears Romano, pears Chantilly, or pears Escoffier. Live entertainment follows, headlining the celebrated "Maestro of Moose County" and his accordion. When you retire after your full day of fun, you will find an individually wrapped square of fudge on your pillow. Sweet dreams!

*Sunday* . . . The excitement begins with a sumptuous breakfast buffet offering 85 items. (Choose any four.) Then it's "all aboard" a specially prepared hay wagon for a ride to Lighthouse Point via the exclusive West Beach Road. See the summer homes of the rich and famous! Photograph the picturesque lighthouse! See where hundreds of ships sank and thousands of persons drowned! Thrill to the sound of gunfire in the woods! After lunch (not included), you board the ferry and bid a reluctant farewell to magical Pear Island, an experience you will never forget . . . And only $149.50, based on triple occupancy! Price includes a short-term life insurance policy *plus* a free cat for each and every visitor to take home. Choice of colors. (Black-and-whites temporarily out of stock.)

Writing the skit put Qwilleran in a good mood for an evening with the Rikers, and shortly before eight o'clock he called for a carriage and picked them up at their bed-and-breakfast.

"How do you like the Island Experience?" he asked.

"It's a dream!" Mildred exclaimed. "The innkeepers are positively charming!"

"But their rates are atrocious!" Arch said. "Do you know what we're paying for that suite you reserved? There's only one other guest registered; that should tell you something."

"But the decor is exquisite," Mildred insisted, "and there's a lovely arrangement of fresh flowers in our suite. Pink carnations and snapdragons."

"Frankly, I think those two women are just going through the motions of innkeeping," her husband said. "They take the inn as a loss for tax purposes, while they spend the summer getting sloshed in the gazebo."

"Yes, they do seem to imbibe quite a bit," said Mildred, who was on the wagon. "Oh! Isn't that a hideous building!" she added as the carriage passed the Domino Inn.

"But it's popular," Qwilleran said.

"Because the prices are right; that's why," Riker snapped.

At the hotel they pushed through a phalanx of pickets, tourists, and stray cats. Mildred said it was a mess. In the lobby she said the black flags were too somber. Then she caught sight of Derek Cuttlebrink at the reservation desk. She had taught him in high school and had applauded him in Pickax theater productions. "Derek! What are you doing here?" she cried.

"I'm playing Captain Hook this week. Next week, King Kong." With a flourish he assigned them to a choice booth in the Corsair Room. Unobtrusively he slipped a scrap of paper to Qwilleran, who dropped it in his pocket.

The three old friends had much to talk about after being apart for a whole week: the shooting on the sand dune, the mosquito controversy, and ordinary newspaper shoptalk. Then Riker asked Qwilleran, "Do you consider this boondoggle of yours worthwhile? You're not jamming the fax machine with copy."

"Did you come over here to check up on your hired help?" Qwilleran retorted.

"The paper is paying for your junket, don't forget."

"Well," Qwilleran began cagily, since Riker was not aware of his real mission, "I have a lot of notes and tapes, but I need time to organize them. I've discovered, for example, that Pear Island is not pear-shaped. It may have been pear-shaped when it was surveyed a couple of centuries ago, but erosion has changed it to an isosceles triangle."

"That's a world-shaking discovery," the publisher said dryly. "Let's see you write a thousand words on that profound subject. Do you recommend changing the name again? It'll sound like a Greek island."

The entrées were served. Qwilleran had recommended the Cajun menu, and all three had ordered pork chops étouffée.

"Why, these are nothing but smothered pork chops, highly seasoned," Riker said. "Mildred fixes these all the time. How much are they paying this New Orleans chef?"

When they settled down to serious eating, Qwilleran told them the story behind the story of the snake-bite incident, with hitherto unrevealed descriptions, reactions, apprehensions, and conclusions. "First aid was the only merit badge I ever earned in scouting, and it finally paid off," he said.

Mildred was thrilled. Even Riker was impressed and wanted to know why the facts had been withheld from the newspaper. "It would have made a great feature: everybody's favorite columnist rescuing an heiress."

"There may be more to the story. They're an unusual family, and I'm invited to tea tomorrow afternoon."

"Speaking of tea," Mildred said, "have you been to the tea room? They serve real tea in fat English teapots with thin porcelain cups and all the shortbread you can eat."

Her husband said, "Qwill and I had enough shortbread in Scotland to last a lifetime. It hardly strikes me as tourist fare in this country. They certainly weren't doing any business when we were there."

"Did you go into the antique shop?" Qwilleran asked.

"Yes, and we recognized the woman who runs it," said Mildred. "She's staying at the Island Experience. We saw her in the breakfast room this morning, but she was rather aloof."

"No wonder the prices in her shop are so high," Riker said. "She has to pay for that suite with fresh flowers and champagne. Moreover, her inventory is questionable. She has some reproductions of Depression glass that she represents as the real thing. There's a lot of fraud these days in scrimshaw and netsuke and pre-Columbian figures. Is she uninformed or deliberately falsifying?"

"How would Exbridge react to this information?" Qwilleran asked. "He seems to run a tight ship."

"Well, I'm not going to be the one to tell him. He's been hard to get along with lately. Thinks he can tell us how to run the paper."

Over dessert—the inevitable pecan pie—Mildred asked about the Siamese.

"Koko is learning to play dominoes," Qwilleran said, "and he beats me every time."

"That shouldn't be hard to do," Riker said gleefully.

"What do you think of the feral cats on the island?"

Mildred was an activist in humanitarian causes, and she said vehemently, "There are too many! Overpopulation is inhumane. To maintain a healthy cat colony in an area like this, they should be trapped, neutered, and released—the way we're doing on the mainland."

Riker said, "Our editorials finally convinced the bureaucrats it's not only humane but cheaper in the long run than wholesale killing."

Qwilleran, who liked to stir things up, made a sly suggestion. "Why don't you send a reporter over here to discuss feral cats with vacationers, businesspeople, and the chief honcho himself? You could get some good photos."

"Don't assign my son-in-law," said Mildred. "Roger will break out in a rash even before the ferry docks."

After dinner, riding up the beach road in a carriage, Qwilleran announced that he was staying at the "hideous" inn to save the newspaper money. Then he had the driver wait a few minutes while he showed the Rikers the four tree trunks in the lounge and the cottage on Pip Court.

"Don't you get claustrophobia?" Riker asked.

The Siamese and Mildred indulged in a display of mutual affection (she had been their cat sitter once for two weeks) and then she said excitedly, "Where did you get those?" She pointed to the gilded leather masks.

"They were a birthday present," Qwilleran said, thinking it better not to tell the truth. "Do you know anything about that kind of work? They're leather."

"Yes, I know," she said. "It's an old Venetian craft that's been revived by a young artist down south. She does excellent work."

Then the Rikers drove back to their B-and-B. Everyone had enjoyed the evening: the usual joshing, frank talk, and exchange of news. To Qwilleran the news about Noisette confirmed his suspicion that she was an impostor. Why was she on the island? He sat on the porch and listened to June Halliburton playing jazz. She had a male visitor again. The voice sounded younger.

The Siamese sat with him; they were friends again. Before going to dinner he had bitten the bullet and given them a can of red salmon. The partying next door was still going on when he retired. It was not until he emptied his pockets that he remembered the scrap of paper from Derek. It was a one-word message: Gumbo. Later, after his lights were out, he heard good nights being said next door, and the beam of a flashlight preceded the departing guest—not to the nature trail but up Pip Court. The tall, lanky scarecrow of a figure was that of Derek Cuttlebrink.

# Twelve

The arrival of two more pounds of meatloaf on Sunday morning steeled Qwilleran's determination, and the standoff between man and cats resumed. "Take it or leave it," he said. They left it.

Sunday was the turning point, however, in Qwilleran's floundering mission. He took tea with the Appelhardts; his undercover agent made his first report; Lyle Compton presented his program on Scotland at the hotel; and Yum Yum found something among the sofa cushions.

While Qwilleran was dressing for breakfast, he heard the musical murmuring that meant Yum Yum was digging a rusty nail out of a crevice, or trying to open a desk drawer, or retrieving a lost toy. She was on the seat of the sofa, thrusting first one paw and then the other behind a cushion. As the mumblings and fumblings became frantic, he went to her aid. As soon as he removed the seat cushion, she pounced on a half-crumpled piece of paper and carried it to the porch in her jaws, to be batted around for a few seconds and then forgotten.

It looked like a piece of music manuscript paper, and he picked it up.

"N-n-now!" she wailed, seeing her prize confiscated.

"N-n-no!" He retorted.

Offended by the mockery, Yum Yum went into a corner and sat with her back toward him.

"Sorry, sweetheart. I won't say that again," he apologized.

She ignored him.

Smoothing the scrap of paper, he found a phone number. The first three digits identified it as a local number—not the cab stand and not the hotel, both of which he would recognize. The style of the numerals had an affectation that he would associate with June Halliburton, and the type of paper confirmed his guess. Obviously she had dropped it while occupying the cottage. Then the question arose: Whom would she be phoning on the island? It was none of his business, but, still, it would be interesting to know. He could call the number and then hang up—or ask to speak to Ronald Frobnitz.

The first time he tried it—when he went to the inn for breakfast—the line was busy. After corned beef hash with a poached egg, plus hominy grits with sausage gravy (Lori was running out of ideas, he thought), he called the number again. It rang several times, and then a gruff voice answered: "The Pines gatehouse."

"Sorry. Wrong number," he said. Why June would be phoning the Appelhardt gatehouse was a question even more puzzling than why she would be making an island call at all. There was a possibility, of course, that he had punched the wrong digits. He tried again and heard the same voice saying, "The Pines gatehouse." This time he hung up without apology.

Qwilleran spent some time that day in deciding what to wear to tea. The role he was playing was not that of an inquiring reporter, nor Sherlock Holmes in disguise, nor a commoner being patronized by the royal family. He was playing a hero who had saved the life (probably) of an only daughter. Furthermore, while Elizabeth was an heiress, he himself was the Klingenschoen heir, and the K Foundation was capable of buying The Pines and the entire Grand Island Club and restoring it to a wildlife refuge. The idea appealed to him. He would not wear his silk shirt nor even his blue chambray that screamed "designer shirt"—another gift from Polly. No, he would wear his madras plaid that looked as if it had been washed in the Ganges for twenty years and beaten with stones to a muddy elegance.

In this shirt and some British-looking, almost-white, linen pants, he went out to meet the carriage that was picking him up at four o'clock. The conveyance that pulled up to the carriage block in front of the inn caused a murmur of admiration among the guests on the porch. A glossy-coated horse, quite unlike the nags pulling cabs-for-hire, was harnessed to a handsome buggy of varnished wood and leather.

The driver in green livery with an apple logo stepped down and said, "Mr. Qwillum, sir?" He pointed to the passenger seat on the left, then sprang nimbly into the seat behind the reins. He was a young version of the gaunt old islanders who drove the hacks.

As the carriage started up West Beach Road, Qwilleran remarked that it was a nice day.

"Ay-uh," said the driver.

"What's your name?"

"Henry."

"Nice horse."

"Ay-uh."

"What's his name?"

"Skip."

"Do you think we'll have any rain?" It was a brilliant day, with not a cloud in the sky.

"Might."

At The Pines, the carriage rolled through an open gate and past a gatehouse of considerable size, then to the rear of the main lodge. It stopped at a carriage block on the edge of a stone-paved courtyard. Beyond were acres of flawless lawn, a swimming pool with a high-dive board, and a croquet green, where white-clad youths were screaming epithets and swinging mallets at each other. In the foreground was a grassy terrace with verdigris iron furniture and a scattering of adults in the same croquet white. They looked clinical, compared to Qwilleran's mellow nonwhiteness.

One of the men came forward toward him. "Mr. Qwilleran? I'm Elizabeth's brother, Richard. We met last Thursday for about three seconds. We're grateful for your help in the emergency."

"I'm grateful there was a doctor in the house," Qwilleran replied pleasantly. "How is the patient?"

"Right over there, waiting to thank you personally." He waved a hand toward a chaise longue, where a young woman reclined. She wore a flowing garment of some rusty hue, and long, dark hair cascaded over her shoulders. She was looking eagerly in their direction.

The two men started toward her but were intercepted by an older woman—buxom, regally handsome, and dramatically poised like an opera diva on stage. Gliding forward with outstretched hand, she said in a powerful contralto, "Mr. Qwilleran, I'm Rowena Appelhardt. Welcome to The Pines."

"My pleasure," he murmured courteously but cooly. As a journalist Down Below and abroad, he had been everywhere and seen everything, and he was not awed by the vastness of the estate. Rather, it seemed to be the Appelhardts who were awed. Had they made a quick background check and discovered his Klingenschoen connection and bachelor status? He became warily reserved.

The matriarch introduced the family: Richard was genuinely cordial; William smiled continually and was eager to talk; their wives sparkled with friendliness. Qwilleran suspected the queen mother had briefed them. She herself was an effusive hostess. Only Jack hung back, his face handsome in a bored and dissipated way. Finally there was the undernourished, unmarried daughter. She made a move to rise from her chaise.

"Stay where you are, Elizabeth," her mother admonished. "You must avoid exertion."

"Mother—" Richard began, but she stopped him with a glance.

Soulfully, the patient said, "I'm so grateful to you, Mr. Qwilleran." She extended her left hand; her right wrist was bandaged. "What would have happened to me if you hadn't been there?"

She had that loving look that women are said to bestow on their rescuers, and he kept his tone brusquely impersonal. "Fortunate coincidence, Ms. Appelhardt," he said.

"It was karma. And please call me Elizabeth. I don't remember what happened after that frightening moment."

"You were only minutes away from home; your brother was waiting with the golf cart; and you were choppered off the island by the Moose County sheriff."

"I love your shirt," she said, scoring several points.

Tea was served, and the conversation became general. The servers were two young men in green seersucker coats—island types but meticulously trained. There was tea with milk or lemon, and there was pound cake. This was no garden party with peacocks and memorable refreshments; this was a simple family tea with seven adult Appelhardts, while the younger members of the family squabbled on the croquet court.

"Richard," came the deep voice of authority, "must my grandchildren behave like savages while we are having tea with a distinguished visitor?"

Her son sent one of the seersucker coats to the croquet green, and the fracas ended abruptly.

"Do you play croquet, Mr. Qwilleran?" she asked.

Mallets, wire wickets, and wooden balls interested him as much as dominoes. "No, but I'm curious about the game. What is the major attraction?"

"Bonking," said Jack, entering the conversation for the first time.

"It's more than a matter of knocking a ball through a wicket. You hit your ball so that it sends your opponent's ball off the field. That's bonking. It takes practice. You can also bop your ball over your opponent's ball, blocking his path to the wicket."

"Jack is a sadistic bonker," said William's wife as if it were a compliment.

"It's changed from a harmless pastime to a strategic sport," William said. "It requires deliberation, like chess, but you're limited to forty-five seconds to make a shot."

Richard talked fondly about his Jack Russells, three well-behaved dogs who mingled with the family and never barked, jumped, or sniffed.

Mrs. Appelhardt asked prying questions, skillfully disguised, about Qwilleran's career, lifestyle, and hobbies, which he answered with equally skillful evasion.

Elizabeth was quiet but looked at him all the time.

Then William said, "How did you like that carriage we sent for you? My hobby is restoring antique vehicles."

"It's a beauty!" Qwilleran said in all honesty.

"It's Elizabeth's favorite—a physician's phaeton, so-called because of the hood design. It's deeper and has side panels, the idea being that physicians had to call on patients in all kinds of weather. In fact, this type of vehicle became the badge of the profession, along with the little black leather bag."

"How many carriages have you restored?"

"About two dozen. Most are at our farm in Illinois. There are five here. Would you like to see them?" To his mother, William said, "Do you mind if I show Mr. Qwilleran the carriage barn?"

"Don't keep him away from us too long!" she cautioned with a coy smile. The corners of her mouth turned down when she smiled, making emotion ambiguous.

He was glad to get away from the chatter of the tea table. "This will be highly educational," he said to the eldest brother. "I don't know anything about America's wheels prior to Henry Ford."

"Wheels built the country," William said. "There were carriage makers everywhere, always improving and innovating. In the early 1900s, there were dozens of models shown in the Sears Roebuck catalogue."

"How do you bring them to the island?"

"Disassembled—on my boat. To restore a vehicle you have to take it apart completely in order to strip and sand the wood parts. It takes hours of sanding to make a finish that looks like glass."

The physician's phaeton stood in the courtyard with empty shafts resting on the pavement. Two other four-wheelers were inside the barn, one of them enameled in glossy yellow with black striping and a fringed canopy.

"We use the surrey to drive to the club for lunch or dinner," William said. "The red wagon is for a pack of kids. I personally like the two-wheeled carts—light and easy to drive and safe. You can make a sudden turn without upsetting. If you ever turned over in a carriage with a frightened horse fighting to get free, you'd know why I stress the safety factor. Here . . . sit in this one."

Qwilleran climbed into a bright green dogcart with carriage lanterns and seats perched high over a box intended for hunting dogs.

"Do you think you might get interested in driving?" William asked. "There's a driving club in Lockmaster—and driving competitions. Are you anywhere near Lockmaster?"

"Yes. Good horse country. I'd like to sit down with you and a tape recorder some day and do an interview," Qwilleran said. "This is good material for my newspaper."

William hesitated. "I'd like that, but . . . it's like this: Mother is adamant about avoiding publicity. I wish we could, but no way!"

"How did you learn this craft?"

"Believe it or not, our steward was my mentor, beginning when I was a kid. He's an islander and a rustic Renaissance man—no formal education, but he can do anything. He taught us kids how to drive, sail, fish, hunt—"

"I'm doing a series on islanders for my column," Qwilleran said, "and he sounds like a good character study."

"I'm afraid Mother would never okay it. Other families would try to get him away from us. Sorry to have to say that."

They started walking back to the terrace, and Qwilleran asked him how much time he spent on the island. "I personally? No more than I have to. There's a limit to the amount of croquet a sane person can play, as someone once said."

"Dorothy Parker, but not in those exact words. How do you feel about the new resort development?"

"It's inevitable, if you want my personal opinion. That's the way our country is going. Mother is vastly unhappy, of course. She wants the islanders to file a class-action suit against the resort, and she'll cover the legal fees, but it's a lost cause, and attorneys avoid lost causes. The courts have ruled again and again that the owner of property can use it in any way that's not illegal."

As they returned to the terrace, he said to Qwilleran, "Talking to you has been a distinct pleasure. If you ever get down to the Chicago area, I'd like to show you the vehicles on my farm." They both looked up in surprise; Elizabeth had dared to rise from her chaise and was approaching them.

She said, "I forgot to thank you, Mr. Qwilleran, for finding the things I lost on the trail."

"I couldn't help noticing the entries in your book. You must be a botanist."

"Just an amateur. I'm fascinated by plant life. Would you like to see the herb garden I've planted?"

Qwilleran appreciated herbs in omelettes, but that was as far as his interest extended. Nevertheless, he acquiesced, and she asked her mother for permission to take him away from the party.

The queen mother said, "Promise not to tire yourself, Elizabeth."

On the way to the herb garden near the kitchen door, Qwilleran might be said to amble while the amateur botanist wafted in her long flowing robe. "Herbs thrive in the island sun and air," she said.

He stared blankly at two wooden tubs, a stone planter, and some large, clay pots, holding plants of various sizes, shapes, and colors. Finally he ventured, "What are they?"

She pointed out sage, rosemary, sweet basil, mint, lemon balm, chives, dill, and more, explaining, "There's something mysterious about herbs. For centuries they've been used for healing, and when they're used in food, something lovely happens to your senses."

He asked about the tea they had been drinking. To him it tasted and smelled like a product of the stables. It was Lapsang souchong, she said.

"Do you grow catnip?" he asked. "I have two Siamese cats."

"I adore Siamese!" she cried. "I've always wanted one, but Mother . . ." Suddenly she appeared weary, and he suggested sitting on a stone bench near the herbs, which were aromatic in their way.

He asked, "Where do you live when you're not on the island?"

"Mother likes to spend autumn at our farm, the holidays in the city, and winters in Palm Beach."

"Have you always lived with your mother?"

"Except when I was away at school."

They sat in silence for a few moments, but her eyes wandered, and her thoughts were almost audible. She had an intelligent face, delicate but wide-browed.

Speaking like a kindly uncle, he said, "Did you ever think you'd like a place of your own?"

"Oh, Mother would not approve, and I doubt whether I'd have the courage to break away or the strength to face responsibility. My two older brothers have suggested it, but . . ."

"Do you have money of your own?"

"A trust fund from my father—quite a good one. Mother is trustee, but it's mine, legally."

"Have you ever contemplated a career?"

"Mother says I'm not cut out for anything requiring sustained commitment. She says I'm a dilettante."

"You do have a college degree, don't you?"

She shook her head sheepishly. He felt she was going to say, Mother didn't think it was necessary, or Mother didn't think I could stand the pressure, or Mother-this or Mother-that. To spare her the embarrassment he stood up and said, "Time for me to go home and feed the cats."

They returned to the terrace, and Qwilleran thanked Mrs. Appelhardt for a pleasant afternoon; he commented that she had an interesting family. She mentioned that tea was always poured at four o'clock, and he was always welcome.

Unexpectedly Elizabeth spoke up. "I'll drive you home, Mr. Qwilleran, and we'll take some fresh herbs for the cook at your inn."

"Henry will drive our guest home," her mother corrected her.

Flinging the hair away from her face, the young woman raised her voice bravely. "Mother, I wish to drive Mr. Qwilleran myself. He has two Siamese cats that I'd like to see."

Other members of the clan listened in hushed wonder.

"Elizabeth, you're not quite yourself," Mrs. Appelhardt said forcefully, "and certainly in no condition to drive. We prefer not to take chances. You're so sensitive to medication . . . Richard, don't you agree?"

Before the elder brother could reply, Jack raised his voice. "For God's sake, Mother, let her do what she wants—for once in her life! If the buggy turns over and she breaks her neck, so be it! It's karma! That's what she's always telling us."

Qwilleran, a reluctant witness to this embarrassing moment in family history, walked over to the daughters-in-law and asked if they had heard about the unsolved lighthouse mystery. Fortunately they had not, so he recounted the story in detail, with a few embellishments of his own. By the time his listeners had speculated on the fate of the lightkeepers, Elizabeth reappeared in culottes, boots, straw sailor hat, and tailored shirt. "The groom is bringing the phaeton around," she said in a voice that trembled slightly.

# Thirteen

The groom handed Elizabeth into the driver's seat, and one of the seersucker coats came running with a bouquet of herbs. She sat straight and square, with elbows close to her body and reins between the fingers of her left hand. Her right hand held the whip. She was in perfect control as they drove away from the lodge.

Qwilleran thought, All we need for this climactic scene is some melodramatic background music with full orchestra, as we drive away into the sunset. And what a cast of characters! Autocratic mother, timid daughter, two obedient sons, plus one who's sufficiently cavalier to deliver the defiant punch line.

Seated alongside the frail driver, he said, "Are you sure your injured wrist can handle that whip?"

"It's only a symbol," she replied. "Skip responds to the reins and the driver's voice. Our steward happens to be a wonderful trainer." They had stopped at the gate before turning into the procession of Sunday sightseers. "Walk on, Skip!" Nodding his head as if acknowledging the request, the horse moved forward into a left turn.

"Mother says you write for a newspaper. Which one?" Elizabeth asked.

"The *Moose County Something* on the mainland."

"Is that really its name? I don't read newspapers. They're too upsetting. What do you write?"

"A column about this and that . . . If I may ask, where were the peacocks today? It was my understanding that you have peacocks."

"Mother sold them to a zoo after Father died. Their screams made her nervous. Actually they were Father's pets. She sold his telescopes and astronomy books, too. That was his hobby. Did you ever see a UFO? Father said they hang over large bodies of water. If he spotted one, he'd wake us up in the middle of the night, and we'd all go out on the roof with binoculars—except Mother and Jack. She said it was foolish; Jack said it was boring. Jack is easily bored."

Elizabeth was more talkative than Qwilleran had expected. As she rambled on, he silently classified the family he had just met. Jack and his mother had the same assertive manner, good looks, and inverted smile. It was a safe bet that he was her favorite. He caused her trouble with his marrying addiction, but she kept on bailing him out. The three other siblings probably favored their male parent. They had wide brows, delicate features, and a gentler personality.

Elizabeth was still talking about her father. "He taught me proper driving form when I was quite little. It's more fun than driving a car." She identified two private vehicles returning from the Grand Island Club: a Brewster and a spider phaeton, both restored by William. When they reached the commercial strip, she expressed surprise and sadness at the conversion of private lodges.

Qwilleran said, "You probably remember the birchbark lodge. It's now the Domino Inn, and I'm staying in a cottage at the rear. It's small and quite confining, but I tell the cats to be patient; it's better than a tent."

"Do you really talk to them like that?"

"All the time. The more you talk to cats, the smarter they become, but it has to be intelligent conversation."

In front of Four Pips, Qwilleran handed her down from the driver's seat. "I hear lovely music! A flute with harp!" Her face was suddenly radiant.

"My next-door neighbor is a musician, and if she isn't playing the piano, she's playing recorded music."

"I wanted so badly to play the flute. I had visions of piping on the nature trail and luring small animals out of the woods. But my mother insisted on piano lessons. I wasn't very—" She stopped and squealed with delight as she saw two pairs of blue eyes watching from the front window. Koko and Yum Yum were sitting tall on the domino table with ears alert and eyes popping at the sight of a large beast outside their cottage. Indoors, Elizabeth extended her left hand to them, and they sniffed the fingers that had held the reins.

Qwilleran made the introductions, mentioning that Koko was unusually smart; his latest interest was dominoes.

"He feels the power of numbers," Elizabeth said seriously. "Cats are tuned into mystic elements, and there's magic in numbers. Pythagoras discovered that thousands of years ago. Do you know anything about numerology? I've made an informal study of it. If you write down your full name for me, I'll tell you something about yourself. I don't do fortune-telling—just character delineation. Write down the cats' names, too, in block letters."

Qwilleran thought, Wait till Mildred hears about this! Riker's new wife was involved in tarot cards and other occult sciences. Soberly he did what Elizabeth requested:

JAMES MACKINTOSH QWILLERAN
KAO K'O KUNG a.k.a. KOKO
YUM YUM, formerly called FREYA

"Notice," he pointed out, "that my name is spelled with a QW."

"That's important," she said. "Each letter has a corresponding number. I'll take them home and work on them. And now I must drive back to The Pines, or Mother will fret. Your little friends are so beautiful. I hope we'll meet again."

"Yow!" came a stentorian voice from the desk.

"He's thanking you for the compliment," Qwilleran explained.

Koko had something else in mind, however. As soon as he had their attention, he nosed the maroon velvet box across the desk until it fell to the floor.

Qwilleran picked it up. "He has a parlor trick he performs. If I place the dominoes facedown on the table, he can make a blind draw and come up with high-scoring pieces, like double-six and double-five. You sit down and watch quietly." He spread the entire set on the table and encouraged Koko to draw.

The four dominoes that landed on the floor were not high-scoring pieces; they were 0-1, 1-2, 1-4, and 3-4. Elizabeth laughed merrily. It was the first time Qwilleran had heard her laugh. "Do you think cats have a sense of humor?" she asked.

"I think Koko gets a kick out of making me look like a fool."

She was toying with the four dominoes Koko had selected. "He's smarter than you think," she said. "If you add the spots on each one, you get one, three, five and seven. If you match them with the letters of the alphabet, you get A, C, E and G. And if you shuffle them, you get *Cage*. That's my middle name."

Qwilleran felt goosebumps on the back of his neck. It had to be pure coincidence, he thought. And yet he said, "I'd like to hear more about numerology. Would you have lunch with me at the hotel some day this week?"

"I'd be delighted!" she said, and her eyes sparkled.

He thought, There's nothing wrong with this girl that can't be cured by a reduction in motherpower and a few chocolate malts.

On the way out, Elizabeth caught sight of the gilded leather masks over the sofa. "Your theater masks are stunning!" she said and then she giggled. "One looks like my brother William, and one looks like Jack."

After the phaeton had rolled away from Four Pips, Qwilleran remembered an episode in his early school years. His teacher, Miss Heath, had a toothy and ambiguous smile that could mean either good news or bad news. Being a domino player at home, although a reluctant one, his private name for her was Miss Double-six. The class was seated alphabetically, and James Qwilleran was assigned to sit in front of a fat kid named Archibald Riker. In dull moments they amused each other by exchanging notes in secret code. It was nothing that would stump a cryptographer—or even Miss Double-six if she had caught them; the letters of the alphabet were numbered 1 to 26. One day, while her back was turned, Qwilleran tossed a wad of paper over his shoulder: 13-9-19-19 8-5-1-20-8 8-1-19 2-9-7 20-5-5-20-8. Arch decoded it and laughed so hard that he choked and was sent into the hall for a drink of water. Forty years later, he still quaked with internal laughter whenever he saw someone with prominent dentition.

And now, after all those years, Qwilleran had a cat who was interested in double-six—most of the time. That was the name of Nick's boat; did it mean that Koko wanted to go home? Or did the twelve pips signify the letter L? And if so, what did the letter L have to do with anything? Kao K'o Kung had some obscure ways of communicating. Often it was merely a matter of nudging Qwilleran's thought processes. In this case, nothing clicked.

The morning plate of meatloaf was still untouched, and Qwilleran's determination to win the argument struggled with his humane instincts—and lost. Just because he had been impulsive enough to pay for ten pounds of meatloaf up front, he could not let them starve. He opened a can of boned chicken. The breakfast that the Siamese had ignored was carried to the trash cans for the strays.

Nick was there, working on the foundation of the building. "Mildew's a problem," he explained. "I'm taking a week of my vacation and trying to catch up on the maintenance . . . Say, Qwill, does the music from Five Pips bother you?"

"It's a little mind-numbing when she practices technique, but I've learned to wear ear plugs for catfights, fog horns, and finger exercises."

"I had to speak to her about smoking this afternoon," said the hardworking innkeeper. "I was repairing one of her porch screens and saw a saucerful of butts. She thinks she's a privileged character because Exbridge pays her rent . . . How about you? Is everything okay?"

"So far, so good. Tonight I meet with my undercover man. Right now I'm on my way downtown for something to eat."

At the hotel he waited for the Comptons to come out of the small auditorium where Lyle had delivered his lecture on "Bloody Scotland." The superintendent of schools had a perverse sense of humor that Qwilleran enjoyed, and Lisa's agreeable disposition was a foil for her husband's orneriness.

She said, "We had a good crowd, with lots of young people. They like blood, and Lyle always pours it on: the massacre at Glen Coe, the atrocities of the Highland Clearances, and the slaughter at the Battle of Culloden."

They took a booth in the Buccaneer Den and ordered burgers, and Qwilleran said, "You talk about the farmers being cleared out of the Scottish Highlands and replaced by corporate flocks of sheep. It wouldn't surprise me if the natives were driven from Breakfast Island and replaced by something like corporate oil wells."

The cynical jest appealed to Lyle. "That would be a juicy rumor to start on the mainland! All I'd have to do is whisper confidentially to my next-door neighbor that XYZ has struck oil behind the swimming pool, and in two days it would be all over Moose County, and Don Exbridge would be denying it in the headlines. Of course, no one would believe him!"

"It would be just like you to do it, too," said his wife, "and that's really sick!"

"I'll tell you what's sick, sweetheart. It's sick what XYZ did with the new elementary school building. It's lousy construction! They keep patching it up, but what we really need is one good tornado, so we can start again from scratch—with a different builder."

Lisa said, "Be careful what you wish for; you may get your wish! The weatherman says there's a peculiar front headed this way." Then the food was served, and she said, "It's so dark in here, I can't tell whether this is a burger or chocolate cake."

"That's because people patronize bars for illicit trysts, graft payoffs, and subversive plotting," her husband informed her. "Nice people like you should eat in the coffee shop."

After a while, Qwilleran asked him if he remembered a student named Harriet Beadle, an islander who attended high school on the mainland.

"No, but we've had a pack of Beadles from the island. Another common name is Kale. Another is Lawson. They're all descended from survivors of the same shipwreck, supposedly. They work hard to get good grades, and some even earn scholarships. Those one-room schools aren't all bad."

"How do the other students treat them?"

"They taunt them about their so-called pirate ancestry, and there are some bloody fights. And who knows whether it's true or not? But I'll tell you one thing for sure: The islanders know more about ecology than we do. They grow up with a respect for the earth and the elements."

Over coffee Lisa asked about Polly.

"She's in Oregon, visiting an old college chum."

"Great country out there!" said Lyle. "Let's hope she doesn't decide to stay. She's a great librarian."

"Everybody loves her," said Lisa.

"Nobody loves a school superintendent. I'm on everybody's hit list —board of ed, taxpayers, and parents."

Qwilleran asked him, "Do you know that one of your department heads has a summer job over here?"

"Wish she'd stay on the island permanently," he grumbled. "June is an independent so-and-so."

Lisa said, "She's certainly not popular with the wives of Moose County. She thinks she's God's gift to husbands—mine included, and Lyle is no Robert Redford."

"Why," Qwilleran asked, "does an educator with her credentials choose a rural county like ours?"

"Horses! She likes to ride. That's how she landed in Lockmaster after a divorce Down Below. Then we offered her a good contract, and now we're stuck with her. But she's good! She sailed through school on scholarships and did a concert tour before coming to us."

The check came to the table, and when Qwilleran reached for it, Lyle said, "Drop it! The hotel's paying for this one."

The Comptons were staying for a nightcap, but Qwilleran groped his way out of the murky bar, bumping into tables and kicking chair legs. In passing the corner booth he squinted into the gloom and saw a man and a woman leaning amorously toward each other. Their faces were in shadow, but he heard the woman say, "Shall we have a replenishment?"

Before riding home in a cab, Qwilleran picked up some beer for Derek Cuttlebrink, as well as crackers and pickles to go with the meatloaf. On the way he pondered several of Lyle Compton's remarks, chiefly his hint that Polly might decide to relocate in Oregon. It was a possibility that had never crossed his mind. It made him vaguely uneasy.

At Four Pips he was met by a highly disturbed cat. Koko was yowling in two-part harmony and running back and forth between sitting room and porch. A casual inspection showed nothing amiss, but after refrigerating the beer Qwilleran investigated with deepening concern. The cat was jumping up and pawing the porch screen as he did when batting down an insect. This time there were no insects—only small holes in the screen. Alarmed, Qwilleran hurried to the inn and confronted Nick in the office.

"Someone's been taking pot shots at the cats!" he said with indignation.

Nick looked up from the bookkeeping. "I can't believe it! How do you know?"

Qwilleran described Koko's behavior and his discovery of the holes. "There's growing hostility among the islanders, I'm convinced, and someone may have connected me with the financial backers of the resort. Someone may be using this method of harassment!"

"Did you look for spent shot on the porch?"

"There was nothing that I could find, but the porch is shaded at this hour."

"Which screens had the holes?"

"Both side panels, east and west."

"Birds!" Nick said. "Bird beaks! They try to fly through the porch, not realizing it's screened. All the cottages have holes in the porch screens."

Qwilleran huffed into his moustache. "Well . . . sorry to bother you, Nick. Now all I have to do is explain it to Koko."

Back at Four Pips he prepared for Derek's visit. He opened a can of mixed nuts and dumped them into a soup bowl, filled another bowl with dill pickle chips, and arranged a platter of crackers and meatloaf slices.

When the young man arrived, the Siamese gave him the royal welcome, prancing with lofty tails curled like question marks. "They like me," he said. "I'm getting a standing ovation."

"Before you congratulate yourself," Qwilleran parried, "bear in mind that these opportunists have an instinctive affinity for dairy farmers, fishermen, butchers, and restaurant employees. I leave it to you to figure out."

Derek's height made the ceilings look lower than ever. He walked around, looking at the travel posters. Then he pointed to the tragedy and comedy masks. "I'll bet those didn't come with the cottage. Where'd you get them?"

"In Venice—from a small antique shop near the Accademia delle Belle Arti" was the casual reply. "How about a beer? Sit down and help yourself to the food. What time did you have dinner?"

"They feed us just before we start the dinner shift, at five o'clock."

"Then you must be hungry. Dig in. The meatloaf is homemade." Then craftily he asked his guest, "Did you have any trouble finding this place?"

"No. I was down here last night," Derek said with youthful candor. "Dr. Halliburton wanted me to audition."

"Did you read a script? Or sing?"

"We just rapped. She wanted to know what acting I'd done, and how I felt about theater, and what kind of role I liked to play. I told her what I'd done in *Macbeth*. We just drank beer and listened to jazz and had a good time. She's very friendly. I was surprised. She may get me the job of assistant entertainment director. That would pay more money than I'm getting now."

Uh-huh, Qwilleran thought. "So explain the note you handed me last night, Derek. What's all this about gumbo?"

"Yeah . . . well . . . I met this girl where I'm rooming, and she kinda likes me. Her name is Merrio. How's that for a name? She's a waitress in the Corsair Room, but she was hired for the kitchen in the beginning. Then Mr. Ex decided she had a good personality for meeting the public, so now she's out on the floor, serving."

"Did the switch—or promotion, whatever it was—occur after the poisoning incident?"

"I guess so, because she was still on salads when it happened."

"Where does gumbo fit into the picture?"

"That's the interesting part," Derek said. "They had several chicken specials that night, but the only people that got sick were the ones that ordered chicken gumbo. The shrimp gumbo—no trouble!"

Qwilleran thought, So it wasn't necessarily contaminated chicken from Lockmaster. It could have been the fault of the hotel kitchen. "Who was working that night?" he asked.

"Well, besides the chef and sous chef, they had some college kids from restaurant schools and some islanders for the support staff— that's what they call the unskilled jobs."

"Who was responsible for the gumbo? Was it a single individual, or were others involved? And was it *freshly made that day?* If so, was it the usual recipe? Did anything unusual happen in the kitchen that night? Had anyone been fired?"

"I'll have to get back to Merrio," Derek said.

Qwilleran said, "It might stimulate her memory if you showed her a good time and spent a little money. You have an expense account, of course."

Derek liked that idea.

"Okay. Now, what about the guy that drowned. Any luck? Have you found a source?"

"Yeah. One of the barhops—his name is Kirk—rooms at our place, and he remembers serving them."

"Them?"

"The guy was drinking with some woman. They were sitting by the pool."

"What were they drinking?"

"Wine. He remembers that, because most people want beer or Pirate's Gold or a straight shot."

"Did they seem like friends? Or was it a pickup?"

"Oh, they knew each other all right. They were arguing. The guy was pretty upset."

"Was he a hotel guest or a drop-in? And what about her?"

"Kirk didn't know her, but the guy was registered, and the drinks were charged to his room. They had a few rounds, and then Kirk took his break. When he got back, the pool lights were off, and the busboy was cleaning up the rim. He's the one that saw something floating. He rushed into the bar; the head barman called security; the police came, and the rescue squad; and that was it!"

"Did the police investigate?" Qwilleran asked.

"They hung around for a while, asking questions, but the boss told everybody not to talk to outsiders—or even discuss it with other employees—or they'd lose their jobs. When I talked to Kirk, we went down on the beach for privacy. He was glad to get it off his chest. He'd been thinking about it a lot. Because of the secrecy thing, he was suspicious, you know."

"What did he remember about the couple who were drinking?"

"Only that they were sharp-looking—young, but not too young—and they were speaking a foreign language."

"That's a big help," Qwilleran said. "The last time I counted, there were five thousand foreign languages."

Derek had another beer and finished the meatloaf before leaving with some extra money in his pocket. As they stepped out of the cottage, music was coming from Five Pips, and voices could be heard, a male and a female.

"Sounds like another audition," Qwilleran said.

Derek galumphed up the lane, wielding his flashlight and swinging a sack of pears for his fellow roomers.

Qwilleran went back indoors and immediately stepped on something small and hard. At the same time he caught Koko with his paw in the nutbowl.

"No!" he yelled. "Bad cat!" he scolded as he gathered up the nuts scattered on the floor. It was no great loss; they were all hazelnuts, and he considered them a waste of chewing time. The walnuts, pecans, almonds, and cashews were untouched.

"Smart cat!" Qwilleran said, changing his tone. Koko sat up like a kangaroo and laundered a spot on his underside.

# Fourteen

When Qwilleran went to breakfast Monday morning, he first detoured into the office. Lori, of course, was busy in the kitchen, and Nick could be heard hammering nails somewhere, but Jason and Lovey were playing with toy telephones. The two youngsters sat on the floor, three feet apart, holding pink, plastic instruments to their ears.

The three-year-old said, "Are you there?"

"You're supposed to wait till the phone rings and I say hello," her brother said.

"Who's this?"

"We're not connected! You didn't dial!"

"How are you?"

"That's not right, Lovey," the exasperated six-year-old shouted.

"You look very nice today," she said sweetly into the mouthpiece.

Qwilleran interrupted. "Excuse me, Jason. Would you find your father for me?"

"Okefenokee!" The boy scrambled to his feet and disappeared into the family quarters.

Nick soon walked in, wearing his carpenter's apron. "Hi, Qwill! What's up?"

"I've received a report that's somewhat revealing."

"You did? Sit down . . . Jason, take your sister into the other room."

"Okefenokee!"

"Thanks, Nick, but I'm staying only a minute. I want to get into the breakfast room before it closes. Here's what I heard last night: The guests who were poisoned were *not* eating Cajun chicken, or chicken étouffée, or chicken Creole. They had all ordered chicken gumbo! It seems to me that an extra ingredient went into the pot, accidentally or on purpose."

"You think Don deliberately twisted the truth when he blamed the poultry farm?"

"Or the kitchen didn't give him the true facts. It may be that chef— Jean-Pierre Pamplemousse, or whatever his name is—didn't want his reputation besmirched. So that's where we stand at the moment." Qwilleran started toward the door but turned back. "Do you know anything about the woman called Noisette, who runs the antique shop?"

"No. She hasn't attended any of Don's business meetings or get-togethers."

"One more question: What happened to the Hardings? I haven't seen them for the last day or so."

"The old gentleman caught cold," Nick said, "and they wanted to get off the island, so I ferried them across yesterday and put them on a plane."

Too bad, Qwilleran thought. They would have enjoyed hearing about the visit to Buckingham Palace, the eccentricities of the royal family, William's antique carriages, and the fate of the peacocks. The vicar would have had his own sly comments to make, and his wife would have rebuked him gently.

For breakfast he had pecan pancakes with homemade sausage patties, followed by brioches filled with creamed chipped beef. The sausages were particularly good, and he attributed their distinctive flavor to fresh herbs from Elizabeth's garden.

There were things Qwilleran wanted to do that day. He wanted to visit the antique shop once again, have a few words with Dwight Somers, and check the post office for a postcard from Oregon—all errands that were better done in the afternoon. Before leaving the inn, therefore, he picked up a couple of their Sunday papers from Down Below—to read in the privacy of his screened porch.

It was warm and humid on the porch, and the Siamese had found a cool patch on the concrete slab: Yum Yum lounging like an off-duty sphinx with forelegs fully extended and paws attractively crossed; Koko with hind quarters sitting down and front quarters standing up. His elongated Siamese body made him look like two different cats with a single spine, and the thinking end of the cat was now alert and waiting for something to happen. Suddenly ears pricked, whiskers curled, and nose sniffed. A few moments later Qwilleran caught a whiff of smoke and turned to see June Halliburton approaching through the weeds.

"Don't invite me in. I'm just enjoying a legal smoke," she said, holding a cigarette gracefully in one hand and a saucer in the other. As usual, a limp Panama drooped over her red hair and white complexion. "The esteemed management will have me shot if I smoke indoors or drop live ashes outdoors."

"I agree with the esteemed management," Qwilleran said. "Today's too warm for anything as uncomfortable as a forest fire."

Peering through the screen at the three of them, she said with an arch smile, "What a touching domestic scene! I suppose the demographers have you classified as an untraditional family: one man, two cats."

"One man, two *animal companions,*" he corrected her.

"And how do you like your cottage?"

"The roof doesn't leak, and the refrigerator works," he said. "What more can one ask?"

"My refrigerator is full of ice cubes, so join me for a drink, any time."

"Yow!" said Koko impatiently, his nose twitching.

"No one invited *you,*" she said. Stubbing her cigarette in the saucer, she walked away at a languid pace, and Koko shook himself so vigorously that the flapping of his ears sounded like a rattlesnake. Then he ran indoors and yowled over the domino box.

"Okay," Qwilleran agreed, "but this is a whole new ballgame. We don't add scores any more; we spell words."

Koko watched with near-sighted fascination as the dominoes were randomly scattered over the tabletop. Instead of standing on the chair with forepaws on the table, however, he elected to sit on the dominoes like a hen hatching eggs.

"What's that all about?" Qwilleran demanded. "Are you getting a gut feeling?"

The cat seemed to know what he was doing. Suddenly he rose and, with a grunt, pushed several pieces onto the floor. Quickly and with high anticipation Qwilleran retrieved them: 0-2, 1-3, 3-4, 2-6, and 5-6. By adding the pips on each piece he got 2, 4, 7, 8, and 11, which corresponded to B, D, G, H, and K in the alphabet.

"That won't fly," Qwilleran said in disappointment. "We need *vow-*

*els,* the way we did when we played Scrabble." He asked himself, What does a cat know about vowels? And yet . . . Koko could read his mind without understanding his speech.

Either Koko understood, or the next draw was a phenomenal coincidence. It produced 0-1, 0-5, 1-4, 2-3, 4-5, and 3-6, all of which corresponded to the vowels, A, E and I.

Qwilleran groaned and pounded his forehead with his fists. It was beyond comprehension, but luckily he had learned to take Koko's actions on faith, and he continued the game. Who would believe, he asked himself, that a grown man in his right mind would participate in such a farce? He took the precaution of drawing the window blind.

After that, Koko's efforts were more to the point. Sometimes he swept pieces off the table with a swift flick of his tail, and from the seven or eight designated dominoes Qwilleran was able to spell words like *field, beach, baffle* and *lake.* (It could also be *leak.*) Unfortunately, the operation was limited to the first twelve letters of the alphabet. Nevertheless, he liked the challenge and kept a record: *fable, dice, chalk, chick, cackle.* Koko pushed dominoes off the table; Qwilleran translated them into words; Yum Yum sat on her brisket and kibitzed.

Eventually the cats lost interest, having a short attention span, and Qwilleran decided it was time to walk downtown. His first stop was the antique shop. Noisette was sitting at her desk, looking stunning, and reading another magazine, or perhaps the same one.

"Good afternoon, mademoiselle," he said pleasantly.

She looked up with a smile of recognition, and he realized that her lustrous brown eyes were a rich shade of hazel. "Ah, you have returned! What is it that interests you today?" she asked.

"The green glass luncheon set," he said. "It would be a good gift for my sister in Florida, but I don't know about the color."

"Green glass can be used with pink, yellow, or white napery," she said. "It gives the most enjoyment of color."

"I see . . . My sister lives near Palm Beach. She'd enjoy your kind of shop. Are you on Worth Avenue?"

Noisette shrugged apologetically. "At the moment I regret I do not know my address. I am moving due to the expirement of my lease."

Qwilleran mumbled something about the luncheon set and his sister and edged out of the shop. He was convinced that this was the woman he had seen, and heard, in the Buccaneer Den. A ripple of sensation in the roots of his moustache told him that she was also the woman drinking with the man who drowned.

Qwilleran's next stop was the post office. He was sure that Polly would have mailed a postcard the day after she arrived. Then, he figured cynically, it would go from her friend's country address to the General Mail Facility in Portland and then across the country to the General Mail Facility in Minneapolis, from which it would be delivered to Pickax and forwarded by his secretarial service to the island, via the General Mail Facility in Milwaukee, which would have no "Breakfast Island" in the computer, so Polly's postcard would go to the dead letter office in Chicago. At least, he thought that was the way it worked. Only one thing was certain: It had not arrived at Pear Island.

At the hotel he found Dwight Somers in his office and asked to have a few private words. They sauntered out to the farthest rim of the pool.

"Something on your mind?" Dwight asked.

"I'd like to ask a favor," Qwilleran said. "I need to know the last name of Noisette, who runs the antique shop. She must have signed a lease or other contract with the hotel. Would it be in the hotel files?"

"Probably, but I wouldn't have access to them."

"You could wangle your way into the vault."

"Is it that important? Okay, I'll give it a try."

"Do that, and I'll owe you one," Qwilleran said. "By the way, I'm bringing the mermaid to lunch at the Corsair Room tomorrow, in case you want to size her up."

Dwight asked, "How are you getting along with your next-door neighbor?"

"I avoid her, but I found out why she's working 400 miles north of everywhere. She came up to Lockmaster because it's horse country, and she's fond of riding."

"Are you sure?" Dwight asked. "When we had dinner at the Palomino Paddock, surrounded by bales of hay, saddles, and photos of famous horses, she never once said anything about riding, and that pale face doesn't belong on an outdoorswoman."

"Something's wrong somewhere," Qwilleran acknowledged. "How's your boss's disposition lately?"

"He's hot under the collar today. A photojournalist from your paper has been over here, questioning hotel guests about how they feel about feral cats on the island. Don had him thrown out and refused to speak for publication."

On the way out of the hotel Qwilleran saw a towering figure occupying one of the rocking chairs on the porch and rocking vigorously. He had to look twice; he had never seen the Pickax police chief dressed in anything but the official uniform or full Scottish kit. He dropped into a rocker next to Brodie and said, "Andy! What are you doing here?"

"It's my day off, and we came over for the ferry ride—the wife and me. I'm cooling my heels while she's off buying T-shirts for the grandkids."

"What does she think of the resort?"

"Same as we all think: too expensive and too built up!" Brodie said. "Nobody on the mainland likes what they've done to our Breakfast Island. We used to bring our three girls over here for picnics when they were growing up. It was a wild and lonely beach then."

"Did the islanders object?"

"Naw, we didn't bother them. We weren't rowdy, and we didn't spoil anything."

As they talked, Qwilleran noticed listening ears in the nearby rocking chairs. "Let's walk down to the docks, Andy," he suggested.

One of the piers, damaged by the boat explosion, was closed for repairs. They walked to the end of the longest pier and looked back at the flat-roofed hotel, the strip malls on either side, and the dense forest beyond. The ancient evergreens were so tall, they dwarfed the man-made structures.

Brodie said, "What's going to happen to that flat roof when they get tons of snow this winter? You know why they made it flat, don't you? Exbridge wanted to be able to land a helicopter on top of the hotel, but he found out they'd have to have special roof construction, and his partners at XYZ didn't want to pay for it. So now there's a pad behind the rescue headquarters, for when they have to chopper out an emergency case. They've had quite a few of those lately. I'll tell you one thing: I wouldn't want to be in that hotel during a bad wind storm. See all those tall trees? You can bet that their roots are drying out because of the drain on available ground water. It takes a lot of water to service the hotel, twelve stores, a big swimming pool, and all those food operations. A tall tree with a dry root system is a pushover in a big blow. No, sir! I wouldn't want to be here. How about you, Qwill?"

"Ditto."

Brodie said, "There was another incident this weekend—the shooting. That was a strange one, if you ask me."

"That makes five incidents," Qwilleran said, "and they have five logical explanations."

"Have you come up with any theories?"

"Nothing conclusive, but I have some leads and a couple of good contacts. You could do me a favor when you get home, Andy. Get me the name and hometown of the hotel guest who drowned. They're hushing it up over here."

Andy said, "If you find any evidence, don't waste time talking to the sheriff's department. Go right to the prosecutor. The sheriff has no background in crime fighting; he's a good administrator, that's all, and if you ask me, it was XYZ backing that got him elected. How much longer will you be here?"

"Another week."

"How's Polly enjoying her vacation? Where did you say she was going?"

"Oregon. She's having a good time."

"When are you two gonna—"

"We're not *gonna*, Andy, so don't plan on doing any bagpiping for us unless we kick the bucket."

"Let's mosey back to the hotel," the chief said. "The wife will be looking for me, now that she's spent all my money. Also, we have to watch the ferry schedule; they've cut back the number of crossings. They're not getting the crowds they expected. Look! Half the rocking chairs are empty. There's a rumor that the hotel may fold. Did you hear that?"

"I'm not up on my rumorology," Qwilleran said with mock apology.

"There's also a rumor that the hotel was planned to fail. Don't ask me how that works. I don't understand financial shenanigans. They say XYZ is too successful to be healthy, whatever that means."

Leaving Brodie, Qwilleran started to walk home and found himself face to face with the Moseley sisters on the boardwalk. They had just stepped out of a horse cab and were headed for the tea room.

"Oh, Mr. Qwilleran! We were just talking about you. Have you any news about our dear Elizabeth?"

"She's fine. She's back on the island. I visited her family yesterday."

"You must tell us about her. Will you join us for tea? We're leaving tomorrow." They were pleasant women, and they looked at him eagerly.

"I'd be happy to," he said, although he usually avoided tea rooms. This one was bright with posters of Scottish castles and displays of ornamental teapots. A cheery, pink-cheeked woman in a tartan apron brought a platter of shortbread and offered a choice of five teas. The Moseleys recommended a tisane, blending leaves, roots, flowers, and grasses.

Qwilleran gave them an update on their former student, and they described their vacation week. They had enjoyed the people at the inn, the sunsets, the carriage rides, and the lectures at the hotel.

"A conservation officer told us that this island was completely submerged thousands of years ago, except for the promontory where the lighthouse stands," said the one who had taught science. "Now all that's left of the wetland is the peat bog in the center of the island. I do hope they won't spray for mosquitoes. Insects, birds, frogs, snakes, turtles and all of those creatures work together to preserve the bog, which in turn preserves the quality of air and water."

"A peat bog," said the other sister, "is a mysterious miracle of nature. Did you know that a human body can sink in a bog and be perfectly preserved forever?"

Altogether, the conversation was better than the tea, although Qwilleran drank three cups of the stuff—not because he liked it, but because it was there. Later, while walking home, he formulated a new theory about the missing lightkeepers. First he thought they had been drugged with island coffee and dropped into the bog. Yet, that would require a motive on the part of the islanders, and motive was the missing piece in the puzzle.

Next, he decided that the lightkeepers had wandered into the bog themselves—but why all three of them? And what were they doing in the woods?

Stimulated by the tea blended of leaves, roots, flowers, and grasses, Qwilleran composed a scenario: The islanders had entertained the lightkeepers with tall tales about chests of pirate gold, buried in the marsh long before the Beadles, Kales, and Lawsons washed up on the shore. The lightkeepers believed the stories. Perhaps they were bored; perhaps they were greedy; perhaps they had been drinking too much ale. Whatever the reason, the head lightkeeper sent an assistant to reconnoitre on one moonlit night. The fellow went out with a lantern and shovel and failed to return. The second assistant was dispatched to look for him. And finally the lightkeeper himself went in search of the other two, with the result that Trevelyan, Schmidt, and Mayfus are honored by a bronze plaque on Lighthouse Point.

That evening, the crew in Four Pips played dominoes again, and the highlight occurred when Koko made one grand swipe with his tail, knocking a dozen pieces on the floor and enabling Qwilleran to spell *hijacked.* Otherwise, the words were ordinary: *jailed, ideal, field* (again), *lake* (again), *deface, flea* (which could also be *leaf*), *lice, bike,* and *feed.* Then, just as Qwilleran was getting bored, he was able to spell *Beadle,* and that gave him an idea. He walked up the road to Harriet's café to get a chocolate sundae and try out his lightkeeper scenario.

It was late, and there were no customers. "Just a chocolate sundae," he said to the island woman who was waitress, cashier, and busgirl.

As soon as his order was placed in the kitchen, Harriet came through the swinging doors. "I knew it was you, Mr. Q. Would you rather have hot fudge? I know you like it, and I can boil some up, if you don't mind waiting a bit."

"I appreciate that," he said, "but you look tired. Just sit down with me and have a cup of coffee."

Her plain face looked drawn, and her shoulders drooped. "Yes, I'm beat tonight . . . Hettie, dish up a chocolate sundae and bring us two cups of coffee. Then go home. I'll clean up. Thanks for staying late."

Qwilleran said, "Your long hours are getting you down. Why don't you take some time off once in a while?"

"It's not that so much," she said as she dropped into a chair. "I'm discouraged about business. All those accidents are scaring people away, and the radio is saying it'll be a bad summer—rain, high winds, and low temperatures. The B-and-Bs aren't getting reservations for the holiday weekend—not what they expected, anyway. And the hotel is cutting down on help. Some of my roomers upstairs have been laid off, and they're going back to the mainland. And then . . ." She stopped and heaved a long tired sigh. "Yesterday I heard something that upset me."

"Is it something you can tell me?" he asked.

"I don't know. It's something I heard when I visited my ma yesterday. I just don't know what to do. I always thought islanders were good people who wouldn't hurt a soul, but now . . ." She shook her head in despair.

"It might help you to talk about it," he said, mixing genuine sympathy with rampant curiosity.

"Maybe you're right. Will you promise not to say anything?"

"If that's what you want me to do."

"Well . . . one of our people was involved in the accidents."

"Do you know who it is?"

She nodded.

"Those are serious crimes, Harriet. This person must be stopped."

"But how can I squeal, Mr. Q?" she said in desperation. "We've always stuck together, here on the island, but I'm getting to feel more like a mainlander. I lived there so long."

"It's not a case of islander against mainlander," he said. "It's a matter of right and wrong. You're a good person, Harriet. Don't wait until someone else is killed or injured. If that happens, you'll never forgive yourself. You'll feel guilty for the rest of your life."

"I wish I hadn't come back to the island," she moaned. "Then I wouldn't be faced with this terrible decision."

"That's understandable, but it doesn't solve any problems. You're here now, and you're involved, and it's your duty to come forward."

"My ma thinks I should keep my mouth shut. She's afraid something will happen to me."

"You won't be at any risk. I've been doing some snooping myself, and if you tell me what you know, I'll be the one to blow the whistle. No one will be the wiser."

"I've got to think about it," she said, wringing her hands.

Qwilleran's moustache bristled, as it did at moments of suspicion or revelation. This was a breakthrough waiting to break through, and it was a delicate situation. These islanders required special handling. He had to be at his sympathetic best.

"More coffee?" she asked.

"No, thanks," he said. Already the drums were beating in his head. There was no telling what wild-growing leaf, root, flower, or grass the islanders put in their coffee. "I think you should call it a day and get some rest. In the morning you'll be thinking clearly, and you'll make the right decision."

"Yes," she agreed with a sigh of relief. "I just have to clean up a bit, and then I'll go upstairs."

"What has to be done?"

"I always sweep the floor, straighten the chairs, and tidy up the kitchen."

"I'll help you," he said. "Where's the broom?" Gripped by the immediacy of the situation, Qwilleran forgot to mention his peat bog theory.

# Fifteen

Qwilleran greeted Tuesday with the feeling that it would be momentous, and so it proved to be, although not in the way he expected. As he envisioned the day's prospects, Harriet would agree to tell all; the post office would have a postcard for him; and Koko would unearth a blockbuster of a clue. To start with, breakfast was auspicious: French toast with apple butter and bacon strips, then a poached egg on corned beef hash. Afterward, the Siamese were in the mood for dominoes: Koko as player, Yum Yum as devoted spectator.

Koko started conservatively, flooring only four or five dominoes with each swish of the tail, thus limiting the play to short words: *lie, die, bad, egg, cad* . . . or *gaff, jail, lice, dead.*

The connotation was generally negative, and it caused Qwilleran to wonder. He said, "Loosen up, old boy. Put more swish in your tail."

After that, words of special relevance cropped up: *bleak,* as in Four Pips; *bald,* like Exbridge; and *fake,* like the antique shop. Certain pairs were linked in tandem: *black* followed by *flag,* and *head* followed by *ache.* If Koko really knew what he was doing, the last one meant he'd had enough!

Qwilleran gave them a treat before leaving for his lunch date with the Appelhardt heiress. Arriving at The Pines in a hired cab, he found her waiting on the porch of the main lodge, and when he handed her into the carriage, he realized she was trembling, as she was on Sunday after defying her mother. He assumed they had exchanged words.

Mrs. Appelhardt had been an effusive hostess before her daughter showed signs of rebellion. No doubt he was now considered a bad influence; beware of journalists!

As they drove away from The Pines, he said to Elizabeth, "That color is very attractive on you."

"Thank you," she said. "I like all shades of violet, but Mother thinks it's less than respectable—whatever that means."

"I've noticed that women of spirit and individuality are drawn to purple," he replied, thinking of Euphonia Gage, who had been one of Pickax City's most original and independent citizens.

Elizabeth was wearing a lavender dress belted with braided rope, and her mermaid hair was rolled up under a tropical straw hat that looked as if it had been drenched with rain and stomped by a horse. "This hat belonged to my father," she said proudly. "He called it his Gauguin hat."

"You have interesting taste in clothing," he said. "Those long robes you wear . . ." He ran out of words. What could he say about them?

"Do you like them? They're from India and Africa and Java—hand-woven cotton and batik-dyed. I love exotic fabrics. Mother says I look like a freak, but it's the only way I have to express myself."

They were approaching the Domino Inn, and he remarked, "Two of the guests here read about your accident in the paper and mentioned that you'd been a student of theirs—Edith and Edna Moseley."

"How wonderful! I want to see them."

"Unfortunately, they left this morning to return home—Boston, I believe."

"Why didn't they let me know they were here?" she said. "When Mother enrolled me in the academy, I was in a very bad state psychologically, and they were so kind! You're a very kind person, too, Mr. Qwilleran. Am I right in thinking you're not married?"

"I'm not married at the moment . . . but I'm committed," he added quickly.

"What is she like?" Elizabeth asked eagerly.

"She's intelligent and comfortable to be with and nice-looking, and she has a melodious voice. She's head of the public library in Pickax City . . ."

"I'd love to be a librarian," she said wistfully, "but I don't have the formal education. Mother convinced me I didn't have the temperament or the stamina for college."

They reached the downtown area, and she was appalled. "How

could they desecrate this lovely island? Those dreadful shops! Those vulgar rocking chairs!"

To alleviate her horror he said lightly, "I have a vision of all fifty rockers occupied and rocking in unison like a chorus line and creating electromagnetic waves that would bring the entire resort tumbling down."

She relaxed and laughed a little.

"The worst is yet to come," he went on. "The lobby is hung with black pirate flags, and we're lunching in the Corsair Room, the entrance to which is guarded by a swash-buckling pirate."

At the reservation desk Derek looked at Elizabeth, and then at Qwilleran questioningly, and then back at the woman in the unusual hat. "Hi, Mr. Q! Do you want your usual corner booth?" he asked, adding under his breath, "Hey! Wow!"

When they were seated, Elizabeth said, "That person in the lobby is *so tall!*"

"That's Derek Cuttlebrink, a well-known figure in Pickax and an actor in the Theater Club . . . Would you have a cocktail, Ms. Appelhardt? Or an apéritif?"

"Please call me Elizabeth," she said.

"Only if you'll call me Qwill."

After a moment's hesitation she asked for a chardonnay spritzer, and he said he would have the same thing without the wine.

"And now I'm dying to know something about your name—James Mackintosh Qwilleran with a QW. Was that your name at birth?"

"As a matter of fact . . . no. Before I was born, my mother was reading Spenser's *Faerie Queene,* and she named me Merlin James. When I was in high school, you can imagine how my peers heckled a first baseman named Merlin! So I changed it when I went to college. My mother was a Mackintosh."

"That makes a big difference," she said. "When I charted 'James Mackintosh Qwilleran,' I knew something was wrong. First I have to explain how numerology works. Every letter of the alphabet has a corresponding number, beginning with *one* for the letter A. When you reach *ten*—for J—you drop the zero and start again with *one.* To chart a name, you give each letter its numeral equivalent, total them, and reduce the total to a single digit. Is that clear?"

"I think so," he murmured, although his mind was wandering back forty years to Miss Heath—she of the toothy smile.

"When I charted the name you gave me, the final digit was *two,* and instinct told me you were not a *two type!* I had a feeling that you are a *five!* . . . So now, if you'll give me a moment, I'll chart your birth name." As she scribbled in a notebook, she mumbled to herself, "Merlin reduces to *eight* . . . add *three* for James and *three* for Qwilleran . . . for a total of *fourteen* . . . which reduces to *five.* . . . I knew it! You're a *five!*" she cried in triumph.

"Is that good or bad?"

Excitedly she said, "It means you like freedom, adventure, and change. You've probably traveled extensively, because you're adaptable and have a lively curiosity about new places and new people. And you have ingenuity, which must be useful in your work."

"In all modesty," Qwilleran said, "I must say you've got it right. But how did you know the previous number was wrong? You don't know me that well."

"It's your aura," she said seriously. "You have the aura of a *five.*"

"And what is your digit?"

"I'm a *seven,* which happens to be the same as your male cat. In charting them I came upon an astounding fact. Kao K'o Kung adds up to *seven,* and so does Koko. In the case of Yum Yum and Freya, each name comes out to the same digit: *one.* That means she's patient and independent, with strong willpower. Koko is aristocratic, scientific, and mentally keen, but rather secretive."

"Remarkable!" Qwilleran said. Pensively he devoured a bowl of gumbo, while his guest nibbled half a chicken sandwich without mayonnaise. Gradually he led her into a discussion of cooking herbs, then medicinal herbs, and then toxic herbs.

"The islanders would probably know about poisonous plants," she said. "They make their own folk medicines. Have you ever been to the Dark Village?"

"Is that what the natives call Providence Village?"

"Yes, and it's a fascinating place. My father used to drive us through the village. If you'd like to rent a carriage after lunch, I could drive."

"Is it true they resent strangers?"

"Ordinarily, but we were always quiet and respectful of their privacy. The islanders liked my father. He'd talk to the fishermen on the beach and buy some of their catch."

She lapsed into a thoughtful silence and he left her alone with her memories for a while. Suddenly she said, "Qwill, would you call me Liz? No one but my father ever called me that. He was my best friend and the only one who ever really listened to me."

"I'd be honored . . . Liz," he said. "How long has your father been gone?"

"Six years, and I still feel lonely. I have no rapport with my mother. William and Ricky are good brothers, but they have their own families and their own life."

"What about Jack?"

"We don't get along," she said sharply. "When we were growing up, he used to torment me—paint moustaches on my dolls and glue the pages of my favorite books together."

"Did your parents let him get away with that?"

"Mother excused him, saying he was naturally playful and didn't mean any harm, and Father—well . . . Father never tried to argue with her. You see, Qwill, Jack was such a beautiful boy that he could get away with anything! He's lost his looks now, from too much partying."

"Does Jack have a profession?"

"Marriage!" she said acidly. "He's been divorced three times, and he's only twenty-six. Mother says she doesn't care how many women he has, but why does he have to marry them all? It's like an addiction. Did you ever hear of such a thing? It's not a subject the family likes to discuss, but I'm sure he's married again and wants to get out of it. Whenever Jack spends a few weeks at home, he has an ulterior motive. He's been married to a rock singer, a figure-skater (she was nice), and an Italian actress."

"Some day he'll marry a librarian and live happily ever after," Qwilleran said.

Liz laughed a little. "I'm doing all the talking, Qwill. Tell me about you. Where do you live?"

"I live in a converted apple barn in Pickax City, population 3,000. I used to write for large metropolitan dailies, but now a friend of mine publishes the small local newspaper. I write for it and get involved, somewhat, with small-town life."

"You seem happy," Liz said with a touch of envy.

"I've achieved contentment, I think. I have friends, and I'm writing a book."

"I'm not happy," she said with bitterness. "You were right when you said I need a place of my own. When I'm at home, I lose all my spirit and ambition and appetite."

"How do you account for that?" he asked gently, although he was eager for particulars. Some day he would actually write that book, and he was always scrounging for material.

"Mother wants to direct my life, choose my friends, and make my decisions. After a while one just . . . *gives up!* . . . There! That's all I'm going to say about it."

"Let's visit the Dark Village," Qwilleran said.

He rented a two-wheeled cart, and they headed toward the east beach with Liz at the reins. It was an expanse of pebbles with picnic tables and rubbish containers at intervals. A few tourists were sunning on beach towels or hunting for agates or sharing picnic lunches with stray cats. Qwilleran said, "I've seen feral cats everywhere except at The Pines."

"No," she said sadly. "They know they're not wanted."

After a while a rutted road forked to the left and plunged into the woods. The hush was almost oppressive.

"The Dark Village," Liz whispered. "Can't you feel its spell?"

Ancient trees spread a dense canopy of branches over the road. There were windswept cedars twisted into grotesque shapes and gnarled oaks with trunks five feet in diameter, crusted with lichens. As the horse plodded through the ruts, the wheels of the rented gig creaked noticeably; otherwise, there was a lonely silence. A ramshackle hut or collapsed roof might be seen in the woods, but there was no sign of humanity. Deeper and deeper into the forest the road followed a tortuous path between the arboreal giants. Qwilleran had to remind himself to take a deep breath occasionally.

Farther on, scattered habitations began to appear—pathetic shelters nailed together from fragments of wrecked ships or structures swept away from some distant shore long ago. Some of them had small yards fenced off with misshapen pickets of driftwood, enclosing two or three crude tombstones. Yet, there was evidence of the living as well as the dead. A few pieces of clothing hung forlornly on a clothesline; an old dog slept on a doorstep; hens pecked in the road, and a goat nibbled weeds in a front yard. Once, a wild cat dashed across the road, dodging the horse's hooves. Some children, playing in a yard, rushed out of sight when the cart approached. Occasionally there was a glimpse of movement in a window, as someone peered out at the strangers. Somewhere a rooster crowed.

At one point the road widened slightly, and there was a small but well-built schoolhouse with outhouses for boys and girls; the siding was government-issue aluminum. Nearby, a weatherbeaten structure looked like the ghost of an old general store; two gaunt old men sat on a bench in front and glared at the cart as it trundled past. One other building made a brave showing with white paint but only on the front; there was a cross above the door.

After that, there were fewer dwellings and more open spaces with more patches of sunlight, until the road came to an end at the mountainous sand dune. Here the road forked right to the pebble beach and left into a tangle of weeds and underbrush.

Liz told the horse to whoa. "It was a hard pull through those ruts. Let him rest awhile."

Now what? Qwilleran thought; there seemed to be more on her mind than the welfare of the old nag. She was preoccupied. He said, "This has been a spellbinding experience. It's hard to believe that people live like this. What is that overgrown road to the left?"

"It used to be the villagers' shortcut to the west beach. It was closed when the Grand Island Club originated."

He was searching for a topic that would focus her attention. "That must be the sand dune where the fellow was shot last weekend." Then he told himself, This woman doesn't even read newspapers; she may not know about the shooting.

Liz turned to him abruptly. "Qwill, I think my guardian angel sent me that snake, so I could meet you."

"That's a charming compliment," he said stiffly, "but you paid a high price for a dubious benefit." He hoped this avowal would not lead to embarrassment.

Speaking earnestly, she said, "Ever since my father died, I've had no one to confide in."

"Is something troubling you?" he asked cautiously.

"I had a horrible experience right here on this spot a few years ago, and I've never been able to tell anyone."

"How old were you?"

"Sixteen."

Qwilleran's curiosity went into high gear, but he said in an offhand way, "If it will help you to talk about it, I'll be willing to listen."

She pondered a few minutes, looking tragic in her father's old hat. "Well, I was spending the summer here with my mother. Father had just died, and I felt so alone! Then my brother Jack came up for a few weeks. Mother had just paid a big settlement to get rid of his first wife, and now he had married again. Mother was upset, but Jack was her pet and could wheedle her into anything." Her mind wandered off into realms of family intrigue.

Qwilleran nudged it back on track. "So he came up to The Pines for a few weeks."

"He was doing penance. He was being sweet to Mother and even to me. We played croquet and went sailing, and one day he took me for a drive through the Dark Village, just as Father had done. We took my favorite carriage and favorite horse and a basket lunch to eat on the south beach. I was so happy! I thought I had finally found a big brother who would be my confidant."

The rented horse snorted and stamped his hooves, but Liz was consumed by her memories.

"We drove through the Dark Village and when we came to this fork in the road, he turned left into the weeds. I said, "Where are you going? This road is closed!" His mouth turned down with a nasty expression, and I can't tell you what he said! I can't tell you what he tried to do! I jumped out of the carriage and ran screaming to the beach road. There were some fishermen beaching their boats, and I told them I was from The Pines. I said my brother had played a trick and driven away without me. They remembered my father and took me home in their boat. It was full of wet, slippery, flopping fish, but I didn't care. I was grateful."

"What did you tell your mother?" Qwilleran asked.

"I couldn't tell her what happened. She wouldn't have believed me. I told her my mind suddenly went blank. Jack told her I went crazy. Ricky said I was grieving for Father, and the ride through the Dark Village triggered a seizure. I had to have a nurse companion all summer, and Mother sent Jack to Europe while she paid off his second wife. That turned out to be poetic justice, because he met an actress in Italy and married again."

There was a distant rumble on the horizon, and Qwilleran asked, "Is that thunder? Or is Canada being attacked by missiles?"

"It's a long way off," Liz said. "Sometimes we hear distant thunder for two days and nights before the storm reaches us. It's rather exciting."

"Nevertheless, we should take this tired nag back to the stable for his afternoon nap," Qwilleran said.

Downtown he checked the post office—there was no mail from Polly—and hailed a cab to take Liz home.

"I feel as if a great weight has been lifted from my mind and my heart," she said. "Would you be my guest for lunch at the clubhouse some day?"

He agreed, hoping the invitation would be delayed until he was safely back in Pickax. He had done his good deed—two of them, in fact. He had listened sympathetically and allowed himself to be adopted as a godfather of sorts. From a practical point of view, meeting the royal family had been unproductive, supplying no material for his column and no leads in his investigation. Furthermore, if and when he ever wrote his book, it would not be about people like the Appelhardts . . . What prompted this asocial thinking was an immediate concern of his own, prompted by Lyle Compton's casual remark that Polly might decide to stay in Oregon. Qwilleran's uneasiness increased as each day passed without a postcard.

# Sixteen

After dropping his lunch date at The Pines, Qwilleran went into the lounge at the Domino Inn to borrow some newspapers. There were few guests in evidence, but that was understandable; it was a weekday, and weather predictions for the next five days were iffy. Thunder still rumbled sporadically. It was not coming any closer; it was simply a warning of something that might never happen.

At the fruit basket he was glad to see that the pears had been replaced by apples. He was helping himself to one red and one green when the vice president in charge of communications and deliveries dashed up to him with two slips of paper, a foil-wrapped package the size of a brick, and an excited announcement in the language that Qwilleran was beginning vaguely to understand. As far as he could construe, either Sherman had had kittens, or Sheba was afraid of thunder, or Shoo Shoo had thrown up a hairball. He nodded and thanked Mitchell and then read his two telephone messages:

TO: Mr. Q
FROM: Andrew Brodie
REC'D: Tuesday 1:15 P.M.
MESSAGE: George Dulac. Lake Worth FL

To Qwilleran the name sounded Slavic. This was the ill-fated hotel guest who had conversed with a woman in a foreign language. The other message was from Dwight Somers: "Leaving the island. Information you want is in the mail." From these few words Qwilleran deduced that the public-relations man had been fired, possibly for snooping in the hotel's confidential records. If that were the case, Qwilleran rationalized, his friend was better off; he was too good for XYZ; he deserved more civilized working conditions; he could start his own agency.

When Qwilleran returned to Four Pips, he found two restless cats. They could hear the far-off thunder, and they knew instinctively what was in store. They might, in fact, know more than the weather forecasters. Koko was prowling and looking for ways to get into trouble. Yum Yum was murmuring to herself as she tried to open a desk drawer. When Qwilleran opened it to show her that it was empty, that was even more frustrating to her feline sensibility. He tried reading to the Siamese from the editorial page of the *Moose County Something*, but they were bored. So was he. All three of them were at sixes and sevens.

Polly was on his mind, along with the reasons why she would decide to move to Oregon: Her old school chum pressured her into relocating; the opportunities for birding were irresistible; a suburban library needed a librarian with Polly's expertise and made her a good offer; she had reached the restless age and was ready for a new challenge. Although he tried to be understanding, Qwilleran found it difficult to imagine life without Polly. True, he had many friends, and two animal companions, and an enviable place to live, and a column to write for the newspaper, and a host of devoted readers, and money to spend. Yet, Polly filled a long-felt need in his life.

"Enough of this sentimentality!" he said to the Siamese, and he made a meatloaf sandwich. They muddled through the evening, hearing sounds of yet another audition at Five Pips. The atmosphere was calm, and the unceasing thunder seemed to be coming from several directions. Shortly before midnight he gave the cats their bedtime treat and retired, taking care to close the bedroom door. When the weather was threatening, they liked to crowd into his bed. He thought he would have trouble sleeping, but . . .

Qwilleran was sound asleep when the disturbance started outside his door—first the yowling, then the urgent scratching on the door panels. He sat up in bed and checked the hour; it was almost two o'clock. Then he smelled smoke. It was not tobacco this time; it was something burning. He checked his own kitchen burners hastily and then stepped outside with a flashlight.

Black smoke was issuing from the cottage next door. Without a second's hesitation he ran to Five Pips and pounded on the door, shouting "June! June! Fire!" The door was locked. He tried to kick it in, but he was wearing only light slippers. He lunged at it, but it held fast. He smashed the front window with his flashlight and then ran up the lane to ring the firebell. He clanged it again and again. Lights appeared instantly in certain windows of the inn, and Nick's voice shouted. "Where is it?"

"The last cottage!"

"Get out! Get everybody out!"

Qwilleran ran back to pull on some clothes—he was still in pajama bottoms and slippers—and stuff the cats into their carrier. He could hear a motor vehicle in the distance and the emergency beep—beep—beep. As soon as he emerged, lugging the carrier, Nick was running down the lane in full firefighting gear.

"Get everybody to the inn!" he yelled.

Now the motors of heavy vehicles could be heard on the still night air. The family in the first cottage—parents and two children—stood outside, confused and frightened.

"Go to the inn!" Qwilleran shouted. "Keep out of the way! The fire trucks are coming!" Already the police car was rounding the building.

In the lounge, where guests were standing around in nightclothes and robes, the Bamba cats hissed and growled at the sight of the caged Siamese invading their territory.

"Take them upstairs and shut them up in any vacant room," Lori said to Qwilleran. She was moving among the guests and saying, "Everything's under control . . . Don't be alarmed . . . The fire trucks are on the way . . . We've got plenty of water in the lake . . . There's no wind tonight, so it won't spread."

From the upstairs window Qwilleran saw the police car floodlighting the burning building. Black smoke billowed from the windows. Then the tanker and pumper arrived, and a line was run down to the lake. Soon his own cottage was being hosed down with torrents of water. An ambulance lumbered onto the scene, and a stretcher was rushed to the end of the lane. When another firefighter came running, helmet in hand, he recognized Harriet Beadle; she went to work as a backup on the hose.

The Siamese, sensing the tension of the emergency, were solemnly quiet when he released them from the carrier and left them alone.

Downstairs Lori said, "I'm fixing coffee for the firefighters. Does anyone want to help make sandwiches?"

"I can do that," Qwilleran offered. While she cut lunchmeat and separated cheese slices, he spread mayonnaise on bread. "I saw her being loaded into the ambulance," he said gruffly.

"We were afraid she'd get us into trouble," Lori said in a quiet voice. "She was so self-willed."

"Today she was walking around the yard with a lighted cigarette and an ashtray, and she told me she was observing house rules. I assumed she had reformed, but she had company tonight, and they may have been careless."

Lori looked out the window. "I don't see flames. They must have contained the fire. Thank God there's no wind. You won't be able to use your cottage, Qwill. We'll make up a suite, and you can spend the rest of the week upstairs . . . Listen! I hear the chopper. They're taking her to the mainland."

The other guests were sent back to bed, but Qwilleran stayed and helped serve coffee and sandwiches to the sooty-faced volunteers, who reported to the inn in shifts to take a breather. Some would stay on duty all night, watching for hot spots. He talked to the chief and then phoned the night desk of the *Moose County Something.*

"Reporting fire at Pear Island resort. Discovered at one-fifty-five A.M. Confined to one cottage at Domino Inn on West Beach Road. Occupant removed by volunteer rescue squad and airlifted to mainland. Check Pickax hospital for condition. Adult female. Check sheriff for release of name. Got it? . . . Ten volunteer firefighters, one tanker, and one pumper responded. No injuries. Water pumped from lake. Calm atmosphere averted forest fire and damage to other buildings. Probable cause of fire: smoking in bed, according to fire chief. Got it? . . . Okay, now listen here: If the victim dies, police will withhold her name temporarily, but I can tell you that she was Dr. June Halliburton, head of music for Moose County schools. Check Lyle Compton for bio. She was also summer director of entertainment for the Pear Island Hotel. Check Don Exbridge of XYZ Enterprises for comments . . . Okay?"

As he hung up, Qwilleran said to himself, Lyle will be shocked! So will Dwight. So will the Rikers. And there goes Derek's job as assistant director—if such a job ever existed.

Lori was finally persuaded to get some rest, but Qwilleran was still manning the coffeemaker at six A.M., when the news was broadcast by WPKX:

"A fire in a cottage on Pear Island claimed the life of one person early this morning. Volunteer firefighters responded to the alarm and were able to contain the blaze that originated in a smoldering mattress. Cause of death was asphyxiation resulting from smoke inhalation. The victim, an adult female from the Pickax area, was airlifted from the island by sheriff's helicopter but was dead on arrival at Pickax General Hospital. The name is withheld pending notification of relatives."

After a few hours of sleep Qwilleran was roused by the yowling of two Siamese, who wanted their breakfast, fire or no fire. He ventured down the lane and salvaged a can of red salmon from Four Pips. The family in Two Pips was packing up and leaving, and most of the guests in the inn were checking out. They said the continuous thunder made them nervous. According to weather reports, the storm would reach Moose County and environs in twenty-four hours.

A pale and weary Lori was serving scrambled eggs and toast, that was all, and when Qwilleran inquired about Nick, she said, "He took the kids and cats to the mainland at eight o'clock this morning. He's dropping them at his mother's house—nine cats, including the new kittens. Then he'll come right back. There's a lot of cleanup to do, as well as securing everything against the storm. High winds and thunderstorms are predicted. That means shuttering windows and removing anything that could blow away."

"I'll help, if someone will tell me what to do."

"First, you might bring all your belongings from Four Pips," she said. "And now that our cats have gone, yours can have the run of the inn."

"But not until I can supervise them," Qwilleran stipulated.

There was no fire damage at Four Pips, but the acrid smell of smoke and a mustiness from the drenching of the roof had permeated everything, including his clothing. Once more he bundled shirts, pants, and socks into pillow cases and carried them to the Vacation Helpers.

Wordlessly he tossed the bundles on the reception table.

"Oh, no! Not again!" said Shelley.

"How fast can you have it ready?"

"Two hours. Is it smoke damage? I heard about the fire. Too bad about the woman who died. Did you know her? Was she young?" In a high state of excitement induced by the approaching storm, Shelley talked nonstop, asking questions without waiting for answers. "Did you hear the storm warning on the radio? Did you see the ladders out in front? Some of our roomers are shuttering the windows. Mr. Ex wants all hotel employees to leave the island, but some of us are going to ride it out. We'll have plenty of beer and meatloaf sandwiches, and we'll have a ball! They predict gale winds or worse, but this building is good and solid. If there's high water, it'll be bad for the hotel. We're on a higher elevation, so I don't worry, do you? Have you ever gone through a hurricane?"

On the way out, Qwilleran encountered Derek Cuttlebrink, leaving with a duffelbag, and he asked the young man, "Are you one of the rats deserting a sinking ship?"

"Yeah . . . well . . . I'm laid off—for how long, I don't know—so I might as well go home and see my girl. How d'you like this thunder? It hasn't stopped since yesterday noon. It spooks me!"

"The ancient gods of the island are having a bowling tournament," Qwilleran said, adding in a lower voice, "Did Merrio come up with any more information? Let's walk down to the beach."

They sat on the steps leading down to the abandoned beach, and Derek said, "I don't know if this has anything to do with the Chicken Stink or not. That's what they call the food poisoning behind the chef's back," he explained with a grin. "But here goes: The hotel doesn't buy all its food from the mainland. Some of the islanders bring the chef fresh fish, goat cheese, and rabbit, but no chicken."

"Do they simply walk into the kitchen and peddle their goods?"

"They used to, but now the back door is kept locked, and vendors have to be on the chef's list. But when the hotel first opened, Merrio remembers a man who used to bring fresh herbs to sell. The chef was glad to get them. He's French, you know, and they always make a big thing of fresh herbs. Fresh or dry, I don't see that it makes any difference."

A connection flashed across Qwilleran's mind: Does the chef know Noisette? Are they a couple? Is that why she's here? Is that why she has a suite at a secluded inn? Is the chef paying for it? Was it the chef drinking with her in the Buccaneer Den on Sunday night?

"So how'm I doin'?" Derek asked.

"Mission accomplished. Next assignment: *Kamchatka.*" He handed Derek some folded bills. "Now you'd better get in line for the ferry."

Qwilleran helped Nick carry the hurricane shutters out of the basement, and then he helped carry the porch furniture indoors. By that time his laundry would be finished, and he walked up to Vacation Helpers. Shelley had two neat packages of folded clothing waiting for him, plus a foil-wrapped brick of something that looked all too familiar.

She said, "This is your Thursday meatloaf, just out of the oven. Would you like to take it with you? It may not be as good as before, because it's all-beef. Do you mind? Midge's regular recipe calls for two parts beef and one part rabbit, but she couldn't get any rabbit meat today."

"I can live with that," Qwilleran said agreeably.

He had a hunch, and it proved to be correct. As soon as he returned to his suite at the inn, he gave the Siamese a taste of rabbitless meatloaf, and they gobbled it, yowling for more.

"Cats!" he said in exasperation. "Who can understand them?"

They were adjusting to their new environment readily. It was the bridal suite. The furniture was new, the chairs luxuriously cushiony, the colors soft. There was none of the overscaled, bargain-priced fabric that decorated the rest of the inn. There were too many knick-knacks for Qwilleran's taste, and the pictures on the wall were Victorian Romantic; he removed two of them over the sofa and substituted the gilded leather masks. He had also brought the maroon velvet box from Four Pips.

"How would you guys like to play the numbers?" he asked.

Koko was in good form. The first dominoes he swished off the table spelled *gale*. Next came one of his favorites: *lake*, which could be shuffled to spell *leak*.

Qwilleran said to him, "If the weatherman is correct, there's going to be a leak in the plumbing of Mount Olympus tomorrow."

After that the words were ordinary: *idea, blade, gable, hack, deaf* (or *fade*) and *deal* (or *lead*). Then five of Koko's favorite dominoes landed on the floor: 3-3, 2-2, 6-6, 2-3, and 4-5. As usual, Qwilleran was able to spell *field*. There was no particular significance to *field* until the next draw, which consisted of 2-4, 1-3, 6-3, 6-6, and 0-5. Although the pips were different, they reduced to the same digits, which corresponded to the same letters: *field*. It had been one of the cat's favorites from the start. A tremor rippled across Qwilleran's upper lip. For the first time it occurred to him that *field* could be shuffled to spell *filed*. He hurried from the room and ran downstairs to have a look at the porch. The crawl space underneath was ventilated with panels of wood lattice. He found Nick hanging shutters on the south side of the building. "How do we get under the porch?" he asked. "I'd like to put Koko on a leash and have him look at the underside of the steps."

"There are removable panels at each end. You need a high-powered flashlight—maybe two. I'll go with you."

Qwilleran never traveled with the Siamese without taking their harnesses. Yum Yum abhorred the idea, but Koko always liked to be buckled up.

Downstairs Nick had removed the access panel and had two battery-operated lanterns.

Qwilleran said, "This is a wild shot, but we might find evidence of tampering." First he let Koko wander about the porch, now empty of swings and chairs. The cat sniffed in desultory fashion for a few minutes and then went directly to the third step from the top. In a low voice Qwilleran said, "He knows the trouble spot. Let's crawl underneath."

He went first, with Koko leading. Nick followed with the second lantern. It was a long crawl through damp sand, detritus, and skeletons of small animals. They made slow progress, as Koko was distracted by many items of catly interest. When they reached the steps, Nick flashed his lantern up at the new construction—treated wood, solidly braced and nailed—but the cat was interested only in the sand below. There were sawed-off remnants of lumber and new galvanized nails dropped by the carpenter. There were also fragments of old rusty nails and something else half-buried in the sand. Koko was digging for it—an old hack saw blade. Qwilleran's moustache bristled as he remembered the dominoes: *hack* and *blade* and *filed*.

He said to Nick, "Do you see what I see?"

"A couple of swipes with that thing would cut through a rusty nail like a piece of cake."

"Don't touch it. It's our evidence," Qwilleran said. "You know, Nick, when my barn was being converted, there were rusty nails in the hundred-year-old timbers, and the carpenter whacked them with a metal file. They broke like breadsticks."

"So now the question is: Who whacked the nails under our steps?"

"Let's get out of here."

They crawled out, dragging a reluctant cat. Nick wanted to finish the shuttering. Qwilleran wanted another look at the domino records he had been keeping. He also wanted to check the post office before it closed.

Upstairs, Yum Yum greeted the returning hero with assorted reactions; he brought with him the scent of untold mysteries. Koko, when divested of his leather trappings, took a half hour to launder his fur thoroughly. Qwilleran checked the records for words and numbers that would trigger a thought process.

*Lead,* depending on how it was pronounced, could refer to a metal with chemically poisonous properties, or it could be another name for *leash.* Words with K, L, and J reflected Koko's preference for high-pip dominoes: 5-6, 6-6, and 5-5. In general he favored doubles—like 1-1, 2-2, 3-3, and 4-4—suggesting a sense of order or balance.

Next Qwilleran examined his own shuffling of letters: *Field* became *filed; idle* could be *lied; lake* and *leak* appeared on the list every day. Why? Because Koko liked 5-6 and 6-6? The letters, Qwilleran now realized, could also spell *kale,* a kind of cabbage of which he was not fond, or the name of a local family. There were Kales, Beadles, and Lawsons all over the island, someone had said.

"Yow!" said Koko in a tone that made Qwilleran's moustache bristle again.

He glanced at his watch. There was no time to lose. "Be right back," he said to the Siamese, who gazed at him with their so-what? expression.

The postal clerk at General Delivery, who had disappointed him so many times, was pleased to hand him two pieces of mail. The postcard he read immediately. It was written in Polly's usual telegraphic style:

> Wonderful country. Good birding. Sarah is fun! She's helped
> me make a very important decision. Details later. Arrive air-
> port 7:35 Friday. Love, Polly

Qwilleran's suspicions were confirmed. So be it! He huffed into his moustache with resignation. It would make some changes in his life. It would never be the same without Polly.

The other piece of mail was a letter in a Pear Island Hotel envelope, with "D.S." inked above the return address. He put it in his pocket. At the moment, and under the circumstances, what did he care about Noisette's last name?

# Seventeen

•:•

Qwilleran was somewhat subdued as he helped shutter the windows of the inn. Nick said, "They darken the rooms completely, so we'll leave one window uncovered in each room—until the last minute. After that, we live with artificial light, like prison inmates —unless there's a power failure. That means no lights, no water, no refrigeration. We're filling the bathtub with water—and also some five-gallon jugs for drinking. Lori has a campstove that's all right for heating canned food and boiling coffee, but that's about all. The radios operate on batteries, and we have plenty of oil lamps and flashlights, but it won't be fun. If you don't want to stay, Qwill, I'll understand. I'll take you back to the mainland while the lake's still calm."

"I'll stay," Qwilleran said.

"Okay, but don't say I didn't warn you. If you want to phone anyone on the mainland, tell them we're on high ground, and the building is solid, constructed with huge timbers and thick planks. No shortcuts or substitutions or imitations."

Qwilleran took the suggestion and phoned the newspaper office, leaving a message with the secretary. It was a relief to find that Riker was out of the building. The editor would have tried to harangue him into changing his mind. Whatever Qwilleran proposed to do, his old friend insisted that it was too reckless, too impractical, too frivolous, or too expensive.

Now he was suffering from lack of sleep and the exertion of ladder climbing, and Polly's postcard had induced a state of numb indifference. He flopped on his bed, narrowly missing two dormant lumps of fur, and slept until he was disturbed by two active cats, who were themselves disturbed by noises in the corridor. There were voices, and sounds of luggage handling, and the opening and closing of doors. Someone was moving in! In the groggy state of first awakening, he wondered why anyone would move into the Domino Inn at a time like this, when everyone else was moving out.

He roused himself, combed his hair, washed his face, and went downstairs, where he was met by a wide-eyed Lori. "You'll never guess!" she said. "A new guest just registered! She has beautiful luggage, and she was brought here in a splendid carriage! She says she knows you!"

"What's her name?" he asked warily.

"Elizabeth Cage. I wanted to ask why she'd check into a place with shuttered windows, but then . . ." Lori looked at Qwilleran slyly. "I thought it might be something private between you two."

"Where is she now?"

"Upstairs, unpacking. She's in the Lakeview Suite across from you."

"This comes as a total surprise. Do we have any meatloaf sandwiches left over from the fire?"

"That's about all—including the whole meatloaf you gave us. I'm not prepared to serve dinner guests, you know."

"She doesn't eat much, so don't fuss and don't apologize. I'll go upstairs," he said irritably, "to see what this is all about."

The young woman who opened the door was dressed in a caftan and seemed very glad to see him.

"Liz! What the devil are you doing here?" he demanded.

"My family left this noon, taking both boats, and I told Mother I didn't wish to go. I told her I'm moving to Pickax City."

"You're a very impulsive young woman! You don't know anything about Pickax." He was thinking, Arch is right; I should mind my own business.

"Will you come in? I'd offer you tea, but I suppose there's no room service today."

"Not today, and not ever! And if the storm hits hard, there may be no lights, no water, and no ferries to the mainland. The only boat left in the downtown marina belongs to Domino Inn, and the storm could reduce it to splinters. Have all the boats left the Grand Island Club?"

"Yes, but . . . if I may use the telephone, I think I can arrange something."

"Go down and tell Mrs. Bamba what you have in mind. She'll let you use the office phone . . . And now, if you'll excuse me, I have an errand to do."

He wanted to walk away from the situation and consider the complications involved if Liz should move to Pickax. Could she handle her own living arrangements, face responsibility, make wise decisions? Or would she require and expect a full-time guardian? That was a role he was not prepared to play. He had come to the island to help Nick, and he had stepped into . . . the peat bog, so to speak.

Qwilleran walked to Harriet's Family Café, not expecting it to be open but hoping to follow up their previous conversation. Two men—who proved to be her cousins from the village—were shuttering the windows, while she supervised with tough authority. When she saw Qwilleran, she walked toward him with a solemn step and an anguished face.

"Isn't it terrible about the fire?" she moaned. "We had to notify the fire marshal. He comes up from Down Below if anyone dies—or if the chief suspects arson."

"But you and the other volunteers did a heroic job, Harriet. It could have been much worse."

"I know, but I feel bad *because I knew her!* I knew June Kale all her life, and I know her pa."

"June Kale? I thought her name was Halliburton."

"She got married once. It didn't last long. Yep, she grew up on the island and went to high school on the mainland, like I did, but she was really bright. Never took piano lessons till ninth grade, and next thing we knew, she was teaching music and playing the piano in big halls. She got kinda stuck-up then—didn't want anybody to know she came from Providence Island, but she visited her ma and pa a lot, and I give her credit for that! . . . My! They were so proud of their daughter! Her ma's dead now, and her pa must be all broke up. I feel terribly sorry for him. He's the caretaker at The Pines."

"Does he live in the gatehouse?"

"Yep, as far back as I can remember. June grew up there—with electric light, a bathroom, telephone, and all that."

Qwilleran was asking himself questions, and answering them. Did June want to live in the north country to be near her parents? *She was too brittle, too worldly for that kind of sentiment.* Did she really rent Five Pips to avoid disturbing her elderly neighbors? . . . Or so her father could steal in to visit her via the nature trail? *Neither. The voices drifting across the yard after dark weren't those of father and daughter.*

*They were young, bantering, teasing, laughing voices. The parties didn't sound like auditions either.*

"Do you want some coffee or ice cream?" Harriet asked.

"No, thanks. I just came to see how you are. You must be exhausted after being up all night. Do you plan to stay here during the storm?"

"Nope. I'll be sitting with my ma in the village. It's gonna be a bad one! My cousins are putting up the shutters to save the glass."

Qwilleran turned away as if to leave and then added as an afterthought, "The fire is the sixth incident in less than three weeks, and the fourth to result in a death. If you have any idea who's involved, now is the time to come forward."

Harriet's face became flushed, and she clenched and unclenched her fists. "The fire was an accident! How could it be anything else? She was smoking in bed. She always smoked a lot. Her ma and pa tried to stop her, but they couldn't."

"Okay, leave the fire out of it," Qwilleran said. "You told me you knew something about the other incidents. You knew someone who was responsible."

"I was wrong. That was a mistake. It was just village gossip," she said, walking away and shouting to the cousins who were shuttering the windows.

Qwilleran walked away, too, thinking, Once an islander, always an islander. Harriet had decided to remain loyal. Actually, her transparent denials only confirmed his suspicions.

The WPKX announcer said, "A storm watch is now in effect for all shoreline communities. The Disaster Center has issued evacuation directives for all occupants of beach property. Two fronts are approaching at the rate of five miles an hour and could converge over northern Moose County and adjoining lake areas by midnight. Severe thunderstorms, winds of seventy to a hundred miles an hour, and rising lake levels are expected."

The storm was indeed closing in on all sides, as four persons gathered around the kitchen table at the Domino Inn. Nick had installed the last of the shutters and had nailed planks across the front and back doors to prevent them from bursting open. He also nailed a towel-wrapped two-by-four across the bottom of each door to keep the rain from pouring across the threshold.

Lori served a pickup supper in the kitchen, around a big square table with piano legs and scarred top. There were meatloaf sandwiches, and there was a homemade soup that was thick and grayish in color, but it tasted good. The only recognizable ingredient was alphabet pasta. She explained, "It's full of chicken broth and veggies, but I puree them so the kids won't know what they're eating, and the alphabet letters keep them from thinking about it too much."

Since the pasta alphabet contained all twenty-six letters—as opposed to twelve in the domino game—Qwilleran was able to spell *papilionaceous,* a word that had once won him a spelling championship and a trip to Washington. Liz had the good manners to be amused by the soup and tolerant of the sandwiches.

Lori said, "Ms. Cage arranged for us to dock the *Double-Six* at the Grand Island Club."

"Yeah, it worked out great!" Nick said. "I took the boat up there, and they rolled it into a concrete boathouse. Then one of the guys drove me home in a snappy little cart. He said he'd always wanted to see the four big tree trunks inside our lodge."

Liz told them that the west beach had never experienced much damage from summer storms. "We might lose a few tree branches or shingles, but we've never been inconvenienced by loss of power, because we have generators. So it surprised me that Mother wanted to leave this time."

It was no surprise to Qwilleran. The queen mother, he guessed, wanted to whisk her daughter away from his radical influence. Thinking the Bambas deserved an explanation, he said, "Ms. Cage has been wanting to relocate in Pickax, and she thought this would be an appropriate time, storm or no storm."

Lori expressed surprise and pleasure. "You'll like Pickax," she said. "The population is only three thousand, but the town has some good things going for it, including a very good theater club. Also, they're getting a community college." She turned and looked brightly and expectantly at Qwilleran, who had authorized the Klingenschoen Foundation to underwrite the new institution. He had no intention of picking up the cue, however, and said not a word about the college or the theater club or anything else in Pickax. He was not going to encourage this impulsive and eager and reputedly flaky young woman to move into his backyard. Instead he said to her, "You might prefer Lockmaster in the adjoining county. They have horse farms and carriage collectors and driving clubs."

"I've never cared about joining clubs," she said. "What I enjoy is a leisurely drive down a country lane. I would have my favorite horse shipped to Pickax; I suppose he could be stabled there. And my brother William would let me have the physician's phaeton."

Lori said, "If you like country lanes, you'll love Moose County. It has very picturesque countryside."

*Shut up, Lori,* Qwilleran thought. He said, "I don't know whether picturesque is the right word. The terrain has a ravaged look because of the strip mining and overcutting of forests earlier in the century. Abandoned mines and abandoned quarries are everywhere. They can be an eyesore."

"Yes, but the abandoned shafthouses are like romantic monuments to the past," said Lori, her eyes sparkling. He wanted to kick her under the table, but even his long legs couldn't reach.

Nick, noticing his scowl and sensing his purpose, said, "There's a lot of industry coming into Pickax—like plastics, auto parts, and electronics—but the major industry is the federal prison covering hundreds of acres and housing ten thousand convicted felons."

Lori said, "Yes, but the prison is famous for its flower gardens, tended by inmates. People come from all over to photograph them."

Oh, God! Qwilleran thought. He said, "Does anyone play dominoes? We may have to play a lot of dominoes before this storm is over."

Thunder claps were coming closer, and lightning bolts made themselves felt like electric shocks. Even the solid wood shutters couldn't keep the flashes from outlining the windows like blue neon.

After dessert—ice cream on a stick—Qwilleran excused himself and went upstairs to the bridal suite, intending to remain in seclusion until the rains came. Then he would go downstairs to offer help and moral support to the Bambas and the uninvited guest. He tried to read, but thoughts of the present dilemma crowded the words from the page. He felt burdened with a sense of failure. In his search for clues and evidence he had nothing to show but hunches, suspicions, and a hack saw blade.

The air was heavy with portent, and the cats, huddled close to him, kept looking at the ceiling. Suddenly there was a clap of thunder directly overhead, like the crack of doom. Koko jumped two feet in the air and went into orbit. Circling madly around the suite he kicked a table lamp, sent knickknacks flying, terrorized Yum Yum, and sideswiped one of the leather masks over the sofa.

"Stop!" Qwilleran bellowed as he rescued the expensive artwork—it was the tragedy mask—but Koko was wound up and continued the rampage until his internal springs ran down. Then he flicked his tongue nonchalantly over random patches of fur. At one point he stopped and, with tongue hanging out and one hind leg held aloft, he stared at Qwilleran's forehead.

"Let's play dominoes," Qwilleran said, stroking his moustache.

At the same moment there was another shattering thunderbolt. The rain slammed into the building, and the lights flickered momentarily, but they played the game. Koko's penchant for white spots resulted in words like *click, balked, jack, deckle, ilk* and the ubiquitous *lake*. Just as Qwilleran was trying to make a word out of 4-4, 5-6, 3-5, 0-1, 5-5, 3-6, 6-6, and 2-3, there was a light tap on the door.

There stood Liz in her caftan, carrying an oil lamp. "I'm sorry to trouble you," she said, "but would you show me how to light this lamp, in case there's a power failure?" She handed him a box of kitchen matches. "These were with the lamp."

"Come in," he said brusquely, "and close the door to keep the cats from escaping. In stormy weather they sometimes go berserk." He removed the glass chimney, turned up the wick, and tried to strike a match. "These are no good. They're damp. Let's try mine. Islands are always damp. Shoes mildew, nails rust, crackers get soggy, and matches don't strike. You should know about that; you've spent summers here."

"There was never any problem," she said. "The air-conditioning controlled the humidity."

The matches in the bridal suite were equally damp. "It will be a joke," he said, "if there are thirty oil lamps on the premises and no matches."

"Would anyone have a cigarette lighter?"

"Not at the Domino Inn! No cigarette lighters, no automatic weapons, and no illegal drugs. Did you hear about the fire last night?"

Liz nodded sadly. "The woman who died was the daughter of our steward. The poor man is almost out of his mind. When we were growing up, she was like my big sister, and I heard something this morning that was very upsetting." She moistened her lips and lowered her eyes.

"Please sit down," Qwilleran said. "Would you like a glass of water? That's all I can offer."

She perched on the edge of a chair and took a dainty sip.

"Where did you hear this upsetting news?"

"I was in the stable, giving Skip his daily dose of affection in his stall. He's such a loving animal! And I heard two men in the tack room, having a very heated argument. I knew the voices. One was my brother, and the other was our steward. They've always been friendly, and it was a shock to hear them shouting at each other. I know it's bad form to eavesdrop, but Jack has never had any respect for me, so I didn't feel guilty about listening."

"Did you learn what the trouble was?"

Before she could reply, there was another violent crack of thunder overhead. A purple flash seeped into the room, and the lights went out! Liz uttered an involuntary cry.

"Well, I guess that's it!" he said. "We'd better go downstairs. I have a flashlight. We'll go across the hall and get the one in your room— and hope the Bambas have dry matches."

Nick met them at the foot of the stairs. "Come into the family room. We're lighting lamps. Sorry about this. We should have a generator, but there've been so many other things to do and buy."

"Qwill," Lori called from the office door, "why don't you bring Koko and Yum Yum down?"

For the next five hours, four persons and two animal companions huddled together as sheets of rain assaulted the building and the wind screamed through the treetops like a hundred harmonicas. At the storm's apex, when the turbulence was directly over the island, the thunder was a series of explosions, each louder than the last, making the ground shudder. There were moments when the building quaked enough to rattle glasses and tilt pictures. At such moments Lori sat quietly with eyes closed and lips moving as she hugged Koko for security. Qwilleran held Yum Yum, mumbling reassurances. Both cats were wide-eyed, and their ears swiveled wildly.

Nick produced a jug of red wine, saying, "We might as well be drunk as the way we are."

Qwilleran had to exercise intense willpower to refuse. "How long can it last?" he shouted above the din.

"It's passing over."

Now there were several seconds or even a full minute between thunderclaps, and the purple flashes were weaker, but the rain still bombarded the building. Occasionally there was a loud crack as a tree limb snapped off, followed by a jarring thump as it landed on the roof. No one mentioned it, but all must have been thinking, What if a tree comes through the roof? What if tons of water pour into the building?

Now at least it was possible to talk and be heard, although there was no conversation as such—merely spoken thoughts:

"It still sounds like a locomotive roaring past!"

"The ancient gods of the island are snarling and gnashing their teeth."

"Thank God we sent the kids to the mainland."

"They'll be getting it over there, too."

"Have you ever seen one as bad as this?"

"The cats are very good. Koko is tense, though."

"Yum Yum has been trembling nonstop."

"Did you look at the wind gauge, Nick?"

"It broke the gauge. Must've reached a hundred."

"Wonder how high the lake is."

"If it reaches road-level, we could have a washout."

"Did anyone ever read *High Wind in Jamaica*?"

Sometimes the wind stopped for one blessed moment, then resumed its attack from another direction. When, in the small hours of the morning, the tumult ceased, there was stunned silence in the small room. Everyone claimed to be weary.

"Anyone hungry?" Lori asked.

It was sleep that everyone craved. The oil lamps were extinguished, and flashlights guided the survivors through the black rooms.

# Eighteen

No daylight filtered through the shuttered windows the day after the storm; even the Siamese didn't know it was breakfast time. Only the sound of the sheriff's helicopter assessing the damage and the sound of Nick removing shutters suggested that it was time to get up.

Lori offered Qwilleran hot coffee, cold cereal, and an orange from the fruit basket. "Look out the front door," she said. "You won't believe it."

The sun was shining; the flood waters were rapidly receding; and a workmanlike breeze was drying the drenched building and terrain.

"We were lucky," Lori said. "Wait'll you hear the eleven o'clock newscast!" The WPKX announcer said:

The worst storm in forty years has done its dirty work in Moose County. Beach homes and fisheries on the shore sustained minor damage, but the storm vented its greatest fury on the south end of Pear Island, commonly called Breakfast Island. The Pear Island Hotel was virtually leveled during the five-hour onslaught, which has been officially recorded as a northern hurricane. Winds up to a hundred miles an hour, plus a lake surge, made mincemeat of a structure that was completed less than two months ago. Uprooted trees of tremendous height fell on the flat-roofed building and adjoining strip malls. Sections of the boardwalk and piers were hurled into the wreckage. All personnel had been evacuated from the complex, and no casualties have been reported. The developers, XYZ Enterprises, could not be reached for comment at this hour, but observers estimate that the damage will be in the high millions. Elsewhere on the island, buildings that have survived almost a century of storms continued to withstand the elements with only minor damage.

Qwilleran asked Lori, "Has Ms. Cage been down?"

"No, but I took some tea upstairs. I was worried about her. She's so fragile for a young woman, and so thin! I'm a perfect fourteen, but she makes me feel fat. She's okay, but tired and a little stunned. Aren't we all? You can't use your shaver, Qwill, but you can take a pitcher of water upstairs for washing. I hear the cats yowling. Do you want to let them out?"

"Let them stay where they are. If I open the door, they'll stick their heads out, think about it for five minutes, and then go back in."

"I'll keep them company," said a small voice from the stairs. "We'll play dominoes." It was Liz, wearing another caftan.

Qwilleran helped Nick with the shutters and porch furniture, while Lori tackled the indoor cleanup as well as she could without water or electricity. Rain and sand had blown into the building through invisible cracks, along with black soot from the charred remains of Five Pips.

Nick said, "Did you hear about the hotel? That should tell you something about modern technology. They laugh at our four big tree trunks and birchbark siding, but we didn't blow away, did we? Sorry about the power and phones being out. If you want to go back to the mainland, say when. Any time."

"Well . . ." said Qwilleran, thinking fast, "there's a lot of work here that I could help you with . . . and Polly's plane doesn't come in until tomorrow evening . . . so why don't I stay until then? *But you might ferry Ms. Cage over today.* I'm sure she'd appreciate it. She's not accustomed to discomforts and inconveniences."

"Be glad to, and I can drive her to the airport, if she's flying out."

"Uh . . . she hasn't quite decided. Just deliver her to the hotel in Mooseville. She can stay there a few days until she makes up her mind."

"Sure. Tell her to let me know when she wants to leave. Lori will be more comfortable, I know, if she doesn't have a guest to worry about while the place is such a mess."

Qwilleran found Liz on the porch, reading a book on the preservation of wetlands, and he was only too glad to relay Nick's offer.

"When are *you* leaving, Qwill?" she asked.

"Tomorrow evening."

"I'm in no hurry," she said. "Being here in the aftermath of a hurricane is rather exciting. I'd prefer to wait until tomorrow evening and save Mr. Bamba a trip. And since I'm going to Pickax—and you live there—perhaps you'll let me ride into the city with you."

"Well . . . yes . . . of course," Qwilleran said, "but there's another consideration: It embarrasses Mrs. Bamba when she's unable to produce decent meals."

"Don't let her worry about that! I'm not particular about food. She's a lovely person, and I'm enjoying my stay. Koko and Yum Yum and I are quite compatible, and I'll keep them entertained while you're helping Mr. Bamba," Liz assured him.

She stayed. Qwilleran cleaned up the storm debris. Lori served canned beans and canned corned beef. Finally, at departure time on Friday, Qwilleran accompanied Liz to the Grand Island Club on foot, and they returned with a dogcart. The luggage was stowed in the dog box, and the two men and two cats perched high on the seat above, while Liz, wearing travel clothes and her Gauguin hat, took the driver's seat. At the last minute Lori ran out with a maroon velvet box. "A souvenir of your vacation, Qwill!"

Aboard the *Double-Six* it was a smooth voyage to the mainland on a lake that had been raging the previous night. At the municipal pier in Mooseville, Nick helped carry the luggage to Qwilleran's small four-door: two suitcases, typewriter, some cartons, the cat carrier, and the turkey roaster—plus five pieces of luggage belonging to Liz. The uninvited guest was busy photographing the *Double-Six* and the seagulls on the waterfront.

"The cats and their commode go in the backseat," Qwilleran told Nick. Even so, the engineer's skill was required to fit everything into the trunk. Polly's luggage, they concluded, would have to go inside the car.

"Qwill, I don't know how to thank you," Nick said. "Sorry the weather was so lousy."

"I wish I could have come up with more answers, Nick, but I'm not through yet. I want to kick it around with Brodie when I get back to Pickax. I know you suspect troublemakers from Lockmaster, but I say the blame lies closer to home. Both the natives and the summer people resent the resort, and something tells me the crimes are being committed by a coalition. The sharpies from Down Below have the brains to organize a harassment campaign, and the islanders have the personnel to sneak around and poison the gumbo or plant a bomb. They're everywhere on the island, in low-level jobs where they can be virtually invisible."

"Gosh, you've really been thinking, Qwill."

"Tell you why I think the summer people are involved. They're angry enough to want to sue the resort, but it's a no-win case, and if they can't do it legally, they'll do it illegally. They're used to exercising their power, and they don't like to be thwarted." Qwilleran lowered his voice. "My immediate problem is: what to do with *this woman!*"

"Don't ask me. She's your woman!" Nick said with a grin.

"Like hell she is! She blew in with the hurricane, and I don't know what she expects . . . Well, never mind, I'll figure something out."

The *Double-Six* chugged back to the island, and Qwilleran faced Liz squarely. "Are you sure you want to go to Pickax and not to this charming town of Mooseville with its quaint Northern Lights Hotel? There's a maritime museum and a mall in a fish cannery and a good little restaurant called the Nasty Pasty."

"No, I find Pickax City more appealing," she said.

Huffing unobtrusively into his moustache, Qwilleran opened the passenger door for her. "We have to stop at the airport to pick up my friend, who's coming in on the seven-thirty-five shuttle. And now that you're here, Liz, what are your plans?"

"I'm going to drop 'Appelhardt.' I like 'Cage' better. It was the maiden name of my paternal grandmother."

"I mean, where do you want to live? What kind of people would you like to meet? How long do you think you'll stay? What do you want to do while you're here?"

"I don't know. Do you have any suggestions?"

He groaned inwardly. He should never have gone to tea at The Pines. "You might take an apartment in Indian Village. They have a clubhouse and golf course, and a lot of young people live there."

"I prefer older people," she said, looking at him appreciatively.

"A lot of older people live there, too. Do you play bridge?"

"No, cards don't appeal to me."

"Wherever you live, you'll need a car. It's a necessity in Moose County. There are no taxis."

"Would there be any objection to a horse and carriage? I could have Skip shipped over here, and William would let me have the physician's phaeton."

"In order to stable a horse, you'd have to live in the country, and you'd still need a car. I assume you have a driver's license."

"I'm afraid it's expired. Mother didn't want me to drive."

"Well, you'll have to renew it."

"Is there a foreign car dealer in Pickax? I'd like a Bentley. William has a Bentley."

Nothing had been settled by the time they reached the airport. Qwilleran parked at the passenger-pickup curb and told Liz to sit tight while he made a phone call and picked up his friend's luggage. In the terminal he called Fran Brodie, the interior designer. "Fran! Have I got a client for you! She's loaded! She's young! She wants to live in Pickax! . . . Don't ask questions. Just listen. She's checking into the Pickax Hotel in half an hour, and I want you to take her under your wing and see that she gets a good apartment, furniture, a car, knives and forks, everything! Her name is Elizabeth Cage. Call her early tomorrow, or even tonight, before she does something impulsive. I've gotta hang up. I'm at the airport. I'm meeting a plane."

When the shuttle taxied to the terminal, eight passengers deplaned, and Qwilleran—in a state of preoccupation—greeted Polly with less enthusiasm than she probably expected. He took her carry-on tote and a long roll of something, saying, "You have one other bag to claim, don't you?"

"That and two cartons. I bought a few things."

While trundling the luggage cart to the curb, he said casually, "I have a hitchhiker who wants to be dropped at the Pickax Hotel."

"Really? I thought you never picked up hitchhikers, Qwill."

"This one is different. I'll explain later."

He introduced Ms. Cage to Mrs. Duncan, and Polly looked at the Gauguin hat and said a stiff how-do-you-do. She was automatically jealous of any woman younger and thinner than she. To his relief, the younger woman had the good manners to relinquish her seat. "Let me sit with the cats," she said.

Polly requested, "When you put my impedimenta in the trunk, Qwill, be careful with that long roll." It looked as if it might be a wall map of the United States.

"I'm sorry, but all your luggage will have to go inside the car," he explained. "The trunk is jam-packed."

As they drove away from the airport, Polly half-turned and asked the other passenger politely, "Did you fly in?"

"No," said Liz in her ingenuous way, "Qwill and I came over on a boat from Grand Island. We were trapped in a strange inn during the hurricane—with no windows or lights or water. It was quite an adventure!"

"Really?" Polly looked at Qwilleran questioningly. "I'm not familiar with Grand Island."

*"How was your flight?"* he asked forcefully.

"Tolerable. Were you covering the hurricane for the paper?"

"Not officially. *Did you see any puffin birds in Oregon?"*

On the way into town the conversation struggled through a quagmire of bewilderment, evasion, awkwardness, and non sequiturs until they reached Goodwinter Boulevard. Then Qwilleran said, "If you don't mind, Polly, I'll drop you off first. We have a luggage problem to contend with in the trunk, and I know you're tired and want to get home."

Her second-floor apartment occupied a carriage house behind an old mansion, and she rushed upstairs to hug Bootsie, her adored animal companion, while Qwilleran brought up her luggage. Then she turned to him and said crisply, *"Who is she?"*

"It's a long story, but I'll make it brief," he said, talking fast and inventing half-truths. "After you left, the paper sent me to Breakfast Island on assignment . . . and I stayed at the Bambas' B-and-B . . . and I happened to meet a wealthy family from Chicago . . . whose daughter is relocating in Pickax. She's a friend of Fran Brodie's. I think she has some interest in the new college."

"Well!" Polly seemed unconvinced.

"And may I ask the nature of the important decision mentioned on your postcard?"

"That's a long story, too. We can talk about it later."

Downstairs, Liz had moved into the front seat again and was enthusing about the neighborhood. "I'd love to live here," she said.

"All these buildings are part of the new college campus," he explained, as he turned back onto Main Street. At Park Circle he pointed out the courthouse, the public library, and the K Theater, originally a mansion that was gutted by fire. *Fire!* His mind did a flashback to Breakfast Island: the fire in Five Pips, the death of June Halliburton, the revelation that she was the caretaker's daughter . . . Liz had known her . . . Liz had heard something upsetting in connection with the fire and was about to relate it when the power failed.

Qwilleran turned the wheel quickly and stopped the car in a parking lot. "Just before the lights went out, Liz, you were about to tell me something you overheard in the stable."

"Yes . . . yes . . ." she said moodily. "It haunts me, but I don't know whether I should talk about it or not."

"Tell it. You'll feel better."

"I'm afraid it's incriminating."

"If it's the truth, it should be told."

At that moment their conversation was interrupted by a tap on the car window, driver's side. "Hi, Mr. Q! Are you back?"

Qwilleran lowered the window but replied curtly. "Yes, I'm back."

An incredibly tall young man peered into the car, regarding the passenger with interest. "I've got my job back at the Old Stone Mill," he said.

"Good for you!"

The fellow was looking speculatively at Liz, and she leaned forward with a half-smile that gave Qwilleran a brilliant idea. He said, "Liz, this is Derek Cuttlebrink—you saw him in the Corsair Room—a prominent man-about-Pickax . . . Derek, Elizabeth Cage is a newcomer from Chicago."

"Hi! I like your crazy hat!" he said with uninhibited honesty.

Qwilleran added congenially, "We'll have to get her interested in the theater club, won't we?"

"Sure will!" Derek said with enthusiasm.

A scenario of the young man's future unreeled in Qwilleran's mind . . . *Exit: the ecologist with camping equipment. Enter: the amateur botanist with trust fund. Botanist and ex-pirate enroll in the new college.*

Derek ambled away, and Liz repeated what she had said in the hotel lobby: "He's so tall!" Her eyes were lively with admiration.

"Nice young man," Qwilleran said. "Good personality. Lots of talent . . . Now, where were we? You overheard your brother arguing with the steward in the stable."

"Yes, I was in the stall with Skip, and they were in the tack room and didn't see me. I couldn't believe my ears! The steward accused Jack of starting the fire that killed his daughter! Elijah said, 'You were married to two women, and you had to get rid of one! You're a murderer! I'm going to the sheriff!' And Jack said, 'You stupid peasant! No one will believe you! And don't forget, I've got the goods on you—enough to put you away for life. You say one word to anyone, and I'll tell them about the explosion . . . and the shooting . . . and the poisoning! That's enough to hang you twice!' Then Elijah screamed at him, 'You're the one told me to do it! You murderer!' And in between they were shouting obscenities that I couldn't repeat . . . Just then, Skip whinnied! There was sudden silence. I almost died!"

She paused to recollect the crucial moment, and Qwilleran urged her to continue.

"The arguing stopped then, and I heard Jack leave the stable, still shouting nasty names at the old man who had been like an uncle to him when we were all growing up. After that, Elijah banged things around in the tack room for a while, and then he left, too. When it was safe, I slipped out the back door and walked all around the poolhouse and croquet court before going home. That's when I discovered that Mother was giving evacuation orders. She said it was going to be the storm of the century. But I think it was Jack's idea to—"

"Leave the scene of the crime?" Qwilleran suggested.

"If it's true what Elijah said."

"Elijah Kale? Is that his name?" Mentally Qwilleran spelled it: 5-12-9-10-1-8 and then 11-1-12-5. "Were you aware that Jack had married his daughter?"

"Well, when we were young we spent summers together at The Pines, you know, and she always had a crush on Jack. Mother didn't like him to go sailing with the steward's daughter, but he always got his own way. Then June went away to school, and that was the end of it—until last summer. She spent the whole season on the island, playing the piano at the club, and Jack spent all his time there. Mother had William investigate, and it was true: June was Wife Number Four! William told me. Mother never tells me anything."

"Did you have any suspicion of a Wife Number Five?"

"William says Jack met a French woman in Florida and wanted Mother to settle with June, but the *steward's daughter* didn't want money; she wanted Jack Appelhardt." Liz said it with scorn.

As soon as Liz was safely registered at the Pickax Hotel, Qwilleran took the shortcut to his apple barn—through the theater parking lot and the dense patch of woods that separated his orchard from urban Pickax. He unloaded the Siamese, put fresh water in their bowl, and unpacked only enough to find his record of the domino games.

The last entry included 4-4, 5-6, 6-6, 2-3, 3-6, 5-5, 0-1, and 3-5—pips that he had translated into H, K, L, E, I, J, A, and another H. He had been trying to unscramble them when Liz knocked on his door, wearing a caftan and carrying an oil lamp like a vestal of Roman myth.

Now the letters fell into place. Discarding the K and one H, he spelled *Elijah*. In that same game Koko had produced dominoes that spelled *Jack* and *Kale*. (Although Qwilleran had thought it was *lake* or *leak.*) Reviewing that final game, he pounded his forehead with his fist and muttered, "Dumb! Dumb!"

Koko, he admitted once again, was amazing. He couldn't spell; neither could he add or subtract. He bypassed the three Rs because he knew everything instinctively. He was psychic! Qwilleran often asked himself, How did I happen to adopt the only psychic cat in captivity? It never occurred to him that Koko may have made it happen, just as he had engineered Qwilleran's presence on the nature trail at a vital moment.

Without further unpacking, Qwilleran phoned the police chief at home. "Andy, I got your phone message, and now I have some information—"

"Where are you?"

"Back at the apple barn, but I was on the island during the storm."

"How was it?"

"Halfway between terrifying and boring. Want to run over for a confidential chat and a nip of the good stuff?"

"Be there in three minutes."

Galloping paws were thundering up the ramps, around the balconies, across the beams, back down to the mezzanine level, from which they swooped to a cushioned chair on the main floor. After two weeks of confinement, they had rediscovered SPACE. Qwilleran said to them, "I swear never to subject you guys to that ordeal again!"

While waiting for Brodie he took another look at the note from Dwight Somers:

> Didn't want to give you this dope over the phone (I used Watergate tactics to get it) and I'm leaving the island on the next ferry. I quit this crummy job! Have an appointment with a firm in Lockmaster—sounds good. Noisette's last name is duLac. Permanent residence: Lake Worth FL. Hope this helps.

Almost immediately a vehicle could be seen weaving through the woods and bouncing on the rutted road. It was an occurrence that always excited Koko. "It's the law!" Qwilleran warned him. *"Please, no catfits!"*

Andy parked at the back door and came blustering through the kitchen. "This had better be good! You pulled me away from a TV special on Edinburgh."

"If it isn't good enough to take to the prosecutor, I'll buy you and your wife dinner at the Old Stone Mill."

Andy's Scotch was ready—with a little water and no ice—and the two men took their glasses into the lounge, where the chief sank into the cushions of an oversize chair. "I hear the hotel got hit bad, just as I predicted."

"The ancient gods of the island have had a curse on the Pear Island resort from the beginning."

"You can't fight nature . . . any more than you can fight City Hall. So what have you got? Hard evidence or soft clues?"

"I've got a hack saw blade, some signals from Koko (who's never wrong), and enough two-and-two to put together and make a case of sabotage, bigamy, arson, murder, and several counts of attempted murder. Everyone tried to explain them away as accidents, but I maintain they were the result of two criminal plots, both masterminded by the black sheep of a wealthy family from Chicago. Finding himself married to June Halliburton and Noisette duLac at the same time, he got rid of one wife and helped the other wife to get rid of her husband. I'd guess that both murders were accomplished by drugging the drinks of the victims. Then June's mattress was set afire, and George duLac fell into the hotel pool, probably with a gentle assist."

"Both of these incidents," Qwilleran pointed out, "made unfavorable publicity for the resort but were actually subplots. The major campaign to harass the resort and undermine its tourist business was engineered by the bigamist and an employee at his family's estate. I'll name names when I talk to the prosecutor."

"How much of this is guesswork on your part?" the chief asked.

"You can call it what you like, but it's deduction based on observation, reports from witnesses, and tips from Koko." Qwilleran went into a few details regarding the gumbo poisoning, the finding of the hack saw blade, and the argument in the stable. He thought it best not to mention the dominoes. Brodie's admiration for Koko's occult talents had its limits. "Freshen your drink, Andy?"

"Just a wee dram."

On Saturday all three of them—the man and his two animal companions—found themselves in a post-vacation, post-hurricane lethargy. The Siamese curled up in their old familiar places; Qwilleran lolled around and refused to answer the telephone. Later, when he checked his answering machine, there were these messages:

From Fran Brodie: "Thanks for sending me Ms. Cage. I'm doing an apartment for her at Indian Village."

From Polly Duncan: "Sorry I was snippy last night. I was travel-weary. I'm dying to tell you about my big decision."

From Mildred Riker: "If you'll invite us for drinks tomorrow, I'll bring a casserole and a salad. Want to hear about the hurricane and Polly's vacation."

On Sunday evening the Rikers arrived with food and bad news: The high winds had damaged the new addition to their beach house. Polly arrived with her roll of papers and good news. "When I told my friend in Oregon that I intended to keep my carriage house apartment in the new college complex, she convinced me I should own my own home. She's an architect, and we spent the whole time planning a house—two stories high, so Bootsie can run up and down stairs. All I need to do is find a piece of land that's not too remote and not too expensive." She unrolled the architect's sketches and spread them on the coffee table.

Riker applauded. Mildred was thrilled. Qwilleran felt much relieved. He said, "There are two acres at the far end of the orchard, where the Trevelyan farmhouse used to be. I'll sell them for a dollar." Then everyone applauded.

When they asked him about the hurricane, he shrugged it off. "When you've seen one hurricane, you've seen 'em all." He captivated them, however, with the tale of the missing lightkeepers.

Mildred said, "Why is everyone mystified? It's perfectly obvious that the men were plucked off the island by a UFO."

No one applauded, but Koko said "Yow-ow-ow" in what seemed to be an authoritative affirmative.

Glibly Qwilleran explained, "He smells the casserole in the oven."

"Okay, Qwill," said Riker. "What was your real reason for going to Breakfast Island? You didn't fool me for one minute, and you've filed only one piece of copy in two weeks."

"Well, you know, Nick Bamba was concerned about the series of accidents on the island, and he wanted me to go over there and poke around for evidence of foul play; but . . . there were three plain-clothes detectives from the state police on the scene, so I told myself, Why get involved?"

"Now you're getting smart," the editor said. "I've always told you to mind your own business."

The Rikers left fairly early. Qwilleran drove Polly home and returned to the barn fairly late. He gave the Siamese their bedtime snack, and then the three of them enjoyed their half-hour of propinquity before retiring: Qwilleran sprawled in his big chair, Yum Yum curled on his lap with chin on paw, and Koko on the arm of the chair, condensing himself into an introspective bundle of fur. Satisfied with his treat and contemplating lights-out, Koko looked like anyone's pampered pet, and yet . . .

Qwilleran asked himself the questions that would never be fully answered:

When Koko tore the month of June off the calendar, did he know that June Halliburton would lose her life next door?

When he ruined my good clothes and stopped me from visiting the merry widows, did he know what lay ahead on the nature trail? Otherwise, I would never have met the royal family or heard their daughter's story of royal intrigue. Or was it all coincidence?

When Koko threw his catfit and dislodged the tragedy mask, was it because it looked like the dissipated Jack Appelhardt?

And how about his raid on the nutbowl? Did he know that the French word for hazelnut is *noisette?*

And how about the dominoes? "Level with me, Koko," Qwilleran said to the sleepy cat at his elbow. "Do you get a kick out of swishing your tail and sending them flying off the table? Or do you know what you're doing?"

Koko squeezed his eyes and opened his mouth in a cavernous yawn —showing his fangs, exposing a pink gullet, and breathing a potent reminder of his bedtime snack.